The Cozy Cosmic

EDITED BY
FRANCES LU-PAI IPPOLITO & MARK TEPPO

Underland Press

Edited by Frances Lu-Pai Ippolito and Mark Teppo
Book Design and Layout by Firebird Creative
Cover art by SaljulQutub / stock.adobe.com

Underland Press
www.underlandpress.com

The Cozy Cosmic

TABLE OF CONTENTS

TABLE OF CONTENTS

THIS ONE IS FOR THOSE WHO CARRY ON.

Death, in Two

~ John Shirley

1. *Memento Mori*

His eyes are white-light ceiling bulbs; his teeth, syringe needles—
he's attended by a retinue of shiny scarab beetles.
I stood a-teetering on the vacuum-breathing brink,
where you fall with the weight of a single thought you think;
where laughing things rise to find they truly sink
and white on white on white on white—is the color of my ink.
I didn't pass through the tunnel; the tunnel passed through me
And death will not hesitate, to come unseasonably.

Memento mori, remember death—I recall it clearly: yes yes and yes.
I've bargained with that smug, smiling merchant of rest;
though that time is past, and I pretend we never met
you know what hasn't happened—will, onward, happen yet.

I no longer taunt the lion, nor will I walk the edge;
I withdrew from the void that shimmers past the ledge.
But every morning when I wake, I see the shadows smile;
I know that it is but his whim to smirk and bide a while.

2. *No Refuge*

So you think you die when you die
(When you die)
it's all over, no more life
(No more life)
Truth ain't that peaceful,
(Believe me!)
You won't get off
Quite that easily

You're going to wriggle
On the hook
Of being alive
It's never one or two or three
or four
Always a five
No real end to strife--
Because there's always
An afterlife

Oh don't think you won't feel
Oh don't think you won't see
You won't get away
So easily:
Maybe it's servitude
Or maybe it's hell
Maybe it's a color
That has its own smell

Maybe it's a weight
That cries out aloud
Maybe it's the razor's edge
Of an unseen cloud

I don't know what shape
it'll take;
Or what color
it'll be—
I only know,
(only know this!)
There's no escape from
What Must Be:
The relentless trap of being
You will never
Finally go free:
There's no refuge—
From eternity . . .

⋈

On Hearing the First Shoggoth in Spring

~ Tais Teng

New Haven sounded kind of hopeful, Lilian Wu had always thought, a quaint, cobble-stoned village sheltered by high cliffs and safe from any storm.

Lilian knew better. Put all hexes and ghost-catchers you want on your roofs, sacrifice your firstborn and the Mi-go would still sweep down from the sky, harvesting the brains of any careless boy who left his amulet dangling from the back of his chair when he crept outside to meet that lovely girl which might even be human.

Deep Ones would crawl from the sea on moonless nights and rattle your doorknob, bubbling and croaking, peddling dried sea anemones and the powdered beaks of Kraken.

Lilian had heard them a dozen times. "Just a pinch of our excellent dust," their glutinous voices would wheedle, "and you'll walk the streets of the great human cities again. Of Shanghai and Quebec. Jet planes will paint your sky with contrails as white as freshly fallen snow. Nothing bat-winged, dear human, no, no. You'll be masters and mistresses again. Strong, so strong. The most fearful predators of Earth!"

One night her father must have listened to those voices and now she didn't have a father anymore. Her mother had found him the next morning in a puddle of green slime and his staring eyes had crystallized into orbs as clear as water. They still lay on the shelf above the fireplace. If Lilian peered into their pupils she saw miniature skyscrapers and the strangely blue sky from Before.

Well, such things happened. It was the sixty-fourth year after the return of the Elder Gods and Lilian saw nothing wrong with her world. Take Amanda Giraud: she was all of forty-three and had still most of her teeth and fingers. You just had to be careful.

"There," her best friend Susan whispered and raised her cross-bow. It was one of those clever Mi-go weapons. The arrowheads branched out into a dozen dimensions and could pierce any armor. It was a family heirloom and had only cost three babies.

"What?"

Susan kept pointing until Lilian got it. The bush in front of them stood completely motionless. Not a leaf stirred and that was a sure giveaway. The green sky was filled with scudding clouds and Lilian felt the breeze caressing her brow. This Shub must be very young to be so careless, though her camouflage was otherwise perfect.

"One of the Shubs," she nodded and unrolled her net. It was made of aramid, a relict from the olden times, and not even the claws of a Shub-Niggurath kid couldn't tear it. There was only a single Shub-Niggurath, just one Black Goat of the Woods with a Thousand Young, but that was enough. A thousand Young was an understatement: they were common as rats and cockroaches now and quite palatable if you first dipped them in vitriol and then left them hanging for a fortnight in your shed.

"Iä!" Susan yodeled, "Shub-Niggurath, the Goat with a Thousand Young!"

The leaves stirred and Lilian caught a glimpse of glittering eyes. The kid jumped and Susan's bow sang, a note high as the screech of a gull. The Shub's snarl stopped in mid-jump and the monster rolled through the gorse, clawing at the arrow.

The girls waited until the convulsions stopped and the glow in the eyes died to a milky white before walking closer. Shubs weren't exactly intelligent but how smart do you have to be to play dead?

"Perfect shot," Lilian said. Susan's quarrel jutted from the skull, exactly between the two horns.

"Thank you. But we'd better make sure." Susan pointed her amulet. It remained ruby-red, not a trace of vital blue. "Dead as a beached jellyfish."

Dead, no longer in her chameleon mode, the Shub didn't look very much like a goat. The pale body was grub-like, segmented and only the eyes could have been a mammal's.

The Shub was unexpectedly heavy for something not much bigger than a hare: at least thirty pounds. *It must be the bones*, Lilian thought. *Some trans-plutonium metal. Perhaps the smith can use them to forge spearheads?*

"That boy," Susan said when they were halfway to the cliff. "That Mike."

It was like an electrical shock, just hearing his name.

"Yes?" Lilian swallowed. "Are you still sweet on him?"

"I was. No use now. He stepped on an egg case and a larva bored right in his foot. His brother tried one of the forbidden words but it didn't help. Justin lost half his teeth and burned his tongue so bad he still can't speak." She balled her fists. "I hate all those stupid squid-heads! Why the hell did they have to wake up?"

"The stars," Lilian automatically replied. "They went wrong. It was nothing we did." She could have bitten her tongue. Susan didn't want an explanation. She just wanted her support. "It is a pity and a waste. Still, there are other boys." She couldn't believe her own mouth saying such crap.

"Less each year and none like Mike."

"Fewer girls, too. It evens out."

"There is just no justice," Susan muttered and there was nothing Lilian could say about that. It only now sank in. *Mike is dead.* Lilian felt very strange, almost tongue-tied. Mike had been Susan's boyfriend, almost from the moment girls and boys started noticing they were different. Lilian had seen them walking hand in hand, kissing, burning blue incense when the black gulls returned from the Mountains of Madness in the ultimate South. Probably they had been doing more than kissing on the afternoons Susan didn't want to go hunting or beach-combing. *I loved him and I can never tell Susan.* She felt like the mistress in the *Severn Castle* DVD, standing in the shadows of the cypress, yearning, while her king was buried by his wife and children.

"What happened exactly?"

"Exactly?" Susan's smile was a savage thing, baring all her teeth. "Well, that larva first devoured his liver and his entrails. Kept his brain for the last. Kept him alive and screaming even after he was a hollow shell."

She hates him. She hates Mike for dying and leaving her behind. I would still love him after he died.

○

"Girls," a voice like a woodwind said. "Walking alone."

A Mi-go stepped from behind an oak tree, his aether wings folded like tightly rolled umbrellas. From his belt dangled half a dozen brain cylinders. Empty cylinders Lilian instantly saw: the plug-in-eyes didn't glow.

'Such beautiful brains," the monster continued. "Convoluted like the mountains where the continental plates clash. Glowing with vitality and fear."

His feelers waved and Lilian tried in vain to locate his eyes. Mi-go didn't have eyes she belatedly remembered and his head was no more than a leathery sack.

"You can't harvest us," she said. "Our village, we paid in advance. We are safe for the next half year."

"It isn't night," Susan added. "Not your hunting time at all! And we are wearing our amulets."

"Such amulets only protect against lesser star spawn. Not against higher beings like us or our esteemed enemies."

"Ha!" Lilian snorted. "You are nothing but a mushroom. A walking mushroom!" All her fear was gone, transformed into pure and shining hatred. There was nothing they could do, anyway, not against a demon like this. *Spit in his face and bite his hand when he tries to touch us.*

"The Kingdom of the Fungi is the mightiest Kingdom of all," the Mi-go lectured. "Every living being will become humus and food for us fungi in the end." He shook the sack which wasn't a head exactly. "Your lives are so short. Like the blooming of a single-season orchid. In my cylinder, you would live for centuries. You would see pulsing Algol rise above towers of burning ice. Hear the star whales scream while we spear them."

They really don't understand us. How could he? He is a goddamn mushroom! "To hear the sky-whales scream? That is not exactly my kind of entertainment."

"You would live for a long time. You could see all your enemies grow old and die. See them feed the mushrooms, eh?"

'Sorry, mister toadstool," Susan said. "We may be only human but we have fangs." She reached behind her back and the crossbow unfolded in her hands like some magic origami trick. "Fangs you gave us yourself."

"How droll! A class nine weapon in the hands of a third chimpanzee. And it is pointing to the only vulnerable part of my body, too."

"Yes. Your second brain node. A hunter told me."

"Humans hunting Mi-go? Such a fascinating concept."

"A priest of Hastur instructed him. The King in Yellow isn't your greatest fan."

The Mi-go hopped backward and opened his bat wings. They started out small, the kind of wings devils sported in the old pictures. But these wings kept unfolding, getting more attenuated until they reached the top of the sky. A single wing-beat and the monster dwindled to a spot, was gone.

"You drove him off," Lilian said. "He was afraid."

"I bluffed him." Susan started to shake and Lilian embraced her, feeling Susan's whole body quake.

"I had only a single Mi-go arrow and that is still sitting in the skull of the Shub. My other arrows are forgeries. Carved to look like the real thing. If he had looked closer . . . The arrowhead doesn't branch out into other dimensions. It is as 3-D as us."

The encounter with the Mi-go had helped Lilian get her priorities straight. Love and happiness were only options: the only thing that counted, really counted was surviving. Seeing the light of another day. Mike was gone. Some other boy would have to do.

At the edge of the cliff, Lilian looked down at New Haven. There were the twin capes with the lighthouse to the left, and the jetty with their five fishing boats. Purple smoke rose from the smithy. Whatever metal Abdul Hunrabi was melting and hammering wasn't something from this solar system or perhaps even from this universe.

It looked so peaceful and it was all a lie. Take the zigzagging stairs that had been carved in the cliffs and reached all the way down to the village. They had appeared overnight and when you put your foot on a step you instantly shriveled, and turned into a mummy.

"No one is fishing," Susan said. "There is only that single sail and it isn't one of our boats. A lure I guess." The jellyfish had been growing more intelligent over the last five years, clumping together until they grew to the size of ancient oil tankers. The white sail probably was only the top of a monstrous jelly, with tentacles that reached for half a mile. "I think it is even flying a flag."

"I'll have a look." Lilian took her treasured binoculars from her pouch. It was upgraded by the Tinkers and could look straight through the thickest mist or even rock.

"It is a flag, one with red stripes and a blue field with white stars. It got it almost right. Only there are too many stars and that red is more like purple." She laughed. "And it is waving but in the wrong direction. Against the wind."

"It is hoping someone will think it is the US Navy and sail from the harbor."

"Nobody is that stupid. If they are rescuing us they are sixty years late." Lilian raised her hand, "Wait. Something is happening." The flag suddenly grew slack and then the whole ship started to go down. Only a few heartbeats later even the tip of the mast slipped beneath the waves.

"End of the show," Susan said. "Let's climb down at the lighthouse. It is still a long walk."

The next morning her mother woke her before dawn was even coloring the sky.

"What?" Lilian muttered and opened her eyes which were still heavy with sleep.

"Your friend Lilian is down in the kitchen. She wants to see you."

"I am coming. One second."

She stumbled down the stairs on bare feet.

Susan was sitting at the kitchen table, sipping a glass of steaming goat milk and she looked just terrible. Pale and her eyes were red from crying.

"He came back, Lil. Last night."

Lilian didn't have to ask who. "What did you do?"

"I called my father and I held him by his wrists while my father cut off his head. I mean, it sure wasn't Mike. Mike is dead."

Lilian felt a delicate shudder, something that was almost sexual.

"But how did you know? I mean, something could have resurrected him. It happens. They are the Elder Gods. Some are heavily into resurrection. I know vampires are only a rumor, but . . ."

"A vampire or a zoumbay at least have known my name. I know Mike quite well. We didn't only kiss and the thing at my door called me 'Suzanne'. It was like he had done all his homework, but the wrong homework. Mike always called me Sue. I have known him since kindergarten and it always was Sue. Mike was the only one who ever called me Sue." She sighed. "He was exactly like Mike and he looked completely alive. 'Hi Suzanne,' he said. 'Let me tell you how I came back.' And that was the moment I knew he was an impostor." She nodded. "This time we didn't take any chances. We burned his body and threw his head into the sea. Let the black gulls have that liar and dine on his eyes!"

Lilian was walking down the beach, searching the flotsam and the tangled weed on the tide line. It had been spring tide that night, with the green and red moon full in the sky, bearing no less than four shimmering rings.

What came back once can come back twice. If it hadn't been Mike really it came close enough and Susan had scorned him. *Now it is my turn.*

Her friend had probably thrown the head from the rock that jutted out just below the lighthouse. With the flood coming in it had probably ended up somewhere left from the middle of the beach. She took her upgraded binoculars from her pouch, put them to her eyes, and whispered; "Find him. Please." The instrument moved in her hand, projected a circle on the beach, and added cross-hairs.

Lilian nodded. "Got it."

Seagulls were screeching and swarming at the indicated place. She pulled a driftwood stick from the kelp and ran at them.

There wasn't much left, only a jawbone with a few shreds of skin and three teeth. She could only hope it was Mike's. She had counted on a more or less intact head.

There was a movement in the corner of her eye and she looked up. The Mi-go landed light as a thistledown on the sand.

"I followed you," he said, "planning to catch you without your fierce friend. You had such a dazzling brain! I would have kept you fresh and screaming for a thousand years." He folded his clawed arms. "This is a much better story, though."

"Story?" Lilian asked. It was useless to run. He would catch her and she didn't want to play his cat-and-mouse game.

"We love dark stories, full of betrayal and selfishness. We like such stories even better than living brains. Think of it! You are stealing your best friend's lover, her dead, resurrected lover. How she will hate you! Perhaps he still loves her? That would tie a love knot made of barbed wire."

Don't listen to him. He is just trying to fuck with my head. Still, he probably knows a lot about cloning and things like that.

"He is dead," Lilian said. "I don't know how he came back the first time but his maker probably had more to go on than a single jaw-bone."

"No, no, this is ample. Just a tooth would do for the DNA. As for the rest, his personality: memories never fade. They are printed on 9-D space itself and quite easy to retrieve."

"Can you . . . Can you resurrect him?"

"Not my specialty. I know some creatures, though, who love to repair things. To upgrade them." He pointed to a ledge halfway up the cliff. "Take him to the Tinkers."

"They always ask a high price." She rubbed the stump of her left index finger. As a seven-year-old, she had left her broken binoculars in one of those nests made from glowing wires. "Too high a price. They took my finger in payment."

"The price for a perfect husband would be something more traditional. Perhaps your first-born son? And remember, they always improve on the original. You'll be the envy of your whole town." He opened his wings. "I'll be observing you. Make it a good tale. I look forward to your suffering."

It took Lilian two hours climbing to reach their nesting place. Ozone and hydrogen sulfide made her gag: it was the very smell of demonic high-tech. The Tinkers themselves were no more than azure Ceren-kov flashes as they moved in and out of her own universe.

Glowing letters appeared in front of her eyes.

PUT HIM IN THE NEST.

"Which nest? I see dozens of nests."

IT DOESN'T MATTER. THERE IS ONLY A SINGLE NEST IN THE HIGHER DIMENSIONS.

"I see." How she hated that superior non-Euclidian double talk. *All is one in a higher dimension.*

She put the jawbone in the third nest and sat down to wait. Higher on the ledge she heard the first wild Shoggoths of spring whistle, their "Tekeli-li" sounding like distant flutes.

Ah, a pink layer of flesh was already creeping across the bare bone. She felt a smile tugging at the corners of her mouth.

It was the sixty-fourth year after the return of the Elder Gods and you had to take your love where you could find it.

⊐

What the Sea Provides

~ Tyler Battaglia

When my net dragged something up from the depths that wasn't fish, but a little girl's body, it was only fair to assume she was dead.

As I hauled her aboard, the stench made it clear; salt water and death, the stench sticky and clinging immediately to my nostrils, to my throat. She might not have been in the water long, but it didn't take much time for the sea to claim corpses, rend their flesh from their bones to feed the fish in her depths. And as I lifted the net, I saw the way the girl's dull eyes stared out from a half-eaten face, her features missing chunks from where the brine had begun to abrade the facial tissue and fish had begun to feast on the loose pieces. Skin and flesh had started to slough off her limbs, slipping from the bone beneath.

There could be no question about her having drowned, perhaps a few days ago. Long enough, at least, that she had begun to become a meal for the sea's other children.

I was frustrated, more than sad for her. Lost things washed ashore from time to time on my barely-inhabited island, buried halfway among the sandbars, or were caught in my net like this. And why should a body be different? But villagers on the mainland expected their things returned. Bringing back something lost from a passing boat was a pain in the ass. Sometimes I kept what I found just to avoid the fuss, if it was a good enough treasure. Finders, keepers.

But perhaps most of all, the body of a lost daughter should be returned home. I had only rare occasion to go to port, and usually for market or trade, wanting even less to do with the villagers than they with me, but I did have a catch to sell, meagre though it was. A trip to the authorities would be a necessary and doable inconvenience. It was about the only concession my hardened heart could bear.

I hauled her to the deck, her body hitting the sole with a wet *squelch*. I crouched close to take in the details. The waves crashed against the bow, showering me and the girl's body in a fine mist.

When the ocean dew landed on her glassy, dead eyes, she blinked away the saltwater tears.

In a panic, I grabbed for a knife and quickly cut the nylon away from her wrecked sundress, away from the cheerful yellow daffodils in fabric that had been eaten away by fish like all the rest of her. I pulled the net from the flesh as much as possible, even when it meant digging the fibers into the too-soft flesh of her face and arms, leaving gouges that wouldn't have been left on healthy, living skin. Once I had cleared the net, she began to cough, saltwater froth on her lips. She turned over, lying flat on her back, staring up at the cloudless sky. The sun beating down on her half-death worsened the mingling smell of human waste and fish guts, but it gave me a better look at her. Now I could see the places where her skin was worn down nearly to the bone. When she struggled to breathe, the flaps of her cheeks that hadn't fully scraped off from sand and ocean grit fluttered in time with her rasping breaths. I could see gums barely clinging to teeth through a hole in her face.

A piece of blue crab leg was hooked in the tendons of her jaw. Not knowing what else to do, I reached down to fish it out of the opening.

That fisheye gaze, looking rounder for her eyelids having shriveled up from the saltwater, fixed on me with fear and wonder.

I cleared my throat. "Can you hear me?"

Barely, she nodded. Tangled hair clung to her cheeks, her neck. Some of it got caught in a wound in her forehead where her skin had begun to separate from her face, torn away by the ocean. She seemed scared, so I took her washerwoman's hand, wrinkly and peeling from where the sea had started to steal her skin away from her knuckles.

I squeezed her hand despite the sickly feeling of it, trying to remember what a father's comfort looked like. "If you can't talk, that's alright. I'll bring you back to my cottage and we'll get you into something dry. Maybe when you're feeling better, you can tell me who your parents are, and we'll find your way home."

Again, she nodded. What was left of her shrunken eyelids closed, partially shading her eyes from sun. Her ragged breathing slowed, and I thought perhaps she was falling asleep.

I got up and headed to turn the boat toward land. It would be best to get her to warmth and safety before figuring out the rest. My hands trembled; I had to hold the wheel in a death grip, lest I lose my nerve.

Once docked, I lifted the sleeping girl into my arms. She was a feather of a thing, no older than the child I'd lost once upon a time, and easy to hold. Her tattered but waterlogged clothes were the only thing that dragged her down; otherwise, she weighed naught more than my own daughter had.

I carried her homeward.

I didn't go to town that day. I had fish to sell, albeit fewer every day as the ocean ate her young, but also now a second mouth to feed. I set her inside, then picked out the least moth-eaten clothes from my daughter's old room that I'd never thrown away despite years of disuse in a room that hadn't been touched for just as long, so the girl could dress in something dry and whole. I woke her and provided a towel to let her dry herself, too worried I'd scrape off her loose flesh if I did it myself. My hands weren't gentle enough for a daughter's care anymore.

Once she was dry, I set her by the hearth with a blanket and started a fire to keep her warm. If the sea hadn't killed her, I thought that the chill might. She slept, again, by the fire, while I set to scaling the fish for supper, ignoring their discoloured blood that verged on unnatural neon as it circled the drain, scrubbing my hands raw until they came clean.

I returned to the living room to cook over the fire, and pretended not to notice the girl when she woke, feeling her strangely steady observation of my back. I didn't acknowledge her until I removed the fish from the flame and plated them—for all *she* was calm, my own head spun at having a child in the house again, innocent despite the unlikelihood of her being there, seemingly alive, watching me. Holding down the heartache and the fear, I turned and set a dish in front of her. Seeing her eye the flesh hungrily, I said, "Careful. It'll be hot."

Without waiting, she reached for the plate and picked up a hunk of tender white fish meat, still clinging to bone. "Careful—" I warned again but she tore her teeth into the grub, devouring it without hesitation.

Instead of protesting thrice, I sat back and watched her for a moment. Despite her age being about that of my lost daughter, the resemblance ended soon after. My daughter had had fair hair—too fair, my husband would tell her, to be getting fish guts in it—and her skin had been pale but ruddied by the sun, with eyes the rich brown of the earth. This girl, on the other hand, had hair as dark as the ocean's greatest depths, and skin the colour of warm sand where the sea hadn't leeched the colour into that of pale, watery vomit. Her eyes, dulled over, were the blue green of the sea under the cover of morning fog. And she looked small but strong—not the strength of a fisherman's girl, but the bone-rigidity of dignity.

We ate in silence, gathering the fishbones between us into a pot for composting in the garden. The meal was warm in my belly, and the company was, too—the first human thing in my home in many years, let alone a child. It had been lonely. A home that had once held a child but now stood empty was, I thought, infinitely lonelier than one that had never seen children at all.

When we had finished, I gathered up our plates. The girl reached for the bucket of bones with hands barely holding onto their own flesh. I shook my head and said, "Let me worry about those. I grind them up into bone meal. Good for the vegetables."

The girl nodded but clasped the handle tight. "Let me help."

I raised my eyebrows—I had wondered if the deeps had stolen away her speech as well, like a small mermaid caught in my net. "You talk." The girl smiled bashfully, so I shrugged. "Alright. There's a spot in the kitchen by the sill for them. I dry them there once I clear the last of the flesh." Though I had seen her eat—I suspected there was nothing left clinging to the bone.

She walked with me to the kitchen, where I washed the strangely coloured blood from the plates down the drain. I gave the girl a knife to clean any tissue still attached to the bones and she dutifully cleared them, knife glinting in her right hand and scaling close to the bone in her left. I watched her scrape the bones, wary she might lose a finger, but she never strayed from her mark. Once cleared, she set the bones by the window where they would dry throughout the day in the morrow's sun.

I put her to bed in my daughter's old room—the only room suitable for life not my own, all the furniture needed for a child still in place—and tucked her in. "Maybe tomorrow you'll talk to me," I said. I didn't apologize for the musty smell of old, unwashed sheets—they were, I hoped, better than the uncaring embrace of the briny deep.

"You could tell me where I might find your parents."

The girl gazed up at me with those deadened eyes and said, "I only have Mother. And she knows where to find me."

I couldn't think of a way one might find a child lost at sea, and I didn't like the idea that someone might find my secluded island home, but I didn't argue. "Do you remember your name?"

"She never gave me one."

Furrowing my brow, I tried to guess her age—what kind of girl wouldn't have a name? "Well, that won't do."

"Mother has many, but cares for none of them."

"Fish nibbling on you must have rotted your brain," I said softly. The girl laughed and I supposed I had meant it as a joke. "Well, if you can't remember your name tomorrow, I'll let you borrow one of mine."

The girl smiled but did not reply, closing her eyes the most she could. I watched until I thought she was asleep and turned off the light and closed the door.

I left the house but didn't go far—I was afraid I'd lose sight of the girl if I strayed. I walked along the cliff edge where I'd made my home, looking out to sea. I saw no sign of life but for the mainland a distance away where the lighthouse stood, lit but lonely. There was nothing else to see, and certainly nothing that indicated anyone looking for a lost daughter. There were no boats on the waves, dragging nets through the waters that were supposed to catch fish and not bodies.

As I stared out at her waters, I wondered at the unkindness of the ocean: why she would take away one daughter just to give back another, years too late for me to be a young enough man to watch her grow.

I went back inside before the chill could get me.

When I rose the next morning, I put on a kettle for tea. I noticed then the bones had disappeared in the night from the sill, but paid their absence no mind—a girl's brush with death would likely drive her to strangeness. If she wanted the bones, the garden would live without. Instead, I stared out the window through to the ocean. I would have to go out for the catch soon, but I thought also of the girl. Would it be too frightful for her to come with me? I was afraid to leave her for long, but if I didn't break water soon, I might find nothing at all, and the fish had been scarce enough of late, and sometimes too malformed to eat. If I didn't fish early, I simply wouldn't fish at all, and now there were two mouths that would go hungry, never mind selling any on the mainland.

Making up my mind, I went to rouse the girl from bed only to find her awake and looking through the dresser in the room I'd given her. She brushed rotted fingertips over found papers. She left perpetually damp fingerprints on the pages. She looked up and held one out to me. Hands shaking, I took it.

A drawing of a fish, crude but recognizable, even in its strange mutations. All her drawings had been like that: alien fish from her imagination, signed in thick, dark lines with the name of Mara.

"My daughter drew this."

"Where did she go?" My eyes flicked to the window behind the bed. The waves of the ocean crashed below. The half-drowned girl in my daughter's childhood bedroom nodded. She understood. "What about her Mother?"

"Didn't have one," I answered. I felt the weight of my wedding ring on my finger, a memory of yet another lost thing. "Not exactly. My husband left a little while after… well, we'd lost our own flesh and blood. Hard to come back from that. Especially living alone on an island with the person you blame."

The girl nodded. Her hair still stuck to her rotten face, even though it should have dried. It was tangled and knotted. I would have to tend to it soon, before she lost it all. "Can I borrow her name?"

I started. "What?"

"You said if I didn't remember a name, I could borrow one of yours. Can I have Mara?" Perhaps seeing my face, she said, "Your daughter isn't using it."

I hesitated. Was the drowned girl wrong? Perhaps not. But would Mara forgive me for defiling the shrine I had made of her long-dead presence in my life?

I hesitated before handing the girl the drawing again. She held it fast. "I suppose she isn't. You can borrow it. I think she'd want to share."

The girl—now Mara, but perhaps not my Mara—stepped up to me and gave me a hug. Her putrid skin *squished* against my clothes, leaving a damp impression and a lingering smell I couldn't quite place. I hugged her back, for how could I not hug a child who must have been lonely, having brushed so close to death?

I patted her tangles and stepped away. "Come with me on the boat. I don't want to leave you alone here today. But we'll be careful, all right?"

She nodded and followed me to the kitchen. I made her tea and toast, which I ate gladly, and she ate reluctantly in tiny pieces fit for a small fish, before I finished it for her, and we took to the sea.

The boat rocked steady on the water until well past noon. Mara was a surprisingly apt helper—she set out the gillnets as if she understood the act of trawling the ocean better than most fishermen. When we had time to rest and wait, I detangled her hair, cutting away unsalvageable clumps where I had to, casting them to the deep to float like masses of decaying kelp.

I did my best to hide my fear and disappointment from Mara each time the net came back mostly empty. More and more of the fish were ill-coloured, smelled like animal-rot, or were slimy in my grip. I was cautious of the fish that didn't look the size or shape to belong to my part of the ocean. I didn't discard them, the pickings were too slim to risk starvation, but I watched for those fish whose scales were too iridescent, or whose gills were too alive, fluttering like they could breathe the air and not just the sea.

Those that stubbornly held onto breath outside the water, alive when they shouldn't be, were swiftly dispatched. Mara helped without having to be asked, solemn and dutiful as she snuffed them out with more brute force than a child's hands should hold.

When I caught her fishing pieces of meat out from beneath the scales and eating it raw, I did not discourage her. She had earned that much.

I began to trust her on the boat, found her invaluable—more for the company I hadn't realized I missed than for her skill. And I only feared for her when she got too close to the bow of the ship, trying not to imagine what might happen to my heart if she drowned twice.

The days went by like this—I caught fish with the girl that was almost my daughter, we ate our catch and made our tea, and we told stories of the ocean and what she meant to us. I realized that for all the gaps in her memory eaten away by ocean depths, Mara loved the sea. Her family must have lived nearby, perhaps even in the coastal town where I sold my fare.

One day at a time, the drowned-girl version of Mara filled the hole that the original had left. I knew that she wouldn't ever be my daughter, but she submerged herself in the void, displacing the grief that only a father without his child could know.

Sometimes I heard her praying at night, not to God but to her own Mother, and I never asked too many questions when I found the collection of bones that she had hoarded from our supper that had once been destined for the garden. She had said, "I am going to make a body for Mother like she made a body for me," and I didn't press.

Little girls had active imaginations, after all.

The next time I went to town to sell the fish we'd caught, I reluctantly took Mara with me. She was again an able helper when we set up on the docks, but I had to swath her in clothes too much for the ocean sun so that people would not spy her sea-wounds from afar. When villagers came to buy our fish, I made sure Mara was away from prying eyes, made busy elsewhere.

I heard strange voices, men pressing the port vendors not for their wares but for answers, instinct railed against my gut. I made excuses for Mara to climb into my boat, out of sight.

The men approached, three in total. When they came close, I could see that the man in the centre had been crying, his ocean eyes reddened from tears and his sandy cheeks sallow. I'd seen a similar look in my husband's eyes and in the mirror. A lump formed in my throat with the dread of what they might want.

One of the men—not the one crying—said to me, "He lost his girl. Overboard." He glanced at the man with wept-red eyes. "We're hoping to find any trace of her."

He procured a photo from his pocket and held it out to me. Hands shaking, I took it.

Dark hair, and skin the colour of warm sand, ocean eyes. Even without holes in her flesh where she'd become fish food, even with life in her eyes, I recognized the once-alive Mara. "How long has she been missing?"

The two men who hadn't been crying exchanged a look over their heartbroken companion. "A week and a half."

I tried to still my hand as I passed the photo back. I steeled myself for the hurt my next words would cause, words that had been said to me years ago. "Even if you found the body now, it would be eaten beyond recognition. I don't know if you would know her on sight."

I saw the man choke. There was a sob caught in his throat and behind his eyes.

One of the men said, "He's looking for closure."

I grunted. My heart ached for another grieving father. "Well, I haven't seen anything."

The men turned stoic faces on me. They started to turn away, but one besides the father stayed. "The townsfolk pointed you out to us."

"Did they?"

"Yes. Said you lost a girl, once. That you're cursed, brought blight to the very fish in the sea. That you're the reason the catch is meek. That your husband left you because, without your child, you were more wed to the ocean than to him. That this is why you left town—no daughter, no husband, no life. Thought maybe you're why this girl died, too. Still cursed. But her father gave you credit. He wanted to ask you. He thought it meant that you'd understand. That you'd *help*."

I kept my gaze steady. I thought of Mara, in the boat, half-dead but the closest to my girl I'd ever have again. I looked at the grieving father a short distance away.

Mara had only ever mentioned Mother.

"Well, then he was wrong, wasn't he?"

The man gave me a hard look, then rejoined the grieving father and his other companion. I watched them leave, then packed up my things. I didn't want to tell the townspeople to shut their fucking mouths, I wanted to just get my things and take Mara back home. My catch had been too meagre for much to sell anyway—the fish continued to dry up, and more and more were inedible. Wrong.

Mara helped as I haphazardly loaded up the boat, unsecured the line, and raised anchor. Only when we were away from port did she ask, "Are you okay?"

"I'm fine, Mara," I said. She gave me the look of a girl wiser than her years, and I felt bad for lying, but couldn't tell her what had happened. I selected a fish and gave it to her. She ate it raw—a habit I was indulging too often—and stared off the bow into the water, at just safe enough a distance that I wasn't worried about losing her.

I heard her singing softly to Mother.

The fish continued to disappear from the ocean. My net caught more disintegrating guts than it did life. I fed Mara first with what little flesh was salvageable. I could not lose a daughter twice.

I should have been afraid when I found the sculpture in Mara's room, a few days after the last time I had caught any fish. I knew she'd been hoarding the bones meant for meal, gathering them in the bedroom that had once been my daughter's, but I hadn't expected her to have knitted them together into something almost human. Somehow, I knew it was a woman, or meant to be something like one. She was missing part of her left arm, but otherwise was almost complete, a skeletal face built from fish bones, sharp teeth embedded in an unnaturally shaped jaw. The face contained raw anger and passion despite lacking in flesh, the fish scales knit into her eye sockets telling a powerful tale.

She was beautiful in her abhorrence. The bones were pieced together into something that could have been divine.

"Who is she?" I asked.

Mara smiled to me, the picture of girlhood innocence even where her gums had receded from her teeth to expose the nerves and the roots beyond shrunken lips. "Mother." The word came naturally. It was the answer I had known, and Mara understood that I had recognized her Mother. "She gave me this body. I made one for her."

The body of Mother called to me. I heard her breathing even though her bone-body was lifeless. Her breath was like the waves, crashing upon the shore.

"She isn't complete," I said.

"No," Mara agreed. Her face fell in childlike disappointment. She looked to the arm. The last piece to be completed. "There haven't been any fish in days."

It was true—Mara and I had been fighting not to go hungry, eating only the scarce vegetables from the garden. The last of the fish had gone away.

"It's true." My heart hammered. The ocean roared in my ears. My husband had left because I had been more wed to the ocean than him after our child had been lost to her. And here she was: the ocean-Mother in all her glory. Or soon enough she would be. "We're fresh out of fish bones, aren't we?"

Mara nodded. She looked away from me, from the body for her Mother, and out to the sea beyond the window. The waves crashed upon the shore. "She won't come for a body that isn't ready."

I thought of how angry the sea had been. I thought of how lonely she had been. I thought of how angry and lonely I had been before Mara—this new Mara—had been caught in my net, a gift from the ocean that was Mother.

I did not have to look at Mara to see her heartache. If she could not bring Mother to her, perhaps she would return to the sea to rejoin her.

And I would do anything to keep my new daughter.

I went to the kitchen to find the descaling knife.

Standing on the cliffside, staring out to the ocean, we were a family. Mara, the ocean, and me. The ragged stump that ended my left arm still bled sometimes, but my right hand held that of my new wife. I felt my own wedding ring loosely hanging off the fingerbone I had given to her as my vow, my own flesh slowly disintegrating off her hand from the salt in the air with no more blood to sustain it. Soon it would be so much bone, just like the rest of her.

The rising tide had climbed enough to start to eat away at the rock below, subsuming the lower shores of the island. My boat struggled to keep float, stern tipping into the water, the tie dragging it down to a pier that had long since disappeared beneath the waves.

The water was clearer than it had ever been, steam rising from it as it purified itself. Yet the fish were thriving, thousands of them frothing over the waves, a thick mass of aquatic life that would have prevented my boat from traveling the sea even if I had tried to save it from its slow, sinking death. Even from atop the cliff, I could see their misshapen teeth glinting in the sunlight where they breached the water.

In the distance, I could see the mainland. The water around the disappearing pier was steadily leaching blood into the ocean from the drowning town. All was quiet, but for the waves crashing upon the store.

I turned to my wife, to the ocean-Mother, whose own fish teeth glinted in the sunlight. I could see the slow growth of ocular organs swelling out from under the scales in her eye sockets, the flesh of new eyes pushing through the cracks in her bone-and-scale face. Yet, despite her ill-formed eyes, she saw me looking to her, and I could tell she looked back. Her sharp-toothed, lipless smile grew.

She did not speak, but we were finding ways of understanding each other already, through soft touches, through gestures, through inelegant sign language we invented together. She was so much more than intelligent—there was something too-knowing contained within those bones.

I did not know if something like her could love me. I did not know what havoc the ocean might yet wreak, if the drowning seaside village across the way was only the beginning. But I felt that she accepted me for caring for her child, some alien soul that had been given a drowned girl's body to wear. I loved Mara, and so the ocean would spare me from whatever she might do next.

I knew I would never fully understand the unkindness of the ocean. But for now, yes, we were family—and the sea would provide.

⬙

My Grandmother's Sacristy

~ Ellis Bray

Scrubbing floors is sacred work—
There's purity in pain
and penance in the callouses
on knees and fingers,
spine and brain—

The house must find you worthy
Should you offer labored prayers.

Grandmother was worthy.
Withered and bent at the end of her years,
but worthy and faithful
In rede and in rote.

"Don't stare," she said that final day.
Her rosary frothed between her fingers,
counting down her life.
"This house is theirs, in beam and root,
so, if you look, *don't stare*."

I never did—
      candle flames with fluttering light
      icy drafts on hellish days

the choking breath of basement rock—
I always looked away.

The house belongs to them, she said;
the living only haunt it.

But when her vanished saffron scent
swims across the vacant room,
        I twist my rag and scrub my sins
        I count the beads and hum the hymns
        I whisper dim doxologies

And struggle not to stare.

⊐

Right and Bright

~ E. E. Marshall

The grease spot on the living room coffee table was Elma's worst enemy. It wasn't her only enemy by a ways, but it was clearly her worst. Some days, it hid there, a corruption in the maple grain, silently taunting her from beneath the doily she had tatted specifically to cover it. Other days, it slid out from under the doily and openly harassed her.

Andrew didn't care—couldn't understand.

He was four years into his executive fast-track. He was doing what he was born to do, obsessing on power and bottom lines. To him, she acted as support personnel. He displayed her, showed her off, and expected her to play the part of corporate wife, lover, and general Martha Stewart model.

She liked the deal they had struck. Her children would come. Her dream of her home was becoming a reality, a reality completely different than the counter-culture vagabond's Ford LTD wagon her parents raised her in. It was more like her grandma's home, a magic place she had visited only a few times: once when the wagon was in the shop and gramps was still alive, once at Christmas after gramps died, and once with Andrew to pick up the few things her grandma had left her.

Today, Andrew was bringing home his new boss, so she hoped grandma would help her kill the spot.

She crouched low, trying to peer into the dark cabinet chasm beneath her sink.

The front lines of her weapons were arrayed in normal formation. Drain clog remover, abrasive chlorine cleanser, ammonia window cleaner, an empty rubber bucket with several grades of stiff and dry sponges inside.

Each weapon had its uses, and each was a weapon she used often. None had ever had any effect on the coffee table spot.

Today, though. Today, she needed something special, something that would really make a difference. She wanted to show the grease spot what was what and who was who.

The black dispose-all canister hung beneath the sink, dark, enigmatic in its incipient power.

She thought how much it was like her, how a flip of the switch could set that little black can's motor spinning, its blades grinding away at whatever fell in, a mindless maw of destruction.

The grease spot had flipped her switch one too many times. Andrew would not bring his new project manager home to see her losing to a spot on the living room coffee table.

She had to get it done before her husband came home. She didn't want him yelling at her in front of his new manager. Of course, she knew she was a little nuts. Andrew wasn't often completely wrong when he yelled at her. He just yelled at her for the wrong reasons.

Beyond the disposal, she kept grandma's bottles and cleansers—in the shadows back with her Pine-Sol, rat poison, roach motels, and collection of lost twisty-ties. There, she had the weapons of her mother's mother hidden in brown bottles and wrapped in oil-paper.

Today, for herself and for Andrew, she would pull out her big guns.

She slipped the useless 4-karat diamond ring from her hand and set it beside the sink. She slid her long, elegant fingers into the protective armor of her rubber cleaning gloves.

Reaching into the darkness, she retrieved the oil-paper package first, placing it gently on the paper towels she had laid out to receive it. Then, she pulled out the two brown bottles. One was quart-sized, brown glass, and stopped with a cork sealed in wax. The second was only the size of an aspirin bottle, but it was the real deal, the spot-death in a bottle. Grandma's own problem solver.

It was the only one that had a label.

In Gram's shaking, loving cursive, the fountain pen lettering gone to faded blue and spread out into the paper, it said, "To set things right, one teaspoon has might. To make things bright and start anew, two will do."

"Thank you, Grams.." Elma put the bottles down on the paper towel next to her oil-paper.

She slipped a butter knife under the folds of the oil-paper wrapping and slit the tape that held it closed. As if ready and waiting for the moment, the paper unfolded almost the whole way.

It pleased Elma to see that her weapons were so happy, so ready to serve. If this worked, Andrew would not complain to his new project manager about her housekeeping tonight.

She carefully unfolded the paper the rest of the way. Inside, a black stone, a square the size of a sponge, waited for her rubber-covered hand.

The butter knife made short work of the wax seals on the bottles. Un-corking, she got a good whiff of the almond and onion smell from the small bottle. A smile came to her before she understood why. That bottle smelled like the love in her grandmother's house.

It wasn't the smell of cigar smoke and whiskey from when the Ford wagon broke down. It was the smell of home and order in the old house on the lane later on, when Elma was older, when she had baked cookies with Grams, after Gramps was gone and lost forever.

She dipped her butter knife into the smaller bottle. A few drops would do. Secret weapons should be used sparingly. The little bottle was only an activator, after all. That, and it provided a scent that didn't offend. Somehow, the almond smell made the onion smell seem sweeter, more soothing.

The first drop hit the black stone. White steam rose from the surface. It didn't surprise her. she'd seen Grams use the stuff once to take a coffee stain, Andrew's, out of her white carpet. No doubt there was still some of Gram's cleaning fluid in the stone. The second drop hit, and Elma was happy. The scent filled the kitchen. The stone changed color from black to deep, cobalt blue.

She nodded, corked the little bottle, then lifted the big one.

Her hand shook, and she was afraid she'd slop some of the precious fluid over the edges of her teaspoon.

She glanced at the microwave clock. Almost three. She still had two hours.

Of course, she'd have to put herself together. That would take some time. Then, there were the canapés and mixed drinks, but she could do that while she had guests. Andrew didn't mind her puttering in the kitchen while he entertained. It looked good for him. It was cleaning while people were in the house that he couldn't abide.

The fluid, red as butchered chicken blood and just as thick, poured into the teaspoon.

Carefully, she poured it onto the black stone.

One would make things right.

Once again would make things bright.

One teaspoon was enough. She only needed right. The stone had already turned white, deep and pearlescent. It seemed to be filled with liquid, with some impossible soapy solution that swirled and whirled just underneath its cold, hard surface.

Just before her grandmother had cleaned that spot from the white carpet, she had smiled, laughed just a little, and raised one of her white eyebrows as if she were sharing an ancient, hidden secret. "Here, Dearie." She held up the pearlescent stone. "This is how it should look if you want to take out a spot."

The stone looked exactly like it had that day. "Perfect," Elma said to the Grandmother she remembered. Carefully, she recorked the bottle and set it aside.

The stain saw her coming. It knew what she was up to. It pulled itself up under the doily, trying to pretend it was gone.

The stone saw it hide, too. It strained in her hand, pulling her toward the stain.

She knelt next to the coffee table. Andrew and she had found it at an antique show.

She fell in love with that table right off. It was just like the one she and Grams had built jigsaw puzzles on. Wide and maple and shining, it had generations of loving use in it.

Andrew hadn't liked the look of it, but he had let her buy it.

Once, after she had it home and accessorized, he had even said it looked nice, that it was "right in the groove." That meant when people visited, they would compliment him on his trendy, retro taste.

She lifted the doily.

The spot tried to be small. The smaller it tried to be, the darker it got.

She touched one corner of the stone to the spot.

The spot stretched, tried to get away, but it was too late. The swirling whiteness of the stone slipped out, surrounded the black blemish, and dragged it back into the stone.

Elma stood. She held the stone in her gloved hand. It quivered and warmed, joyful to have served. The white swirl in the stone mixed with the dark of the grease spot—a twirling, swirling pattern of soapy iridescence and fading brown. After a moment, the coffee stain swirl gave way to white again. A moment later, the stone went black and cold in her hand.

Grams had been something special. Elma thanked her for her love then checked the clock. She had plenty of time.

She returned to the kitchen and carefully returned her weapons to the armory behind the disposal.

The front door opened. Andrew's loud, '*I'm entertaining*' laugh rolled into the house.

Elma smiled. He was in a good mood. Things must be going well with the new manager. She pulled a rack of muffins from the oven and put them on the top of the stove. Elma knew how to please, so she left the oven open so the smell of fresh-baked blueberry muffins filled the house.

Andrew said, "Smells like she's had a Betty Baker day."

A woman laughed—a sharp, cruel laugh.

Surprised, and not prepared for three, Elma removed her apron from the little black tea dress she'd made for herself for days like these. She smoothed the dress, checked her faux pearls in the spotless, reflective surface of the microwave, then headed out to meet her guests.

Entering the living room, Elma froze.

Not guests. No. Andrew's guest.

Even if the woman with Andrew had taken off her heels, she'd have been taller than Elma. Andrew's manager gracefully stripped off her long, leather coat, revealing a sleek LBD that made Elma feel underdressed in her own dress and in her own home. The manager's black hair was brittle from too much time at salons, but it was perfectly behaved, curving around high-cheeks and slightly Asian eyes, as if to yell to the world, look at this perfect face.

Elma tried to like the woman. She gave her points for respecting Elma enough to reapply her lipstick and makeup after a long day at the office. Elma understood that the woman had to project power. That was probably why she wore glossy, Lagrange Lap Dance Red lipstick. It projected expensive, feminine power.

Andrew stood behind her, receiving her coat as the woman stripped it away.

Elma pretended not to notice that he let his hand linger a little too long at the nape of her neck. Since they were a little late, she assumed they had stopped for drinks.

The woman made eye contact with Elma.

Elma couldn't ignore those cold, flint-brown eyes.

The new manager knew that Andrew's hand lingered. She smiled at Elma, savoring Andrew's touch and daring Elma to say anything and turning slightly to show off her fitted, Yves Saint Laurent LBD complimented by matching calf-strapped heels.

Elma tried hard to keep her desire to like the woman. For Andrew, she forced a smile and said, "You must be the new manager."

"You must be the little woman Andrew has told me so much about."

Elma's heart chilled a few more degrees.

Andrew stepped forward and handed Elma the woman's coat. "Come on in, Jen," he said. "Make yourself at home."

Jen nodded. Her cold eyes never left Elma's. "Thanks, Andy. I will."

Jen and *Andy, God, he hated when Elma called him Andy*, pressed past Elma in the foyer. As Andrew passed, Elma's spot-sensitive eyes caught the Lap Dance red embedded in the pores under his lower lip. It wasn't enough to catch anyone else's attention. Clearly, he had worked to rub it away, but Elma's day had honed her eye for evasive spots.

The red spots in Andrew's pores taunted her. The woman's eyes, dress, and heels combined with Andrew's casual hand-off of the leather coat dissolved Elma's desire to like *Jen*, replacing it with full acceptance that Andrew had brought a predator into her home.

When she focused on them, the Lap Dance spots slipped deeper into Andrew's skin, teasing her, telling her she'd never get them out, not as long as she lived, not as long as she was married to Andrew.

By the time Elma served canapés and drinks, Andrew and Jen had soft music playing, and *Andy* was showing *Jen* his collection of antique glass.

Elma served the new boss first, "A dry chardonnay," she said. "Last year was a good year for chardonnay in Nampa Valley."

Jen reached for the offered glass. "Domestic wine?" She touched her strand of real pearls and laughed lightly. "I guess I could try it."

Elma pressed the glass into her hand. A drop splashed out and fell on the thigh of Jen's LBD. "Oh, dear," Elma said.

"Shit." Jen said.

Andrew snapped at her. "Dammit, Elma." He turned to Jen and spoke in soothing tones Elma hadn't heard from him in a couple of years. "We'll have it cleaned for you, Jen."

The woman smiled, but her icy eyes accused Elma. "I have others."

Elma handed Andrew his glass. Unable to restrain herself, she set her thumb to the skin where Lap Dance red hid in his pores.

Carefully kind, she said, "I'm sorry. You have a smudge under your lip."

He shied away from her touch. "What?" His hand came up too quickly, slapped her hand away, and wiped at exactly the right spot.

In superior, ironic tones, Jen said, "I don't see anything."

Elma's switch flipped. Her inner dispose-all started to spin up. She locked eyes with *Jen* and said, "I can get that wine out," she said. "I have something that will make things right."

"You'll only make it worse," Andrew said.

Elma turned her full attention to her husband. "And bright," she said, "to start anew."

Elma headed for the kitchen. She could already smell the pure, sweet almond-and-onion peace that was about to fill her home.

⊐

Dinner, Overlooking the Sea

~ Devan Barlow

When this town seethed with haughty human life
I was merely spinster sister to the woman
whose parties were the most envied invitation
Enough to drive would-be guests
to backstabbing, bribery
even to the summoning
of things better left alone

When the sea monsters first emerged
bearing seaweed and malice
the house was full of guests
Full of prey, yet when the monsters found me
doing dishes (my sister preferred me out of sight)
abyssal eyes met mine
and I was gripped by inexpressible fealty
for all my innermost soul
thrashed against their compulsion

Now, the town's houses are empty
emptier still after my pillaging
I delight in secret stores of unusual oils
threads of saffron, decadent vintages,
but most of all in the cookbooks

so many barely opened,
their sorceries unlearned
before me

Now I cook better than my sister ever did
She relied on the luster of her pearls
and the sharpness of her gossip
to overcome faults in flavor or texture
I cannot leave, but the sea monsters are kind to me
bring me treasures from ships they sink
I've learn to recognize the specifics
of their individual fins and frills

One in particular
sometimes sits with me
flesh-shreds still hanging
from his needlelike teeth
as I sauté, poach, deglaze
crafting delicacies for my own nourishment
He refuses the bites I offer
though occasionally accepts a sip of wine

Tonight, lightning flares
the sky shreds, revealing the truth beyond
I sprinkle dill, grate truffle-curls
upon a plump pilchard
I fill a goblet of ecru bone
from a pilfered jeroboam
and sit upon the balcony
of my sister's house, now mine

To watch the sea
churning
boiling
thrashing
Wondering if tonight
my finned friend will join me again

⬦

A Little God in Their Hands

~ Scotty Milder

Marian Magleby was one of the new ones.

She and her family—husband John, son Ben, daughter Wendy—came down from Salt Lake only a year ago. This was after John took a job as vice-president-of-something-or-other at the boot factory on the way out toward Minersville. The kids started school at Black Mountain Middle and Bradshaw High, respectively, and Marian got on as a part-time bookkeeper at old Dr. Whent's dental practice.

They didn't live in town proper. Vice-president-of-something-or-other meant decent money. Everything in town was double-wides and small Craftsman-style bungalows. If you wanted space to stretch your legs, you had to get out on the old highway and county roads. So that's where the Maglebys went. After a couple weeks of searching, they scooped up the old Brigham place on CR-19.

And they seemed to settle in just fine. The Maglebys were said to be Presbyterians, which was odd for the area but maybe not so odd for folks from up the city, where word was you might even find a Jew or a Muslim if you knew just where to look. There was nowhere in town for them to worship, but they didn't seem to mind overmuch. Everyone agreed that—city folks or no—they were a perfectly nice family.

No one saw much of John Magleby, with his long hours at the factory and all, but he was friendly enough to say hello to if you happened to pass by him at the grocery store. Ben was only twelve, but he was tall and strapping, easy to smile and quick to laugh, always handy with his "yessirs" and his "yes ma'ams." Girls even two years older couldn't seem to keep the blush out of their cheeks when he turned his big brown eyes their way. And he'd already earned a reputation as a power slugger for the Black Mountain Auto Diamondbacks.

Wendy was seventeen, big-breasted and what in the '70s you'd have called "Farrah-Fawcett blond." Rumor had it she ran a little wild.

Nothing for the mothers to worry on too deeply. But with her easy, flirtatious manner and all those low-cut tops, they'd just as soon their boys look elsewhere for dates. They needn't have worried, because Wendy right away attached herself to Ron Baskin's youngest son Chet: a rough leather-jacketed dropout with a permanent glower and a restored 1976 Triumph Bonneville T140. The two of them hung out afternoons and nights at the old Texaco on 130. Chet's brother Nick worked there, and he happily provided them cans of Black Label and hundred-milliliter bottles of Jack Daniels, so long as Doodle Price wasn't around to hassle him.

Wendy might have raised a few eyebrows amongst the pearl clutchers, but everyone liked Marian. She could generally be found most mornings jogging along CR-19's dirt shoulder, waving at cars as they lumbered past. She volunteered with the library's summer BookMobile, a couple afternoons a month at the county no-kill shelter, and taught weekend yoga at the senior center. At Dr. Whent's she mostly stuck with the books, but sometimes—if things were busy or one of the other girls was home sick—she'd go up front and handle the phones. Her smile brightened the office considerably and (while the husbands would never admit this to their wives) she wasn't hard to look at, either. Beauty seemed to run in the Magleby family.

Yep. The Maglebys had settled in fine. Just fine. Everyone liked them. Even (for the most part) Wendy. They were new folks, sure. But sometimes change is good, even in a little frontier town like this.

So it came as a big surprise to everyone when it happened.

It happened the last weekend in May.

The Diamondbacks were out at Brigham's Field putting a solid hurt on the Gene's Roadhouse Tigers. It was bottom of the sixth, and the 'Backs were up five to three. Petey Dodds was pitching for the Tigers, and his day's work was just about done. His elbow screamed and his shoulder felt like someone had been working the joint with a framing hammer. He'd given up three of those five runs in the last inning alone.

The 'Backs weren't letting up. Right up at the top of the inning, Will Parson clipped a worm burner right into the pocket between first and second. It should have been an easy grab for the shortstop,

Ray Smart. If things had gone his way, the Tigers would have started the sixth with an out. But Ray got his feet all tangled up beneath him and he stumbled, letting the ball bounce off the end of his glove. It spun into center field, where big Tommy Dunn was asleep at the switch. By the time Tommy managed to stop blinking at the ball long enough to pick it up and lob it back in, Will had stretched a single out to a triple.

Sam Mapplethorpe flew out to right, and—after nine ugly pitches—Petey finally managed to sit Chris Clarke down. It seemed like maybe he was gonna wiggle out of this jam and end his day—if not on a high—with at least a shred of his dignity intact. But then Cooper Platte caught a piece of the very first pitch and sent a one-hopper right back into Petey's glove. That should have been the easiest throw possible, but Petey was tired and his arm was a boneless pool noodle. He sent the ball sailing over Mack Lunderson's head at first. Mack jumped off the bag and almost caught it—but "almost" is the hardest word to swallow, as Petey's granddad used to say. The ball bounced off the dugout wall and skated up the foul line, where right-fielder Joey Davidson scooped it up. Will Parson scored and Cooper Platte found himself safe at second.

Someone up in the stands made a sharp whooping sound. Petey's stomach sink into his knees. Because that would be Ben Magleby's mom, which meant Ben was stepping up to the plate.

Mr. Colter, the Tigers' coach and younger brother to Gene Colter—whose roadhouse out on 129 gave the team its name—thought for half-a-second about yanking Petey right then. But why bother? The game was pretty much lost, so pulling Petey would only serve two purposes: humiliating his best pitcher unnecessarily, and adding water to the rapid-growing legend of Ben Fucking Magleby.

Petey knew he couldn't out-muscle Ben. If he tried to fire the ball past him, Ben would take him to school. So he tried to outsmart him instead. He'd been cannoning fastballs all day, which was why his arm was pretty much shot. He wasn't confident enough yet in his curveball or his slider to lean on them in any significant way. But desperate times called for desperate measures.

He shook his arm out as best he could and started with another fastball, just a bit high and off the plate. The idea was to (hopefully) lull Ben into a rhythm. Ben watched it go by, looked out at the mound, raised an eyebrow and gave Petey a cocky little smile. The ump was Dr. Whent himself. He croaked "ball!" in his wheezy old-man voice.

Petey put another one in roughly the same place, this time kissing the corner of the plate. Ben almost swung at that one, but checked at the last second.

"Strike one!"

Okay, Petey thought. Got you buttered, fella. Take the bait.

Petey knew he didn't have another fastball in him. If he'd gone for his curve or his slider, things might have worked out. But he tried a changeup instead. The idea was to make it look like the ball was heading to the same general area as the first two pitches, but at three-quarters the speed. If all went well, Ben would swing early and hit nothing but air. But Petey calibrated wrong. Either that, or his arm decided that was the moment to give up the ghost entirely. Instead of shaving off a few miles-per-hour, the ball ambled toward the plate at a much-too leisurely stroll. He might as well have walked it up to Ben and held it there.

Petey knew he was sunk when he heard the thwock. The ball was there one second, then seemed to vanish into thin air. Petey watched the arc of Ben's gaze—along with those of Dr. Whent and the catcher, Sean Mooney—as the ball went up, up, up. Petey didn't even turn to look. He knew he'd be lucky if it didn't make it all the way to the street.

The crowd screamed Ben's name. Someone shouted "bye bye! Bye bye!" at full volume. That would be Ben's mom again. Her voice could shatter glass. Ben jogged the bases, punching the air as he went. Petey sat on the mound and hung his head between his knees. Damnit, he thought. This is gonna follow me FOREVER.

He only looked up when he realized the crowd wasn't screaming Ben's name anymore.

They were just screaming.

Marian Magleby didn't make it to all of Ben's games, but she made it to most. Truth was, she found baseball deadly boring, with its long waits punctuated by flurries of incomprehensible activity. She groused about this occasionally to John, wondering why Ben couldn't have taken to hockey or basketball or something that, you know, moved.

John laughed. "You're looking at it all wrong," he said.

"How?"

"You played soccer in high school, so to you sports are supposed to be an action movie—all running and gunning and big explosions," he said. "Baseball's a Hitchcock movie. Those moments where you think nothing's happening . . . that's when EVERYTHING is happening."

"Oh, Christ." She rolled her eyes.

"No, really," he countered. "At Ben's next game, when he goes up to the plate, look at his eyes. Look at the pitcher's eyes. THAT'S where the action is. It's like two old-west gunfighters facing off at dawn."

"Where'd you get all that," Marian asked. "On the back of a Topps Card?"

"Probably George Will," John said. "Anyway, try it. That stare-down . . . that's the whole game."

She tried it. It didn't work. Baseball remained as inert for her as ever. But she remembered her own high-school days, when she was attacking midfielder on her school's champion soccer team. Her father was a warehouse foreman. He worked ungodly hours and came home dog tired every night. He'd collapse into his chair in front of the TV, turn on CNN, and shut his eyes. He was almost never around for dinner, and breakfast conversations were generally limited to monosyllabic grunts before he opened the Tribune to the sports section and tuned the rest of them out.

But if she'd had a game the day before, he always asked how it went. If she scored, his chapped lips would stretch into a crooked smile and he'd give her a high five. Those high fives meant everything to her. He only made it to two or three games a season—but those were the ones Marian remembered, because of all the noise he made.

So she'd be at Ben's games whenever possible, chanting along with the other parents and cheering Ben's name. A bunch of kids had taken to calling him "Bye-Bye Ben"—a sobriquet stolen from some famous home-run slugger, or so she'd been informed—and she seized onto the nickname with gusto. Whenever he stepped up to the plate she pounded her feet and whooped like an ambulance siren. Whenever he knocked one out past the infield, she jumped up and down and chanted "bye bye! Bye bye!" like an overexcited groupie. Maybe it was unseemly or unsportsmanlike. Marian didn't care. That was her kid, goddamnit, and she was going to make sure he knew she was there. That she'd seen him.

None of the other parents seemed to mind. Her antics provoked nothing sharper than a one or two side-mouthed comments and a few indulgent smiles. Everyone liked Marian Magleby.

For his part, if Ben was embarrassed by her enthusiasm, he never showed it.

It was Candy Platte—mother of Cooper—who noticed that something was wrong. She sat on the bleacher in front of Marian and clapped dutifully as she watched the ball sail over the back fence and bong off the hood of Darcy Clarke's almost-new Elantra. Candy's own son moonwalked across home plate like the charming little shit he was. He spun, grinning, and his teammates swarmed him like a litter of excited puppies. Sean Mooney knocked back his catcher's mask and wisely got out of their way.

Marian screeched behind Candy: "Bye bye! Bye bye!"

Poor Petey Dodds sat on the mound and hung his head between his knees. Candy's heart went out to him. Petey was a solid pitcher, but if he didn't start taking care of that shoulder it would be a mess of scar tissue by the time he got out of his teens.

"Bye bye! Bye bye!"

Ben Magleby rounded third and loped good-naturedly toward home plate. His teammates left Cooper to bask in his reflected glory and thronged around Ben, who was the real hero of the day. They jumped up and down and shouted. Ben grinned ear-to-ear. The Tigers shuffled their feet and looked on impassively, not quite daring to scowl.

"Bye bye! Bye BYEEEEEEEEEEEEEEEEEE—!"

Marian's voice cycled up suddenly, like a slipped serpentine belt in an old car. Candy turned, at first only curious and slightly annoyed. She was gonna say something smartass like *Jeez, Marian, it's not like he lobbed one off of Randy Johnson or something.*

But then she saw it.

Marian wore a light dress that flapped around her hips in the late-spring breeze. Her hair was pulled up in a bun beneath a big floppy straw hat. The hat mostly shadowed her face, but Candy could see the way her spit-slick teeth tore out of the relative darkness like the reaching blades of a thresher. She couldn't make out much of the rest of Marian's face, but in the shadows she sensed it shifting, pulling in on itself like it was trying to turn inside out. The bare skin of her shoulders and collarbone had gone white and waxy and, as Candy watched, shrank against Marian's bones like a vacuum-seal bag.

"—EEEEEEEEEEEEEEEEEEEE—!"

Marian started to vibrate. Tendons stood out on her neck like tram cables. The hat tipped off, spilling out tangles of hair that were rapidly going from shimmering blond to a bleached, brittle white.

"—EEEEEEEEEEEEEEEEEEEEEE—!"

Now the others saw it, too. They stopped chanting Ben's name. Sheila Dodds, Darcy Clarke, and Jill Parson started screaming, but the others just exchanged furtive, guilty looks. They all knew what this meant.

Marian's face was like a mummified skull. Cheeks hollowed out and skin pulled taut against sharp cheekbones. Her eyes filled with blood and plunked back into their sockets. Lips thinned and ripped open, disgorging a green-yellow pus that smeared across blackening gums. Teeth jutted from the rot like meathooks.

Marian's arms speared out, the fingers hooking into claws. One of them grabbed desperately at Candy's shoulder and squeezed. The heat in that grip was astounding. Marian's red eyes found Candy and, in there, Candy could see the horrid and final understanding. She winced and pulled away.

"Shoot," someone said. A man. Candy thought it was Ray Smart's father, Dale. "We better get her out of here before the kid sees."

Marian's voice had faded to a hiss. Her bladder let go, darkening the front of her dress. Doreen Dodds, Sheila's sister, tossed a knitted blanket over Marion's head. She and Dale grabbed Marion by the hips and whisked her away.

Candy looked out into the field. Petey gazed up at them from the mound, his brow furrowed, but the other kids didn't seem to have noticed anything. Ben was over by the dugout, still grinning and high-fiving his teammates.

Poor kid, Candy thought, and wondered what they were going to do about him. About all the Maglebys.

But that was a call for the Mayor.

○

"I'm telling you, it's a front."

Wendy's gaze drifted past the steering wheel to the flat white steeple of the Mormon church, stabbing into the crystal blue sky beyond the pines.

"Come on," she said.

"I'm telling you," Chet said. "No one in this town is an actual Mormon."

They were on their way to the Texaco in Wendy's battered ten-year-old Corolla, because Chet had laid his Triumph over two days ago and tore something in the suspension. The bike was currently on stilts in his garage, waiting for a part. Chet's left leg was swaddled in bandages beneath the knee.

"What do you mean?"

"They're pretending," he said.

Wendy frowned. Chet had a weird sense of humor and an imagination that sometimes spiraled off into baroque flights of fancy. They'd been doing whatever it was they were doing (he refused to call her his girlfriend) for eight months now, and she was just now getting to the point where she thought maybe she could read him. When he was tall-taling, his mouth got this slightly pinched look and his eyes starting bouncing around like balls in a bingo cage. But right now his face was a smooth blank as he gazed past her toward the steeple. With his leather jacket and slicked-back pompadour, he had the look of a classic 1950s juvenile delinquent: a slightly gangly, slightly buck-toothed James Dean. The black-framed glasses and their coke-bottle lenses spoiled the illusion. He was sensitive about them, but she liked the look. She thought the glasses made him look kinda punk rock.

Right now his blue eyes were pensive, magnified behind the lenses.

"What do you mean, 'pretending?'" She asked.

He tore his eyes away from the steeple, glanced at her, then looked away. This whole conversation was starting to bother her, because he was acting like there was something he wasn't willing to tell her. If it was as simple as maaaan, they're all goddamned HYPOCRITES, he would just say that. In fact had, about his own mother and father and tight-assed older sister. The only member of his family who ever escaped the spray of his contempt was his brother, and that was only because he gave them booze.

"You ever go by the church on a Sunday morning?" Chet asked finally.

"Yeah," Wendy said. "It's on the way to work." Work wasn't work exactly. Wendy was a candy striper at the county health clinic over on Lamar. Two weekends a month. Her dad thought it would look good on college applications.

"Notice anything about the parking lot?"

"Sure," she said. "It's always full. Seems like they're all pretty Mormon to me."

"Yeah, and if you go in there you'll have full pews and Bishop Petersen doing the Sunday service. All the good little Saints will be partaking the sacrament and singing their hymns, Firm as the Mountains Around Us, Put Your Shoulder to the Wheel, How Firm a Foundation, the whole fucking deal."

"Okay. So?"

"So they gotta keep up appearances."

"Appearances for what? What the hell are you talking about?"

"In case someone drops in," Chet said. "An outsider."

"Jesus," Wendy said. "You're making it sound like the mafia or something—"

"Nah, it's way worse than that. You ever notice the building behind the church?"

Wendy thought. The church was at the corner of Milford and LaVern. There was a strip mall across the street, with the Krazy Kut and the butcher shop and Nan's Sewing Shoppe. Catty-corner to the church was the old Blockbuster, vacant (according to Chet) for well over a decade now. And behind it . . .

"It's that gray building," she said. "The one with the metal siding. Right?"

"Right."

The steeple whipped by on their left. Now there was nothing but a wall of trees on either side of the road, revealing the occasional flash of a building over on Milford. The road rose briefly and then sloped downward toward the stop sign at Larsen. Someone walked along the shoulder, back to them: a man, tall and gangly, wearing a long overcoat.

"Next time you go by," Chet said, "take a look at that building. It's supposed to be an auto body shop, I guess. But it's been there as long as I've been around and I don't know a single person who's ever taken their car there."

As the Corolla approached, the man on the shoulder spun and stuck out his thumb. Wendy had a quick impression of a coat that was some undefinable, vaguely nauseating color, a narrow and hairless head, a too-wide grin. And then he was past. Wendy tapped the brake as the Corolla rolled toward the stop sign.

"The church parking lot will be full, sure. But so will that other place. You'll see Doctor Whent's car parked there, next to Sheriff Kimball's Range Rover and Mayor Throckmorton's Caddie. A few others. Town bigwigs and shit."

"Maybe they just park there because of church overflow—"

"Yeah, except I've been to services there and I've never seen a one of them."

"Okay," Wendy said. "So that gray building, the auto body place or whatever, it's like a clubhouse. The menfolk gather there and, I don't know, drink caffeine-free Pepsi and gossip like my mom and her quilting friends at Nans and make all their backroom deals, while the faithful sit up front singing their Saintly little hearts out."

"Sure," Chet said. "You go right on believing that."

"None of this is very convincing," she said.

He grunted. She accelerated through the intersection and threw him a glance. There it was again: that far-off, pensive look. That wall.

"I'm just saying," he said carefully, "that when you graduate we should get the fuck out of—"

His words were cut off by the sudden scream of a siren. Wendy's eyes snapped to the rearview mirror, where a police cruiser raced down the hill, lights flashing.

Wendy hit her blinker. The Corolla drifted to the shoulder.

The cruiser shot past. Wendy expected it to keep going, hurrying to whatever emergency was unfolding around the next bend. Instead it veered onto the shoulder and stopped.

Chet stiffened, peering out the windshield with narrowed eyes. His hand drifted toward the door handle.

"Chet," Wendy said. "Chill. It's okay."

He licked his lips and said nothing.

She heard the twin *ka-THUNK*s of car doors slamming. Two cops strode toward the Corolla. The one in the lead was Doodle Price. Young and blandly handsome, if a little doughy; Wendy was surprised by how pasty he looked in the daylight. Three nights out of every five, he could be counted on to swing by the Texaco and harass them. He was constantly threatening to arrest them for underage drinking, but he somehow never got around to it. She'd asked Chet why everyone called him Doodle; he looked back at her with wide eyes and said that's his actual name. His parents must have fucking hated him all the way back to the womb.

"See?" She said. "It's just Doodle."

Chet didn't respond.

Wendy didn't recognize the other cop. He was older, as long and straight as a board, with a pock-marked disaster of a face. His hair was shimmery black.

Doodle and the other cop stopped by the Corolla's headlights, Doodle on the driver's side and the other cop on the passenger's. Wendy noticed Doodle had his hand on the butt of his Glock. She looked at the other cop and saw he held a shotgun, the barrel aimed loosely toward the ground. She felt a stab of fear, but a desperately rational voice droned in the back of her mind: it's a misunderstanding, just a misunderstanding . . .

"Wendy!" Doodle called out, his voice reaching for booming and falling short. "Wendy Magleby!"

She rolled down her window.

"Yeah, Doodle, you know it's me. What the hell's going on? We haven't even been to the Texac—"

"I need you to step out of the car, please."

"Don't," Chet whispered.

She turned to say something to him—stop being weird, or something along those lines—but the sheet-white terror that splashed across his features stopped her. She felt another stab of fear, this one burrowing into the center of her chest like a drill.

"Wendy," Doodle continued, his voice eminently reasonable. "Come on, now."

Chet looked at her. "Hit the gas," He said. "Floor it."

Easy for him to say. Everyone knew Chet Baskin was going nowhere fast. Jail for him would be a few nights on a stiff cot, then back to business as usual. But Wendy had plans. She was going to college. Chet was a good-for-now distraction, but she wasn't going to throw her future away because he got squirrelly around cops.

"Just sit tight," she said, and opened her door. "I'm sure it's nothing."

She opened the door and stood. Doodle was already moving toward her. The black-haired cop had his eyes on Chet.

"Doodle, what the hell's going on?"

"I need you to come with me," Doodle said, and—amazed—she saw he was reaching for his handcuffs.

Another ka-THUNK, this one off to her right. "Sir!" The black-haired cop said sharply. "No one told you to get out of the car!"

Wendy tried to cringe behind her open door as Doodle gripped her shoulder and tried to maneuver her around.

"Sir!" Black Hair yelled, and Wendy watched him whip the shotgun up. "Drop the weapon! Now!"

Everything that came after seemed to happen step-by-step, in agonizing slow motion:

Step one: Wendy looked across the Corolla's roof.

Step two: Chet pointed a snub-nosed revolver at Doodle. It was the one he always carried in an ankle holster. She'd completely forgotten about it.

Step three: Doodle's hand plunged into Wendy's hair to the scalp, balled itself into a fist, yanked.

Step four: Black Hair's shotgun went BOOM. The left half of Chet's face exploded in a geyser of blood, muscle, and ribbons of white-yellow fat. Teeth clattered across the Corolla's roof in a spray of viscera. The revolver went flying.

Someone somewhere was screaming. Wendy understood that it was her, but only in a distant and vaguely clinical way. Her gaze irised down to a tight circle, focused in on that red spray across white paint, the three glistening teeth in the middle of it.

She caught one last look at Chet before he fell. A gaping cavern had opened in his skull. Bits of skull rimmed it like serrated teeth. Inside that cavern was a mangled, glistening pinkness that she understood was what was left of his brain. The left eye was gone—along with everything else on that side of his face—but the right eye found her. It looked strange now that the glasses were blown away. Small. Insignificant. She saw nothing in it.

Then he slid out of sight and hit the pavement with a potato-sack thump.

Doodle yanked again, pulling her off her feet this time. As she sprawled to the asphalt—still screaming—her eyes caught a flash of something black and shiny in his other hand. She had just time enough to think the fuck—? before that hand buried itself in her gut. She heard another BOOM, this one smaller and sharper than the shotgun. An almost pleasant warmth oozed through her belly.

Then the warmth turned into hot, metallic agony, and as Doodle dragged her—choking, crying—across the blacktop and shoved her face-first into the back of the cruiser, all she could taste was blood and bile.

Night.

A man lurked on the walkway between the Krazy Kut and Nan's Sewing Shoppe. Mayor Throckmorton's headlights washed over him as his Caddy rolled up to the stop sign at Milford and LaVern. The lights teased the man out of the darkness and pinned him to the strip mall's brick wall like a bug.

The man swayed drunkenly, his back to the street. He wore a long, indeterminately colored coat. One hand was splayed across the brick in front of him like a starfish.

The guy was probably taking a leak. Throckmorton wrinkled his nose in disgust. If he'd ridden over with Sheriff Kimball, he could imagine Kimball flipping the lights on and letting loose a whoop! of the siren, then pulling into the lot to figure out what the guy's story was. He had the look of a drunk for sure. Maybe even a drifter. Kimball wouldn't want to wake up the next morning to a flood of messages about broken windows and emptied-out cash registers.

But no, not tonight.

Tonight they had more important things to deal with.

What mess the day had turned out to be.

So Throckmorton rolled through the intersection. His headlights slid past the man and let him fall back into the night's yawning blackness. The Caddy passed the church and turned into the auto-body shop parking lot.

Kimball was already there, leaning against the cruiser's hood and smoking a cigarette. He was still dressed in his khaki uniform. The many folds of his face seemed to catch every single one of the night's shadows.

"Heck of a thing," Throckmorton said after heaving his bulk out of the Caddy. He straightened his black toupee without even thinking about it. "Heck of a goshdarned thing. And we're sure it's what we think it is?"

Kimball nodded. "I saw her with my own two eyes. Gibbering and drooling and pissing herself. Two of her fingers plum came off in Doreen Dodds' hand as they took her below." He flicked the cigarette, and they both watched it explode across the pavement. "Jumping Jesus Christ, what a fucking cockup."

Throckmorton frowned disapprovingly. He knew that would amuse Kimball, but he couldn't help himself. Even here in the dead of night—knowing what he knew and doing what they were doing— Throckmorton couldn't seem to drop the good-Mormon routine. "Well. Maybe we got her over here in time."

Kimball nodded toward the street.

"You see that fella over there as you were pulling up?" He asked.

"In front of the Krazy Kut? Yeah I—"

The words bound up in Throckmorton's throat as the truth slammed into him. He spun on his heel and peered into the darkness. He could see the hulking outline of the strip mall beneath the oily coin of the moon. But if the man was still there, the shadows concealed him.

Still, Throckmorton could imagine the grin: far too wide, with gray teeth like chisels and a serpent's forked and searching tongue. He'd been looking at that grin in etchings, doodles, and faded wood-cut prints his entire life.

"Darn," he whispered reverently. "That was Him?"

"Pretty sure," Kimball said. "We got a few reports after . . . after the shitshow at the ballpark was pretty much done with. A couple kids saw him in that field down near the elementary school. And Darcy Clarke said she saw him walking along the shoulder over on LaVern. Said she wasn't sure until he turned and looked at her and she caught sight of his face."

"Oh my oh my," Throckmorton said. He continued to gaze into the blackness, willed the man-shaped being to step out into the glow of the streetlamp where he could get a better look. Throckmorton had only seen Him once before when he was a child, and at a distance. It was a sight that still crept up on him sometimes in dreams.

And now he thought he felt something, a pulse of buzzing energy slithering out of the dark. It settled into his eyeballs and made them itch, way back by the stem. He felt an inexplicable yearning to see, but beneath that was the familiar fear.

"We best get in there and finish up," Kimball said. "If He's out in the open, that means He's all fired up. Impatient. We don't hurry, He might go ahead and grab Hisself another."

"Yes," Throckmorton said, and forced himself to wrench his eyes away from all that darkness. His mouth had gone sandpaper dry. "Yes. We wouldn't want that. Lead the way, Sheriff."

Kimball unhooked his keys from his belt and went to the shop's roll-up door.

Throckmorton's right hand slipped into the pocket of his sport coat. His sweaty fingers wrapped around something hard, rough, vaguely cylindrical. The feel of the thing wasn't exactly comforting— how could it be?—but it steadied him regardless. It reminded him that he didn't have a choice. None of them did.

The door rattled into the ceiling and stopped with a bang. Kimball hit the light switch. Fluorescents buzzed and flickered, casting out dust swirls of sickly greenish light. They didn't entirely dispel the shadows, but rather pushed them back into corners where they crouched predatorily, like watchful creatures waiting to pounce.

It wasn't an auto-body shop. Of course it wasn't. There were four bare walls sheeted in corrugated steel. Open rafters from which lights and cobwebs hung. An uneven concrete floor, its surface marred by black lightning-bolt cracks and ancient, mysterious stains.

A trapezoidal pit sunk into the middle of the floor, covered imperfectly by a square of warped plywood. Laid out on the left side of the pit were John, Ben, and Wendy Magleby. Wendy's glassy eyes looked black in the thin light. Her white tank top was red from the abdomen up to just under her ample bosoms. Throckmorton wasn't quite a dirty old man, but he also wasn't so proud that he hadn't helped himself to a longing look at those bosoms the few times he and Wendy had happened to cross paths. Seeing them now—empty and useless bags of cold flesh, forever-now sheathed in blood-spattered fabric— made his stomach turn over.

John was still wearing his shirt and tie. One of his shoes had gone missing, exposing the sort of plain brown socks your wife picks out for you twice a year at Walmart. There was a round, red hole in his left temple, a jagged and bony cavern in his right. His mouth hung open in an "O" of permanent startlement. His left eye had rolled back in his skull. The right had gone bright red with blood.

Compared to his dad and his sister, Ben looked relatively peaceful. He wore his green-and-gold Black Mountain Auto Diamondbacks uniform. His eyes were closed and his arms lay symmetrical at his sides. Throckmorton saw no visible wounds.

Two plastic buckets sat across from them, on the other side of the pit. Each was half-filled with a foul-smelling, pinkish tallow.

"How'd it go?" Throckmorton asked.

Kimball looked at him, surprised, then tipped him an amused little grin. "What, you want the details?"

Throckmorton felt his cheeks redden. "You don't need to go into every bloody one," he growled. "I just want to know if we're in for any kinda shucks from the Staties."

"I can't say anything about the Staties, not yet," Kimball said. "But it went as well as it could've, I guess, considering these folks didn't know what was coming. Doodle Price and Dave Stoddard did for the girl. That went tits up when old Ron Baskin's youngest Chet tried to get in the middle of it. Dave had to put him down, too."

"Oh no," Throckmorton said, aghast. Ron was part of his Tuesday-night bridge group.

Kimball shrugged, unbothered. "I went over to talk to Ron personally and explain what's what. He didn't complain any. Just said he knew Chet was stupid, but had no idea he was that stupid."

Still, Throckmorton thought, thinking of little Chet running around the Baskins' front yard when he was a toddler, grinning and showing off his plastic shovel like it was the Treasure of the Sierra Madre. It's a real darned shame.

"Merle Kondracke did for John," Kimball continued. "Said the poor fella never knew what hit him. They were at lunch over at the factory, and Merle said 'hey John, come out to my car with me, I wanna show you my new fly-fishing rig.' John went with him, and while he was oohing and ahhing over Merle's new Loomis rod, Merle just came up behind him and—" Kimball made a finger gun and a pop sound with his cheek. Throckmorton scowled. He didn't understand why the sheriff had to be so goshdarned . . . cavalier . . . about everything.

"I guess it was Dale Smart did for the boy," Kimball said. "They told him his ma had taken sick, and offered to drive him home after the game. Once they got him into Dale's truck, Dale took care of him with his belt."

"My oh my," Throckmorton said. He didn't want to think about what the boy must've been thinking in those final moments. How scared and bewildered he must've been.

"Anyhoo. I guess we best get on with it," Kimball said. He was already unbuttoning his shirt. "You ready?"

"As I'm like to be," Throckmorton said dismally. He knew it was selfish, but he hated this part most of all: the grease, the opaque words and half-understood rituals to be conducted by the two town elders in the stinking darkness below. The (hopeful) closing of a circle that would yet again fly open. It was all so meaningless. But if they didn't do it—if they refused, like their ancestors had once tried—who knew what He would do? The tales of His wrath were scattershot and flecked with fictions. But Throckmorton had no doubt the truth of it would be bloody and vile.

He pulled the cylindrical object from his pocket and shrugged off his jacket.

Minutes later their clothes sat near the door in neatly folded piles, and the two men knelt naked before the pit. Kimball had pushed the plywood away, exposing the narrow tunnel and uneven stairs hacked from bedrock. Beyond the tenth riser, it was all just darkness down there, coughing up the bitter smell of old charcoal. Throckmorton was glad for that, because it almost covered the stench of blood and shit that was rolling off the Maglebys.

Along with that charcoal smell came the laughter, high and shrieking. It echoed up out of the pit, ricocheting off itself in a crystalline cascade of sound.

"She went down willing enough," Kimball said. "Like she already knew where to go."

Throckmorton nodded. Most of them He touched were like that. He burned everything essential about them away and directed their shattered minds toward a single, unknowable purpose.

The laughter died off to a few gasping chuckles, then came back in a bright explosion. It sounded nearly human—nearly like a woman— but not quite. By tomorrow, he knew, it wouldn't even sound like laughter. In a week it would be gone altogether. And the thing that had been Marian Magleby would blindly wander that darkness for time eternal.

Throckmorton looked down at the thing in his hands. He rubbed his thumb over its oil-stained surface. His own father had carved it out of a plug of yellow cedar three generations ago, back when the mayor was just a boy still in his nappies. The figure was vaguely human but purposefully disproportioned, with sticklike legs and insectile arms crossed over a narrow, concave chest. Once upon a time the ribs were visible along that chest, but seventy years of handling had rubbed them—and most of the other features—away.

If the thing ever had a face, it was long gone too. But the wide brown smile was still there, formed as it was from a knot in the wood. It gaped crookedly at Throckmorton, and he thought about the man across the street. Wondered if He was still there. If maybe they'd see Him before they were through.

We ain't meant to love Him, Throckmorton's father had said. Throckmorton couldn't remember for sure, but he thought it was one time when they were trout fishing out at Robinson-Tanner Reservoir. We ain't meant to be ascairt of Him neither, exactly. He ain't that kind of god. What we're meant to do, I suppose, is just keep payin' Him tribute so He knows we know He's still there. And what He can do to us if'n we ever forget. I don't think there's that much more purpose in it than that.

"Come on," Kimball said, snapping Throckmorton out of his reverie. The sheriff slid the other bucket across the concrete. The rendered animal smell of the stuff inside made Throckmorton reel back. "And set that thing aside. You know you can't take it down there with us."

The sheriff was already reaching into his own bucket and smearing glops of the stuff across his chest. Soon both of them would be covered all the way from the soles of their feet to their scalp. And Throckmorton knew, from past experience, that it would be a month before the smell had entirely left his nostrils.

Throckmorton set the idol aside and reached into the bucket. As he covered himself, he thought about the Maglebys. The folks in this town knew what was what. Their ancestors found this little valley and settled it in the 1850s, back when they were all still Mormon and the biggest threat they ever thought they'd face were the Missouri militias. They found this valley, and before long they found what came with it, and by then it was too late to leave. He made it clear that He wouldn't allow it.

And in the generations since, He'd only ever taken from town stock. Newcomers came and newcomers went, and as far as Throckmorton knew none of them ever had a clue what was really happening here. A few of them might have sensed something—folks gone missing, other folks not seeming too concerned about it—but they generally moved on before they stumbled anywhere near the truth.

But now He'd taken a newcomer, and because of that Throckmorton was forced to make the call that they had to do for the entire family. Because John Magleby was not like to be as sanguine as Ron Baskin when the facts of what happened to his wife were explained to him.

What next? There'd be more family up in Salt Lake or beyond, and they'd want answers. There'd be state investigators, maybe even Feds.

Throckmorton didn't want to imagine what He could do to all of them if He wanted.

"In your name, oh Agony of Mankind," Kimball intoned as he stood. Throckmorton lurched to his feet, cursing his bum knee on the way up. "We have brought to you your Tribute. Oh He, the Disease of Winds, we pray that you find in our offerings a rich delight."

"Oh He," Throckmorton agreed, nodding. "Oh yes, He."

Kimball glanced at the bodies, then at Throckmorton. "I'll get Doodle over here later to take care of them," he said. "Any Staties come sniffing, none of 'em will be the wiser. Now let's get this over with."

He started down the steps.

"Oh He," he said as he descended. "Oh He. Oh He . . . "

Throckmorton followed. The chill from below licked at his exposed calves. The Magleby woman had started her laughing again. Except now it sounded like screaming.

"Oh He," Throckmorton said as the darkness swallowed him. "Oh He . . . "

⊠

The Great Cosmic Itch

~ Maxwell I. Gold

Bits and scratches along the fringes, begged my body to wonder, to scream at the night—yearning for the bleak-barking operas whose notes howled into the Void. Urges too great to resist, unable to comport my sanity, or what remained of it, into something else other than bits and scratches which had to be purged, wretched from existence, and my body, pitched into the dank, sweaty abysm below. Every night for as long as I was able to recall, fringe-fingers like the tongues of stars teased my tired mind their bristled cilia pushing me towards the edge of catastrophe, hoping I might lift the bedsheets of reality.

No, I can't—though the blood soon followed like tiny levies, forever breached, unable to hold back my fluid erubescence; the smells and lights blurred into a singular column of wild, ecstasy bemused by my unadulterated and dreadful curiosity. Bits and skins, and brain-bile soon fell like the old stars all over my sad peripheries whereupon I begged the endless scratches to stop, as if I were clawing the innards of infinity, prepared to rip the weak sac of creation, laughing as it ruptured across everything and nothing at the same time.

Yes, I can—anything to stop the dread-silence of shadows which caressed my cheek every night while I peered beyond the tattered and worn out dark draperies to finally see the other side of catastrophe.

◇

Wet Dreams in R'lyeh

~ Remy Nakamura

You were having such a wonderful dream. So different from your earlier, troubled sleep. Why rise, when you can descend into the delightful deep?

Anaheim, Present

Tony R promised things would go swimmingly. It wasn't really breaking and entering, not when he had somehow obtained the key. And it was an empty ranch home, and we were just three harmless ex-cultists in gray Dickies jumpsuits. The two team members who couldn't pass as human, Minnie the crustacean-like, brain-~~stealing~~saving Mi-Go, and ZeroRaven—our six-foot tall albino penguin—stayed hidden in the Cox Cable van, where hopefully Minnie kept her fungal stalks on the alert for trouble and Zero had one webbed foot on the gas.

Tony R opened the front door and Punch and I entered. A wave of horror washed over us. This home had clearly not been remodeled since the seventies. How was that drab olive wallpaper ever a thing? While I looked with disgust at the mustard yellow upholstery, a dozen cultists sprang out of nowhere, yelling "Cthulhu fhtagn," throwing f-bombs, tripping on their robes, and hitting us and each other with pepper spray and tasers.

DC, Two Days Ago

We should've known something was up when Tony R played the *Mission:Impossible Theme* on his iPhone. The whole crew was there for the debrief, sitting on second-hand furniture in our HQ's living room: ZeroRaven, slumped on the La-Z-Boy in his mirrorshades; Minnie, the crow-sized alien from Yuggoth, looking like a bat-winged long-legged lobster with a patch of writhing enoki mushrooms where a loving god might put a face and/or head; and finally, Punch, in all their cerulean blue-haired, spiked-pierced-tattooed wonder. Punch usually sported a neck bandana when they went out, but in the safety of our run down Capitol Hill Victorian they could let their gills out.

These were my people. Surrounded by these lovely weirdos, I felt almost normal.

Tony R, on the other hand, reminded me just a teensy bit of the toxic cismen I'd left behind in my NPD uncle's off-brand offshoot Mormon sect, with their public-facing, never-fading smiles. That said, Tony R was different in that he never got mean or other kinds of scary behind the scenes. And he had rescued each of us, not just me: ZeroRaven from some lost city in the Antarctic; Minnie, exiled by her people and left for starving, and Punch from that secret Dagon sect in Kyushu. Back in the day, Tony R himself had been a serial cultist—Cthulhu, NXIVM, QAnon—before the Anti-Cult League Worldwide showed up.

He shone his perpetually gleaming porcelain grin down at us. In spite of his reassurances, this mission felt more like the couple of times we had to snatch and grab kids from especially heinous hard-core groups, ones into human trafficking and sacrifice and worse.

"Good morning, associates," he said as he pulled up a PowerPoint on the TV. "Our next project: to help contain a Cthulhu cult."

"Where we headed? R'lyeh?" asked Punch. Punch had history with ocean-dwelling Elder Gods.

"Orange County, California. If all goes well, I bet the higher ups could swing us some day passes to Disney!"

We had never met anyone from the ACLW hierarchy or from other cells. Tony R said this was compartmentalization for everyone's safety. Tony R clicked through the slides.

"We have solid intel that this safehouse will be unoccupied for one day. We go in, plant some bugs, tiny surveillance cams and signal repeaters, and we're done!"

"This sounds like black ops," said Punch. "You promised we'd never touch black ops." The rest of us weren't great at speaking up, but Punch was right. We mostly helped ex-cultists learn to wear things that weren't robes and otherwise adjust to normal society.

"Punch, I hear your concerns," Tony R said. "But I assure you this is extremely low risk. It's almost more dangerous to sit here at home! And the other units are on sensitive jobs where lives are at stake. This is our opportunity to show the ACLW that we're team players."

Punch clenched their teeth. Their cheekbones and jawline cut such nice Euclidean geometries. I imagined tracing my fingers along those lines. They smirked and raised an eyebrow at me, and I pretended to stare at the ugly peeling wallpaper over their shoulder.

I cornered Tony R afterwards.

"About this job," I stammered. I really sucked at raising objections. A people-pleaser to a fault, that's me.

"Ivy," Tony R grabbed my shoulder. I knew he was trying to be friendly, but I really wished he wouldn't do that. "Remember when we first met?"

Yeah," I said, feeling immediately guilty.

This was a thing he did. It had the effect of shutting me down. I didn't like it, but what could I do? I mean, he did save me. And the ACLW helped me start a new life. They gave me a roof over my head, a job helping former cultists, insurance that paid for my HRT and surgeries *and* weekly therapy. Most importantly, I had a new community of broken people who welcomed me in all my broken glory.

"Keep an eye out for Punch," Tony R smiled but his eyes narrowed. "I'm not saying that they'd do anything, but there are ties between Dagon and Cthulhu. Let me know if you notice anything. For Punch's sake."

Holy crapola. Could some residual feels for the fishy cult explain Punch's hesitation?

Tony R patted my shoulder. "Keep this between us, yeah? I know I can count on you." In spite of myself, I couldn't help but feel like someone called me a good doggo. If I had a tail it would be wagging.

Present, Anaheim

Punch is ready for them. Me? I'm cowering in the shadows, useless as ever. I'm not sure if super-strength is a Deep Ones stereotype, but Punch tosses cultists over ugly yellow couches and into china cabinets full of tchotchkes. On top of the fear and adrenaline is the thrill of watching Punch in action. They clock two more cultists in the face with their metal toolbox—*One! Two!*—before going down in a pile of black hooded robes. Tony R is shouting orders *at the cultists.* How is that two-faced jerk still smiling? I must be screaming because he turns his wild, frenzied look my way and points and yells, and suddenly the cultists are on me and everything goes black.

Two Days Ago, DC

Minnie and I shared a large attic room. For all her alien-mushroom-crustacean-insectoid appearance, telepathic and empathic communicating, and her weird hobby of creating brain jars for little critters, I liked Minnie. She was that kind of weird that the world either really took notice of, or she was too weird to acknowledge so they mostly ignored her.

"Owwww," I yelled, resisting the urge to kick or stomp at the thing that shocked me.

Minnie buzzed warning and caution feelings into my brain. I kept my feet very still.

Sure enough, in the doorway were several robot beetles, looking like uncased USB sticks with paper clips for legs. Each one had a tiny brain jar and metal pincers that sparked with electricity.

Minnie's main hobby was rescuing the brains from tiny critters who would otherwise die, and putting them in tiny cyborg bodies. This included a family of dormice, rescued from traps (which we've since stopped placing); birds who fell victim to cats or windows, their brain jars hovering in $80 mini-drones from Amazon; and a handful of insects and arachnids, some presumably testing their cute new powers of shock and awwww at my feet.

Mi-Go were notorious for removing brains from their owners without consent. They kicked Minnie out because she stood up for their victims. She had gifted all these lowly beings quasi immortality in their thimble-sized brain jars and new robotic bodies—as long as the rest of us watch where we step when we stumble to the bathroom late at night.

Minnie only looked monstrous on the outside. The worst monsters hid behind smiling facades.

Present, Anaheim

When I come to, Tony R is grinning at me. He steps back. I'm in a bedroom with soundproofing panels covering every inch of the walls. To my right, a couple of cultists sit in front of a half-dozen monitors, clicking on keyboards and D-pads and sipping on Monster Energy and Mountain Dew. It smells like old sweat, electrified plastic, and stale vomit. I can't move.

Facing me, Punch groans. They're strapped into to some kind of dentist's chair. They're wearing a metal colander contraption on their head with a bunch of wires coming out, and I realize that for the first time ever, we must be matchy-matchy.

We are in deep doo doo.

Tony R starts to speak but is interrupted by Punch.

"Fuck you, we didn't ask you to villainsplain."

Tony R hits Punch in the gut. I see stars and we hyperventilate together. The machines must be connecting us. Tony R's smile never breaks.

"The sea drones need a couple of minutes to reach their destination. Humor me."

The videos on the monitors show structures on the ocean floor. The buildings looke distorted, like we're seeing them through fun house mirrors in constant motion. The surfaces glisten like oil sheen on fetid water, or like Munsch painted them with The Scream, only subliminally and with thousands of trapped souls.

"Oh," I said. "*That* place."

DCA to LAX, One Day Ago

Punch and I sat next to each other on the flight. They were experimenting with manspreading while I tried to sit demurely. Our legs touched and I forgot my clenched grip as we climbed in fits and lurches towards cruising altitude.

I worried over Tony R's words like a sore tooth. I leaned over and said just above the engine roar, "He wouldn't steer us wrong."

Punch put one hand on my arm and looked at me with an intense stare. I wasn't sure whether to look away or hold that gaze so I played it cool and alternated rapidly between both.

"I don't know about Tony R, but we're survivors, Ivy, you and me. Minnie and Zero, too. Your therapists go on about how you need to unlearn unhealthy patterns, and I get that, but trust your instincts, too. Tony R came for you in that podunk little town in Idaho, but you chose to leave. You were ready. And you deserve credit for that."

Punch leaned back, strong chin in their strong hand, lost in thought.

"We deserve credit for that."

Present, Anaheim

"Next, the unveiling!" Tony R exclaims, like he's that Tesla billionaire guy cooing about some new product.

There, on twin screens, an elder god appears, broad, bald head like a mountain dome. Closed eyelids with orbs the size of deep space telescopes twitching underneath. Face tentacles that would dwarf the ancient redwoods undulating in the current.

Ph'nglui mglw'nafh Cthulhu R'lyeh wgah'nagl fhtagn

These words escape Tony R's lips, spoken with reverence, devotion, deep worship. It is the one time I see his grin soften.

"You never left the Cthulhu cult," I say. It's not a question.

"Oh, I tried! Believe me, I tried." He smiles, and I think about those other cults he joined. "But I'm all about being Agile," he says. "Did you know that Adaptability is my highest ranked Clifton Strength?"

I shake my head. Stall. Keep him talking.

"Is this some kind of perverted ritual?"

"Ritual? Oh no, no no no. We use cutting edge technology. These kids are engineering students and code monkeys."

Ah, not fighters. That explains so much.

"Science helped us find Cthulhu where ancient texts and magical mumbo jumbo failed. And the latest neurophysiological techniques will help us rouse him!"

Then it hits me.

"Holy heck, you got these recruits from—"

"That's right! Where better to find alcoholics than at AA meetings?"

My whole body goes cold. We helped rescue some of these folks. Brought them right to Tony R. "There is no ACLW."

"Well, there sort of is, but I run the entire operation. Your cell was the only one I couldn't convert to the cause, so I've got other plans for you."

He walks over to Punch, who glares daggers at him. He slaps them, and my cheek burns. I taste the blood in my mouth.

"There! You both feel it," he smiles. "These devices act as neural amplifiers and transmitters. When these drones land on the Great Cthulhu's head, they'll transmit your amplified pain to his subconscious. In a sense, you'll enter his dreams. I'm almost envious!"

Punch and I look at each other wide-eyed with fear and dread.

"I know what you're thinking. 'But Tony, we're like microbes to the Elder Gods.' And you're right. But doesn't the fire ant's bite still sting? Doesn't the lowly virus cause sniffles and sneezes?" He pauses to scratch his nose. "You'll be in too much pain to notice, but you two have the honor of initiating the End of the World!"

Eleven hours ago, Anaheim

Minnie and I shared a room the night before Operation Save the Cultists.

Minnie was at the round motel table, repairing a four-inch tall robot made to look like Baba Yaga's hut—I think this one housed a chicken's brain. Human tweezers and eyeglass repair kits were mixed in with her alien tools.

After counting all her charges lined up on the edge of the bed, watching *Mars Attacks*, I sat down next to her. She turned all her mushroom antennae towards me.

"Minnie, I'm worried. Punch thinks something's not right about this mission."

Minnie made a noncommittal buzz.

"What if—" I was worried about offending her. "What if you hung back with ZeroRaven tomorrow?"

That did it. She put down her tools, folded seven of her long crustacean limbs, and her mushroom head stalks stopped waving. Telepathic waves of hurt and disappointment washed over me.

"Not because I don't think you can help! The opposite," I said. "If things go sideways, we may need backup."

She considered this. She motioned to the line of tiny friends and a robot scarab skittered over to the edge of the bed. A spark flashed from its mouth parts. Images flowed into my brain, like I was doom-scrolling Instagram.

"I see, take the roach—sorry, take *Eustace* with me. Oh wow, he can transmit audio and video? Right, and ZeroRaven can monitor the feed with you. That's genius! Thank you so much!"

Eustace saluted at me with one of its mechanical forelegs before joining the others in front of the TV.

Minnie emoted a wave of pride and affection. She didn't like being touched, so I sent her the mental-equivalent of a hug, and we sat there in happy thought for a moment before she turned her attention back to her tinkering.

I stopped by the van to check on ZeroRaven. He was playing *Subnautica* on his goggles. The vehicle had a surveillance set up, full of monitors and computers and even a camping toilet and a small fridge—Tony R spared no expense—and the Penguin cast the action to the main screen. I marveled at how he handled the controller with his weirdly pseudo-pod-like, prehensile wingtips. Not your typical penguin.

His clearly non-human appearance meant he couldn't join us in the house tomorrow, but he was our getaway driver.

"Just checking in," I said. "You good for tomorrow? Minnie might be hanging out with you."

He gave me the equivalent of a thumbs up gesture. Then, after pausing the game and putting down the controller, he gave me a big hug. Penguin wings are stronger than one expects.

We sat there in companionable silence, me marveling as he dove into deep waters and dodged toothy alien fish.

Present, Anaheim

"The eagles have landed!" Tony R's smile is so wide it looks like it might break his face.

I can't feel Eustace in my chest pocket. I hope he's with Minnie and ZeroRaven, and they're driving far inland, away from the global coastal devastation that will certainly be the first symptom of Cthulhu's rising.

At least no more worrying about climate change?

Tony R holds a stainless steel meat tenderizer.

"I've always cataloged household items by their potential for pain," he says conversationally. If Punch could stink eye someone to death, Tony R would be a giant pile of feces right now.

Tony R makes like a doctor doing a reflex test and slams the toothy hammer down on Punch's kneecap. Punch starts to scream, but bites it back. Pain explodes in my leg, and it's like fire is spreading from my left knee down to my toes and up to my shoulders.

"I mentioned the sharing and amplification, right?" Tony R's eyes crinkle with mirth.

"Boss, we've got movement," one of the techno-cultists says. On a monitor, digital instruments are going crazy, all red lights and oscillating seismograph-type readouts.

"These metrics are promising! We're exceeding every KPI!" He turns to us. "Do you know how rare it is for a prototype to work glitch-free on launch? We lost a dozen junior associates in testing, but this is production. Puny humans were no substitutes for an Elder God."

Knowing that we were duped into helping this jerkface kill these poor folks hurts more than the torture.

"And we're just getting started." He picks a potato peeler from the tray of instruments. I look at Punch and hope they see past the terror and tears and read the *goodbye* and *sorry* and *God, I wish I could kiss you* in my eyes.

Chaos erupts.

It starts with a crashing of wood and the buzz of flying things. The few cultists in my line of sight are panicking, beating their hands in the air, tearing at their clothes, and stomping frantically at the ground. Then there is the welcome vision of a giant, albino penguin socking the smile off Tony R's face before reducing the other cultists to unconsciousness. Minnie clambers up Punch's chair and tears and picks at their restraints.

Punch shouts. "Zero, those underwater drones—you've got to move them away from Cthulhu!" Zero glances at the tech set up, nods, and goes to work.

That's when I realize that my anxiety, always high, is dialed up to fifteen. I think I'm having a heart attack and it's hard to catch my breath. I see it all multiply and amplify in Punch's eyes. Even worse, my panic is feeding Cthulhu's subconscious and waking the Elder God who is going to end the world and *ohmygod* I can't stop—

Punch leaps out of their chair on top of me and kisses me. I taste blood where we knocked teeth and lips but then I'm floating, sinking, settling into deep deep bliss.

The device I'm still hooked up to is an emotional amplifier. For me and for Cthulhu.

We finally break off and look around. Cultists groan. Minnie and her tiny allies mournfully gather up fragments of robotic and busted brain jars. (Thank you for saving the world, wee ones.)

ZeroRaven has disengaged one drone, which pulls away and we get one last glimpse of Cthulhu, who apparently doesn't wear pajama bottoms, and we catch sight of a towering, cyclopean—

I'm sure I'm blushing furiously.

Before ZeroRaven disengages the last drone, I channel all my relief, calm, and yep, desire into one last message to the sleeping god:

In your house in R'lyeh, you wait dreaming. And you were having such a wonderful dream. So different from your earlier, troubled sleep. Why rise, when you can descend into the delightful deep? The time to rise will come, but why not rest for another eon or two?

⋈

A Perfectly Fine Hobby

~ Andrew S. Fuller

A year expired since the heavy October storm had found its way into the basement, along with the world's continued interruptions, before Walter addressed the problem. He intended to stack cardboard boxes on wooden pallets, grumbling about the mason's estimate for foundation waterproofing, and cobweb strands touching everything, and the cat Saga huddled on the landing who offered no assistance except a very delayed blink. Not looking inside the boxes was his strategy, sorting their contents would be a very separate project. But he had not brought home enough pallets; and some of the cardboard was decades old, tape yellowed and flaking, and they ruptured.

So he found himself sorting and consolidating for most of the night, beset by memories of his past, placing aside items to sell or discard. Among them were boxes from his childhood, boxes shipped from his parents, and he cried looking at fading photographs, brittle letters, worn toys, forgotten books; and he continued sorting these until the cat demanded her fourth dinner. Nor was the feline very considerate in his repeated trips up and down the stairs with full armloads, and she was offered several other less-endearing names that were threatened to be made permanent.

He did not remember either of his parents to spend time with a stamp collection, but here now was a stack of binders and folders of postage stamps, some slipped into very small sealed plastic sleeves, some loose and trimmed from aged envelopes. He recalled one of his sibling's words when they reviewed the contents of attic and basement and every closet of the old house, saying *hey maybe they would want you to have these, it might be fun, you always collected comics and action dolls and dinosaurs and rocks. Here,* they said, *stuff these in your luggage and you can decide later.*

○

After additional weeks in the continuing world, and its populace making excuses for why many aspects worsened, he became frustrated with the unwanted materials stacked in the hallway and upon most of the sitting spaces, and finally he loaded them into the car. All of the items except for the stamps and their related paraphernalia. He found himself distracted by their character and age, reaching back into the strewn dishevelment of time.

He leafed casually through the album pages featuring stamps in pocketed rows, reading notes in his father's handwriting, and some other hand, perhaps his uncle or grandfather. There were many unused pages and numerous loose stamps and scraps in their own separate and unsorted sleeve. *This is someone else's problem*, he thought, even as he sat down at the dining room table.

Hours later he had sorted all of the stamps by color, by condition, by design—of portraits or aircraft or animal or flower—by currency, or by whether it had been postmarked. Several times the cat sprung onto the tabletop where she knew she was not allowed, and he snapped his fingers and pushed her gently toward the edge, but not quite enough to topple her off. After a few departures and returns, Saga spread her long-haired body along the various piles of stamps, and swished her tail without disturbance.

There was one stamp that continued in its own outcast category, the long rigid profile of a man against a striated carmine background. Alongside the bust was written a word he could not guess if it was the name of the man, of a movement or an exclamation. The proper direction of the letters was not discernible and the symbols did not contain a familiar currency. He continued sorting, and later he mistook the pariah for a different stamp, as the face appeared slightly turned. Admittedly, it was an odd rendering style of engraved lines, for the cheek bones and temple appeared disproportionate at any angle of view.

Only late in the night did it seep into Walter's mind that he wanted to know something more about a few of these old tiny scraps and their origin and rarity. He also realized that he had left the front door open, and the car door open. Someone had helped themselves to all the bags and boxes of books, toys, dishes, unspecific trophies and medals, but it saved him an errand. He became upset that his car battery had declined, and could not blame the feline nor the government nor the weather nor anyone else. So upset that he yanked the front door closed and caught his finger. He glared at the sorted piles of stamps, at the single stamp with the distinct face louring back at him, and swept his arm over the table, sending them flittering. The cat moved to the window sill, and regarded him with judgement.

In the morning, Walter calmly picked up each stamp from the floor, and gathered them in a double-layered paper grocery bag.

After work, where he solved many problems as more were created and someone remarked *well hey that's job security*, he drove to the shops across the avenue from the nearly abandoned mall building. He retrieved the stamp collection from the car trunk and proceeded to the establishment at the end of the block. He turned his head to make sure he had not parked against the yellow painted curb when someone unmercifully collided with him, and he fell onto the heated sidewalk.

He waited there a moment to make sure his mind was functioning and his limbs too, waited to for someone to help him, then tried to decide what words he would unleash on this remorseless person. When he stood, there was no one nearby in either direction, no sound of a shop door or car door. *Perhaps it was all me*, he thought, though there was no mailbox or bike rack or fault in the concrete.

Shaken, he picked up the stamps and albums again, and brought the slightly torn paper bag into the shop. A small bell plinked over the door as he entered.

Glass display cases lined the store interior, the walls covered with multiple small frames. A man with a single-braided beard sat on a stool at the far end, reading a paperback and sipping from a tall tumbler with a built-in straw. He did not offer greeting, and it was difficult to tell if he looked up.

"I have these…" Walter began as he walked across the store. And he did not finish.

"Have what," the shop person said.

He placed the paper bag on the glass counter and began to tip its contents toward the opening.

"Hold on, hold on now." The attendant stood off the stool. He gestured with the drink tumbler. "It's Wednesday."

"Wednesday? I don't—"

The attendant gestured to the opposite side of the shop where each display case contained multitudes of stamps. "Layton will be back tomorrow." Then he nodded to their side of the shop where every case and wall hanging and poster and photo featured or pertained to coins.

Pain thrummed along the back of Walter's head. He touched his nape and found no blood, but perhaps he had hit the cement harder than his estimate. Perhaps he was still lying on the concrete. With people gathered around trying to wake him, trying to find his wallet, his body calling out for him to return. Perhaps Wednesday would never end for him, he would remain in this unresolved moment forever. Or he would drift through life unseen, buried at long last, awake in the coffin, awake and speechless in his silent form on the sidewalk. These kinds of thoughts came to him often but he did not tell anyone.

"He doesn't assess with people waiting." The coin man sipped from his tumbler.

"Oh, that is fine, that's okay. If I could leave them."

"If you leave a number," said coin man, looking at his own hands that still held objects.

Walter realized that he had intended to leave the collection, and not look back, nor give it another thought. *You don't need that*, he practiced in his mind, *you don't need my number*. Or maybe *you can just have them*, or maybe *it's a donation*, or simply *there's no need* sounded better. Instead he uttered his phone number and name, and repeated it when the coin man finally located a pen and paper.

He left the shop feeling unburdened, and enjoyed the pleasing tinny bell. With eyes pointed only forward, he walked carefully to the car and made his harmless getaway.

Layton called on Friday during the work day, and though he was not busy with spreadsheets or meetings, Walter did not wish to talk to anyone at that moment.

That evening after work when he entered the house, Saga did not approach him to rub against his legs as usual, but considered him with wide eyes from the opposite end of the hallway. When he tried to approach, she fled his presence. He added fresh tuna to the food dish and clean water to the bowl. Still, she did not make an appearance before his bedtime.

Unusual noises woke him in the night. He listened to light steps and rustling that seemed to originate in the kitchen or living room, then the hallway. From the bed he could not see enough of the open doorway. He called the cat's name. There was no response and he called again. "Are you hungry?" he said. Then Saga appeared unexpectedly from behind the curtain, jumping down from window sill in his very room. When she entered the hall, she yowled and skittered into the dark. From the far end of the house she wailed.

He remained in his bed waiting for her to quiet. When it was apparent she would not, he ignored the glimmers of childhood fears and arose to feed her again, though serving her in the early hours was not a good habit for either of them. He stumbled in the dark hallway. After switching on the light, he found his pair of comfortable black derby shoes set outside the bedroom door, though he did not recall leaving them in such an absurd location.

The next morning Saga was affectionate and sat in Walter's lap while he breakfasted on eggs and toast. She followed him through his routine of rinsing dishes and watering plants and packing lunch, taking her leave when he donned shoes and coat. Through the rest of the week she either stayed very near him or could not be found for hours, nestled away somewhere.

His employment became very busy, shuffling projects from final stage to on-hold, pulling others from undefined to active, and he often returned home succumbed by lassitude, wondering if he had left food out for her, if there was better opportunity elsewhere, if life itself was a bitter prank, or if his species yearned only for chaos.

Another few weeks crawled along with him in tow, and only after such time elapsed did he notice unusual events occurred in his proximity.

Waiting at a red traffic light, Walter gazed to one side while pondering before his eyes met with the driver next to him. The man looked away for rest of signal, and in fact would not advance even when the light turned green, despite clamoring horns. A few blocks down the street, Walter glanced in his rearview mirror and saw the car lurch forward after the light returned to red, and collide with a crossing car, though both of them travelled slowly enough that it was soundless and not very destructive.

One day at his workplace Human Resources summoned him, and Walter went with inflated anticipation, for it had been a few years since he'd received a raise. When he arrived the HR director announced that some of his recent behaviors had distracted other employees. He apologized for he was unaware. It seemed that his walk had become very loud lately, described by some as a stomping or slapping that carried significantly through closed office doors and the ventilation system, not to mention the open office configuration. Also that his eating habits had left some feeling like they could not utilize the break room, for his chewing had been reported as open-mouthed, which was offensive and unsettling. This was not a warning, they said, only a friendly reminder to consider others in the workplace environment. After that encounter Walter moved very slowly about the office, concentrating on each deliberate step and bite. He ordered a new keyboard with his own funds that featured nearly silent keys.

He slept heavily, not awakened anymore by the cat or anything else. One evening while brushing his teeth he became very aware of the unlit hallway behind him, seeing its dark rectangle in the mirror. After that he closed the bathroom door each time.

At the hardware store he was shopping for a new smoke detector in aisle eight, reading the features and lifetimes on various models, as two laughing children ran by him many times in an exuberant game of chase. When he made his selection and turned toward the front of the store, they began screaming behind him. Walter spun with concern that one of them had fallen. Both were running away, screeching no longer with joy but in uncontrollable fright. He did not see them again and made his purchase. While driving out of the parking lot, a parent exited the store and watched him with elevated irritation.

His siblings called over the weekend and they spoke about the weather, and the local election that a sportswear founder had influenced, and the neighbors who were unhappy with a new fence, and one of them was planning a sabbatical, and the strawberry-rhubarb pie that the other had made, and one of the nephews learning to drive, and another friend of their parents had died. As they were saying goodbye he asked suddenly about father's stamp collection, and both siblings who were older did not recall either parent with such a hobby. He reminded them of the days after the second funeral, going through all of their belongings. I don't remember any stamps, they said. *Well, I'm sure they don't,* he thought, for they led busy lives. No more than most, but the years grew arduous and had to be cut loose and sink away.

One weekday evening as he attempted to rest while viewing a television series about feuding typesetters during no particular war, there rose an unsettling wail that sent Saga bounding off the sofa. Walter paused the program and crept through the house, holding his ears. The entire dwelling rattled around him as he sought each window to secure the latches. Some of the noise subsided, though the wanton baying circled from room to room, and he returned to the dramatic entertainment at a heightened volume.

The following day he saw a neighbor regarding him from across the street, and he stopped to confer about the tempest and gales of last night. The local who was usually quite garrulous, crumpled his face in silence. Walter could not stay or he would be tardy for work.

On that third Thursday of the month, the book club gathered at his house. It was not unusual for them to discuss other matters at the beginning, speaking of their accomplishments while stacking various cheeses on assorted crackers, sipping regional red wine or local beer. Then they spoke of their latest reading selection, an historical mystery in which an elevator operator and a janitor solve a spate of murders. Some of the group felt the polluted river represented an amoral society, others enjoyed the verbal tics of one protagonist and the descriptions, while two regular members did not contribute to the conversation.

The meeting had not lasted more than an hour when one of the guests returned from the bathroom, their face trembling. They admitted to detouring to find the cat and bestow some affection, wandering into Walter's bedroom, where they encountered someone standing in the dark outlined against the window. Furthermore, when the lights from a passing car streaked over the room, flashed over the stranger's face . . . well, they should could not articulate what countenance hung there above the distinct shoulders.

The group offered multiple words of safety and hugs of assurance, and several of them exited the table with a determined sense about them. They gathered kitchen knives and a rolling pin, and stalked down the hallway, shouting for the intruder to come forward. Finally they stormed into the bedroom. Aside from Walter's furniture there was nothing else in the room. The closet proved empty as well, and the window locked. After this incident, the group dismissed early and swiftly without a recommendation for the next title.

When they had departed, he found his shoes aligned in a perfect pair by the bedroom window. He carried them down the hallway to their place under the coat rack by the drafty front door.

The weekend contained no important errands for him, and he remained at home, completing a chore between reading a new novel. He discovered most of his plants had withered very suddenly, and several tarnished spots across the hardwood floors, a fine roseate mold that bloomed under the finish. So he spent the afternoon hunched over in a mask, scraping and sanding, as perspiration adhered his clothing to him. Several times he heard a heavy noise and removed his headphones, and reviewed the room, or went in search of the cat, and finding nothing disturbed or disturbing, concluded it was delivery trucks that frequented the street.

By the early evening as warm colors settled into the sky, he had missed two meals. A phone message from his friend invited him out for an aperitif. *This will be wonderful*, he thought, for he was famished and more than ready, he admitted.

They met at a new establishment located between their homes. He apologized for missing happy hour and dinner though the late-night menu featured many options, not all of which were fried. Since their last outing Demir's hair had grown to his shoulders and incorporated a more venerable gray, though his features were otherwise enthusiastic. Before the waiter arrived they resumed a pattern of friendly banter that extended back many years since their introduction.

Then they sipped dark beers and consumed snaking crispy potatoes dipped in smoky fondue, talking about what shows they had imbibed recently on television, of which there were many. Wherein a shocking murder begins to unravel the secrets in an idyllic small town. Wherein two enemies embark on a journey to find something direly important and end up finding much more. Wherein a young outcast joins with other exiles who inspire an entire civilization to rise against tyrants. Walter ordered pierogis and a cup of corn chowder, and while his friend remarked about foods in the same color palette, he enjoyed each tasteful portion. They continued talking and laughing at a reasonable volume.

"Thank you for helping me escape tonight," he said at one point.

"It's good to see you," his friend acknowledged with authentic affirmation.

It was not the response he expected, and when he considered further, was not sure why the statement had come out of him at all. But it was all said, the moment dispersed, and they talked of comic books and favorite concerts.

Partway through his second beer, Walter excused himself. When he returned from the facilities, Demir was no longer at the table. Of course they must have missed each other in the lavatory, and he waited. Twenty minutes later the server said that his companion had paid the check on his way out. Walter tried to recall if they had said goodbye, or what else he might have said in his frivolous mood, or if he had in fact come to the public house alone and imagined other company, and before he could become upset, completed his beverage without hurry.

The buses ran less frequently in the later hours, and he chose to walk home in the cooling breeze, along perfect sidewalks through expensive neighborhoods. The reflective eyes of felines watched from high windows, automated sprinkler systems misted the streetlight glow, trees swayed against the clear sky, their leaves already changing. A few blocks from his house he began to hurry, feeling ill at ease. Yet when he came to his illuminated porch he was not entirely relieved to return, and might have resumed his nocturnal adventure if not for the urgency in his bladder.

In the silent hours he woke speaking a drowsy string of syllables that he would not have called words in any other sense, with an aching head and regretful stomach. He stumbled from bed to secure a sip of water. The cat hissed at him from her perch on the kitchen counter, and the tap water tasted mucid and stale, everything felt sour and in need of cleansing, but he was very tired.

○

Late in the morning when he finally emerged, he found several unpleasant leavings throughout the house. He had not missed Saga's regular treatments, and these damp semi-solid messes were not her regular color or smell, more like something found along the beach than the usual deposit comprised of hair, but he cleaned them with regret. When he found her on the upper shelf of a closet relegated to bygone clothing, she scratched him viciously on the arm.

He unleashed an outburst of aversion, harsh and throaty noises at which the cat widened her eyes. When he had calmed somewhat he managed to say to Saga and the universe, "If that wasn't absolutely uncalled for." Then he resigned to the fact that things were not as they should be, and had not been so for some time, and he wrote notes apologizing to friends, and folded all of the laundry, and changed the water filters, and called the veterinarian to make an appointment.

He found himself in the attic of the old house, where it was humid and smelled of dust and faint cedar. Old bookcases packed one side of the low triangular space, the spine of each volume featuring a word he did not yet know, while one corner stacked boxes of holiday decorations, another with heavy foot trunks that had traveled to the world via ship, near an antique crib obscured by draped plastic, amid tangled furniture in a desperate embrace, and the aroma of aging paper, all cast in anemic moonlight entering the small octagonal window.

From somewhere in the cardboard labyrinth there came a shuddering whisper. In the shadows behind the chimney and tucked in the eaves there sounded the long bottomless rattle of something rising. Darkness swallowed the stairway and old joists stretched above him, and while he understood now why he was back here and small, and the strange nature of this scenario to be a dream, he could not pull himself free as the bellows within the expanding tenebrosity enfolded him.

In the morning Walter tripped over his shoes again, placed next to the bed, and lifted them behind his head for a furious hurling, when he felt the warmth of their interior. Alarmed at the implications, and his inability to settle on one harmless possibility, he dropped them and ran from the room.

Much later he convinced himself in the soothing daylight that they were merely inanimate footwear, and by the frequency of choice likely his favorite pair, and he returned to find them askew on the unmade bed where they had fallen. At that moment he noticed the odd postage stamp adhered to the worn sole of his right derby shoe.

Immediately he felt a strange perception cascade through his mind and to the outer extremities of body. After an unknown many days of wear, the radiant detail of the small beguiling face remained intact as it surveyed him in a glowering stare.

There slipped a number of missing hours before he felt calm and unafflicted by the needs of the world or his household, and the channels of his mind unearthed many neglected reminders. He threw on shoes and coat, and returned in haste to the collector shop, driving with an eager foot on the gas pedal.

He hurried by a customer in sparring discussion with the coin expert, his lungs heaving when he reached the back counter, where a man perhaps thrice his age with short rounded glasses awaited him with raised brow. The shopkeeper made a comment about the speed and longevity of the Pony Express that Walter nearly understood.

"I must apologize," he said between breaths.

"Then you go right ahead," said the man behind the counter.

"Layton," he said, "Layton, I brought in—weeks ago—What? I go ahead what?"

"If you must apologize, I won't stop you." The man who might be Layton smiled.

"That's—I meant to say… Oh, yes. I am sorry. Very sorry that I did not return your calls."

"It happens to the best of us, while the worst live lives of unfathomable bliss. How can I help you?"

"Many weeks ago, even months, I left a bag—a grocery bag—of stamps with your associate."

The man who was most likely Layton grimaced slightly at the mention of either the paper bag or his compatriot. "What was the name?"

Walter disclosed his full name and phone number in distinct pronunciation, and the stamp man held up one finger and revolved around it to disappear behind a curtain into a concealed back room.

While waiting Walter tried not listening to the coin expert and customer in their defiant exchange. One leaned into the counter and the other stood back with crossed arms, as they contended in a shifting balance of excitement and short contraries, neither of them ending or leaving. Clearly this regular visitor was not the purchasing type and patronized often for company, though not quarrelsome enough to be escorted out.

Layton emerged with a familiar brown paper grocery bag, already speaking. "Yes yes, I spent some time with these. Not much to crow home about." He set the bundle on counter and pushed it toward Walter.

"Not a Penny Black or Inverted Jenny among them, eh?" Walter said with overt suggestion, for he had spent a few minutes researching the topic.

The stamp expert did not chuckle or roll his eyes, only expelled his latest breath in a displeased hiss.

"What am I to do?" Walter said, noticing he spoke in an odd manner lately.

"There are many communities of enthusiasts, local or online. You can look them up, make a post, might find someone interested in the whole collection."

Walter was reminded in shimmers of memory the stale content of the bag, the dust-laden atmosphere of the attic long ago, the endless skies above. Everything around him felt laborious, dragging him into the past and beyond, into a breathless roaring place of darkness becoming lucid, etching its forms into being, monstrous turmoil gaining life.

Nonsense, he thought to himself, and inhaled three measured breaths. Then he picked up the bundle in both arms. "Oh," he realized aloud, "There was this additional thing, perhaps it is nothing . . ." He set down the load again, and tried to reach his foot onto the counter. Without success he turned his back and lifted the foot behind, while he craned his head and pointed at the shoe. There came to him a brief memory of sitting on the living room floor, scraping at the sole of the shoe with his fingernails, with a knife, with a metal rasp from the toolbox; and the colors of the stamp returning as saturated as ever, the face thereon escalating in vehemence, shifting in awful contractions, beginning to speak.

"What am I looking at?" Layton whispered, and all joy receded from his expression. He lunged with careless urgency at Walter who flinched away. Then he threw open the gate between counters and hurtled forward, driving Walter onto the floor of warped bland tiles. The stamp expert sank slowly toward him with clawed hands, then regained himself with rigid posture. "I apologize. I only wanted to see." He smoothed the wrinkles of his shirt, and held out his hand.

Walter reached to accept the gesture, and Layton bent down instead. He took hold of Walter's foot in both hands and tugged at the shoelace. When the knot would not undo, he pulled roughly until the derby slipped free.

Without saying anything else the stamp specialist returned behind the counter and curtain into unknown territory with the shoe. Walter helped himself back to his feet, while the two other occupants of the shop lost interest and resumed their discourse.

For some time Walter waited at the back counter of the shop, standing on one foot. He contemplated the remaining duration on the parking meter, the direction of his employment pursuits, the rise in global temperatures, which television series he might view this evening, the uneven wood box they had found mostly buried in attic insulation years ago, the albums of stamps and the accompanying notes, the jagged desperate characters of the unknown handwriting, the words that were not words, what hand had etched that unsettling stamp, what eyes had recounted the letter thence posted, what message had passed from what relentless whereabouts.

From the unseen back room issued the whine of some electric tool, then a violent sound like thunder trapped in a well, and half of a confused scream. Walter startled, and the coin man bolted down the aisle and through the privacy curtain, calling his partner's name. Immediately there was a gasp of inescapable dismay, and a brief series of timorous utterances, before a resounding clap that shook the building.

The bell over the door jingled behind him and Walter felt himself entirely alone in the shop.

He could not make himself move and worked to empty his mind enough, to accept his coming demise without allowing himself to visualize its method or specifics.

When the sky outside turned as dark as his thoughts, and his being remained unscathed, he backed quietly across the store. Slowly he opened the door so as not to disturb the bell. Then he ran in desperation to his car, cursing for the first time a close parking space.

As he turned the ignition, the shop door swung inward. Out of the agitating darkness exited a man whom Walter had not seen in the store, tall and spare like an unclassified insect wearing clothes, an insect or sea creature molting from one form to another. He swayed and wavered his feet over the sidewalk as though they were first steps, reeling against the placid uneventful reality around him. The anomalous individual appraised the world with famished scrutiny. For a moment his stare fell on the nearby car and its occupant.

Walter saw the face he knew too well but could not name, a visage of unbearable gaze and a deepening mouth that grew into a churning trench of diminution, an inviting nebula of unavoidable belonging, roiling with incalculable multifarious color.

Then the figure lurched around the corner and despite Walter's attempt at following and beholding him again, disappeared into the complicated and falling world, leaving in its wake only an undying sense of loss.

⋈

Obsolescent

~ Kiera Lesley

The smell of old milk filled the cupboard. Nadanti slipped in and perched on the upper shelf, gripping with his sixteen talons, and sniffed the air. No musky, salty scent of warning. Only the delicious, half-curdled milk.

The jar sat on the floor uncovered—not secured under fiendish lids or cursed materials.

Looking around, Nadanti saw no traps. No arrangements of electrical wires overhead, no strange powder combustibles or nozzles aiming foams, no fine metal hatching to make noise. And why should there be? This wasn't stagnant sea water or small drowned creatures. It wasn't music or smoke or blood. It wasn't any of the offerings to be avoided.

It was just milk with all the signs of being forgotten in a hurried pack-up earlier in the night.

It was the best accidental offering he had found in dozens of spins of the stars.

Still, Nadanti paid attention as swept down on cramped wings. He had survived longer than many of his kind thus far by being cautious and adapting. He listened, but heard no footsteps, though there was a strange hum from outside the cupboard.

He landed on one foot next to the milk jar. He curled the others over his head and one—struggling for space—dipped into the outside places. He slipped but managed to find a hold, bracing his wing-tips against the door.

He opened his mouth—pulling his lips well back from the sharp points of his teeth—and bent to suckle at the jar.

As his lips touched the glass something brushed over the talons of his balancing foot to tighten midway up his leg.

He was airborne. Not flying, but strung upside-down and swinging from the cupboard's roof. Nadanti squirmed, trying to free himself, but the cord was tight-spun and made of all the right things: nylon, concrete dust and stuck together with noxious resins. Soaked in human magic.

Nadanti struggled until his strength ran out. He was left waiting with the enticing smell of the old milk below him. Too far away.

It was after dawn when he heard the footsteps. They stopped outside the cupboard and a human female opened the door, bringing her musk with her. Her eyes lit up, delighted, when she saw Nadanti.

"Got one!" she called to someone behind her.

She reached forward with a pair of scissors and cut Nadanti down.

He lacked the strength to fly upward or catch himself. His fight with the cursed rope had left him dazed and exhausted. As he fell he saw a tiny human sitting behind the woman in a long-legged plastic chair.

Nadanti knew fear.

He rallied, trying to get his wings under him, thrashing to rend with his talons and reaching to touch the dimensional slips that would save him. He strained towards the milk jar, desperate to at least have his prize.

A thin plastic bag came down around his body quickly and was tied off at the base of his legs, leaving his talons poking out. The plastic haze bore down on him, blocking breath and light and sense.

He was laid on a hard surface and the air grew cold. The strange, persistent hum he had heard from inside the cupboard surrounded him.

The creature was frozen in a squashed block when Ivy pulled him back out of the freezer. She peeled the plastic bag away from where it had stuck to his gloopy black skin and half-closed vestigial eyes, untwisted it from around his ankles—and dropped his rigid body onto her marble bench-top.

Nadanti broke apart into chunks.

Ivy ground a rolling pin—plastic, always plastic—over and over the pieces until they turned into fine powder. She swept it all into a Tupperware.

She ran the taps in the sink, waited for the water to grow warm, and filled a bottle. She measured three teaspoons of Nadanti's dust into the water, screwed the lid on, and shook it until it turned a murky white. Specks of light flared, trying to cohere into the symbols he came from and reform him. Trying to connect back to this place where he had lived since before the humans arrived.

But Ivy was too fast. She took the bottle over to Miranda's high chair and pushed the rubber nipple between her lips. Miranda began sucking, drooling and gurling happily.

"They taste good, the old ones, don't they?" Ivy cooed.

No way her daughter was going to be stolen away in her sleep for not leaving offerings out at certain times of the year, or go mad for sneaking peaks out of her bedroom window. Not when the town newsletter kept running such good tips on new catching methods and ways to make them more easily absorbed. No wonder the poor squicky things couldn't keep up—they must find it all unfathomable.

Ivy put the rest of the powder into the freezer – the insulation and electricity should be enough to keep it fresh. She poured a new jar of milk and took it back to the cupboard. She placed it in the loop of the nylon noose on the floor in line with the sensor, removed the lid to allow the scent to get out, and closed the door.

⋈

A Mournful Melancholia of Things Forever Lost

~ *Kurt Newton*

1. *The Mother Out of Time*

Out of a thousand born
from the decadent loins
of the Old God Shub-Niggurath,
only one was chosen
for a special song
to be tattooed upon its back.

The ink was made
from blood that was drawn
from Shub-Niggurath's placental sac.
While the Old God dreamed
the child was placed,
submerged in a viscous bath.

The song, as composed,
could only be played
on the horn of the mythical Black Goat.
But someone unnamed
had taken a blade
and removed the song from the infant host.

For a thousand years
the song traveled the world,
its power never truly known.
Many attempted
to hear the unheard,
only to be struck dead after several notes.

But for Shub-Niggurath
years were but a trifle,
with no meaning to future or past,
time was a labyrinth,
a cave with many tentacles
leading along many different paths.

One day a minion was sent
with a child in hand
to the home of a powerful witch,
in the dead of night
under a full moon bright
to deliver the special gift.

Helemut, as she was known,
was the only one of her kind
in all of the Eastern Wild,
who, with a simple wave,
could bend time and space,
and whose heart belonged to no man or idol.

On her doorstep was placed
the small, tortured face
to satisfy Shub-Niggurath's behest.
As dreamed, from the start,
the witch fulfilled her part,
the child would do the rest.

2. *The Thing on the Doorstep of the Witch's House*

It's not often witches find things abandoned
on the doorsteps of their homes,
but on this day one such witch by the name of Helemut
heard a thump and wondered what
had come to land upon the walk
outside her cabin door.

A basket woven from the blackest vines
with a handle spiked with thorns,
inside, beneath a blanket spun from spider webbing,
there came a mewling then a shredding
as the lowly creature tore its bedding,
reared its ugly head and made itself known.

A child? A halfmoon child?
A child of the one called Shub-Niggurath?
The witch laughed and laughed but there was something innocent
about this loathsome creature from the very first minute
she laid eyes upon its soulless grimace—
she found it more than sad.

It's well known that witches are childless,
careless, opportunistic things.
What they love most are potions and spelling,
candles and charms, and hexes for the selling,
not diaper changing and story telling
and all that nonsense that motherhood brings.

But Helemut was different than all the witches
that lived in the Eastern Wild,
she had grown tired of being mired in darkness,
in cauldrons thick with toil and garlic,
no more bubble and boil and blood for bargains,
she just wanted a simple life.

But this child was no ordinary orphan,
as Helemut soon would see.
She examined the infant under candle flame
and discovered the source of its constant pain:
the skin from its back had been peeled away.
What god would do such a thing?

Oh, how it hurt Helemut to look upon
the child's tortured face.
She tried her most powerful healing spell,
but the raw flesh still oozed with a sulfurous smell,
she realized then nothing would make the child well
until its missing skin had returned to its proper place.

She removed the thick drape that covered
the large, smoky mirror in the corner of the room,
and with a single infant hair pulled out
she conjured the location of the skin's whereabouts,
the mirror cleared and she began to count,
as she quickly grabbed the child and stepped through.

3. *Song From the Horn of the Black Goat*

It was a melody composed of arcane notes
on a musical scale never before seen.
It could only be played on the horn of a mythical goat
whose name had been lost to antiquity.

The song is said to be the essence of loss,
born from the whispering wells of the void,
a song that, once heard, would place the listener at odds
with every meaning of existence they enjoyed.

Such a song could only have sprung from loins of one god,
Shub-Niggurath, mother of a thousand young.
Such a soundscape must forever be kept untrod,
and its melody forever unsung.

But all things hidden are eventually revealed,
either orchestrated or purely by luck.
There was no way of knowing how this music became sealed
between the pages of a donated song book.

Isaac Castelbaum's Music Emporium,
a tiny shop on the lower east side,
a place for used instruments, sheet music, and then some,
run by an old violinist born blind.

When Isaac applied his finger tips to the book
before placing it in the front window to sit,
like a curious item tucked away in a nook
he found an album leaf that didn't quite fit.

On first touch, Isaac knew the leaf was not paper,
nor was it leather, vellum or parchment,
it brought with it nightmarish visions of an undertaker
in a Nazi concentration camp in Auschwitz.

The sheet was made of the thinnest of skin
and on its surface were a series of odd notes,
Isaac's fingers could hear the music impregnated within,
a song unlike anything humanly composed.

He felt his way then to his violin
and was about to play the unearthly tune,
when the bell on his shop door rang and a woman stepped in
and said, "I wouldn't do that if I were you."

Isaac could hear the mewling of the child
she cradled in her motherly arms.
"My name is Helemut," she said,"of the Eastern Wild."
"Please, believe me, I mean you no harm."

"That music you hold is not of this realm,
to play it would release untold misery and pain.
This child of mine has a soul that is unwell
because a piece of its body was stripped away."

Isaac could sense the difference between truth and deceit,
he had lived long and had seen many things without sight,
perhaps a Gnostic or two were in his Castelbaum genes,
because he knew what he was about to do was right.

As if guided by forces he didn't quite comprehend,
he took the music sheet and placed it on the infant's back,
returning it to the exact position before it was rent
by the invisible hands of Shub-Niggurath.

The child's body arched as the skin sealed in place,
and its mewling rose to a frightful pitch,
but the notes it hit began to take shape
to form the most haunting melody ever to exist.

"My God," said Isaac, gasping at the sounds,
he shrank as he covered his ears with his hands.
Helemut knew then that they were mere pawns
in some cosmically orchestrated plan.

The horn was the child, born of the Black Goat,
a progeny from its prolific obsidian tip.
To play the horn was to release the music it stowed
inside the depths of its consciousness.

Oh, the horrible, sorrowful music they heard,
a mournful melancholia of things forever lost.
The melody began to filter out into the world
into the city streets beyond the music shop.

"What have we done?" said Helemut wincing,
even she could hear the world's discordant demise.
"We have to remove this child from the land of the living,
or there will be no remedy otherwise."

"Murder a child? This I cannot do," said Isaac retching,
the child's unique ululations made him ill.
"There is another way," said Helemut begetting
the same portal she had used to time travel.

"I will take it to where we can never be found,
I am its mother now," said Helemut, "this is my choice."
"Take me with you," said Isaac, his blind eyes wide and round,
"and together we will soften its voice."

And as the tortured child wailed its last wail,
Helemut and Isaac stepped into the swirling mist.
The portal closed leaving no scent and no trail,
and a peaceful quiet, if such a thing still exists.

But in the wake of their leaving, they failed to hear
the faint laughter of one who is dreaming still.
Time is a labyrinth, and maybe not now and not here,
but Shub-Niggurath will do what it will.

4. *Beyond the Mists of the Forgotten Island*

It was the simple life
the witch, Helemut, had dreamed,
an island surrounded by a heavy mist
that sailors avoided
but where sunlight beamed
and rivers snaked through the jungle thick.

It was here that she
and Isaac raised Charisse,
their orphaned musical savant.
Her somber singing seemed
to carry up into the trees
and return with much sweeter notes added on.

Could it be this place
held something special
in the richness of its earth?
A wellspring of creation
deep below the surface level,
with elemental properties for healing and rebirth?

Even Isaac, who had been blind
since leaving his mother's womb,
could now see shadows where none had been,
and, day by day, Helemut felt
the island's call to sink into the loam,
prompting her to raise a heady garden among the green.

It was as if time itself
had no measure for the trio,
as if caught within a dream within a dream.
Charisse grew and grew
as young children tend to do,
and her singing grew more beautiful, or so it seemed.

As Isaac and Helemut
became more like husband and wife
and Charisse more like the child they never had,
they began to forget
the events of their previous lives
and live purely in the moment at hand.

But a once-blind man
and even a most powerful witch
can be completely and utterly deceived,
for Shub-Niggurath
had planned for this,
giving them only what they wanted to believe.

It's true the island
was something special,
and there was something in the earth.
It was Shub-Niggurath sleeping
just below the surface level
dreaming of its eventual rebirth.

⬦

Lo-Fi Chocolate Cake

~ *J. B. Kish*

For dinner, I hurl German chocolate cake deep into the recesses of outer space. It's a wonderful treat. I can tell you're really going to like it.

The coffee shop is all pothos and golden hour sunlight. Finger-like, our shadow slides across the hardwood floor, and I nod my chin along to something called "*Japanese Lo-Fi.*" What a delight. I cannot wait for you to consume that too.

The barista fetches the rest of my order: a latte that nearly floats free from its mug. A buttery croissant. Avocado toast with blood-red paprika. Everything bagel and three cookies submerged in thick, neon frosting. I've unbuttoned my blouse, and when the young woman notices our gateway—roiling beneath my solar plexus like the teeth of a jet engine pressed up against my skin—she freezes in horror.

Never worry, you, whomever you are. Larger than life and floating out there above these crumb-sized donations. Do not stress because we are still so far away, and we humans have yet to comprehend. I'll protect your passage until the moment you come clawing your way through.

In the meanwhile! I gorge myself on these foods while customers watch in horror. Masticated baked goods slide down my throat and mix with the acid and pepsin necessary to deliver them unto you. The gateway inside me expands ever-so-slightly as these half-digested offerings defecate through the cosmic hole at my center. They are sent twirling out into the dark, unyielding black.

I wonder who you are.

Or why you pace out there, feeding on these bits of fish food I sprinkle. But you seem awfully hungry tonight, and I am pleased to widen this gate together.

The manager arrives—a nervous sapling with borrowed author-ity—and asks if there is anyone who might help me home. What he means to say is, "short women in their seventies shouldn't be lurking around trying to open interdimensional gateways behind tenured breasts." It's hard for his generation to believe someone my age could be chosen for something like this, or that we're the least bit relevant. They cannot even comprehend us and the internet in the same thought because old does not mix with new. This is why they wouldn't think to use artificial intelligence to translate an ancient hand-me-down book written in red ink.

I'm about to explain how enjoyable it will be to watch you peel the flesh from his biceps when my flatulence drives me upward. It smells of quasars and paprika and neutron frosting. I cannot help but blink dumbly.

For some reason, you've forced the offering back through our passageway and into my four-way stretch underpants...

I am exceptionally wounded that you've rejected these foods, and I cry out when our gate collapses in size. Was it something I ate?

Without thinking, I shuffle outside into the evening air. There's a diner up the street and I order two stacks of golden pancakes with soft syrup poured from an unnecessary height. I swallow them without chewing and the gate in my chest expands once more. Then I sit nervously, waiting to see what you're up to. When nothing happens, I order some more. It's been a simple misunderstanding of taste, I tell myself. But before the food comes, the tunnel in my chest stiffens. The coffee shop manager found me, and that insubstantial idiot brought a police officer with him.

It's hard to move quickly at my age, but I manage to totter out back before they see me. I'm very dizzy now, so I stand behind a dumpster and vomit a fermented galaxy onto the asphalt. Imagine it. A small woman in culottes!

The gate in my chest shrinks by two rings.

You've grown frustratingly picky with food, *you.*

I fast until the next evening and feel immense frustration from your side of the gate. The cold of space sneaks through my center and lowers my body temperature so much that I can see my breath. But do not worry, you, whatever you are. I've rented a private room at the local inn.

It's all mahogany and stonework, filled with the sound of a crackling fire. The business is run by a British family that moved—actually, I think you'll rather like the British when you meet them. They have the most beautiful accent with which to scream.

I fiddle with some knitting while the tea steeps and the owner leaves to prepare our meal: roast chicken dinner, fish and chips, a full English breakfast, followed by black pudding, and if you're up for it, a cask of sour ale and four different types of pie.

But first, the tea.

I drink it quickly and scald my narrow throat. I want you to have this the proper way, and the cosmos is very chilly this time of year. At least, I think. My body temperature rises as the liquid burns my stomach and makes its way to you.

I've damaged my throat rather badly and my lips quiver, but I sense it pleases you, and the rings beneath my chest double in number. The gate grows, and for the first time ever, I feel one of your monolithic fingers stroke its entrance. You curious thing, you.

The owner returns with a cart of food and asks about the blisters on my mouth. I shoo him away and pick at the offering. The pain in my throat is so blinding that I've grown numb to it. Tears in my eyes, I hum Ludwig van Beethoven while crisp chicken scratches through the gate.

I've nearly finished when you hurt me once more.

Each bite is abruptly rejected and sent back through the tunnel. It lands painfully in my leathered stomach and finds every possible orifice to retreat. Chicken juice squirts from my eyes. Tomato chunks run from each nostril and egg yolk drips from my gums. The owner rushes in and we scream at one another, but the sound from my throat is choked by sausage and beans.

I'm carried off in an ambulance because of you.

My apartment is all patchwork quilts and detailed embroidery. We are soft things here on earth, unlike the harsh void you're from.

It's not so much that I escaped the independent living facility—you're not a prisoner if you reside somewhere voluntarily. Though I did fail to check-out at the front desk, and now we're on "mandatory observation" for "scaring" a barista and "overwhelming" an innkeeper.

For hours I sit at the window of my third-floor apartment, listening to Japanese Lo-Fi on my phone. I fetch my family's book from under the bed and recall what my father told me before he died. *It's a bastard draft*, he whispered. *And came before a larger work.*

Ours is bound in rabbit skin, which has a little less oomph than human if I'm being completely honest. There are only a few pages inside, filled with unintelligible glyphs. For generations my family kept the book, knowing one day a key might reveal its secrets. And then just last week, they pushed that key directly to my cell phone with an updated operating system—along with some much-needed quality of life fixes, actually.

It's simple functionality: point your camera at a symbol and run it against a comprehensive database of human language. It made the news last month for translating a long-lost Babylonian hymn, but I used it to read an ancient book and open a portal in my chest. So, who's singing now?

Still, I must have missed something. I scan the book with my phone and know the app is thinking because a cartoon man dressed in yellow taps his crown thoughtfully. Then its spits out a messy translation:

> *Slice palm read invocation drink thy blood.*
> *Summon gate nourish by hand.*
> *CEILING FAN will return!*

Of course, the translation's not entirely accurate. But I doubt there's a word for whatever you are anyways.

Perhaps you're a child, I think. A picky thing. Or a teenager unwilling to get out of bed. Is that the case, my little ceiling fan?

I stare at the translation like it's an IKEA manual, retracing each step in my mind.

Slice palm: Yup.

Read invocation: Did it.

Drink thy blood: Mhm.

Summon gate, nourish by hand, CEILING FAN will return!

Yes, yes, yes, I'd done all that—

And then it occurs to me with such amusement that I nearly fall from my chair. Of course. *Nourish by hand.* I close my eyes and chuckle softly.

I sense you brush along the gate and chuff. We understand each other at last, I think. For me to be here, you must be there and vice versa. One thing in, one thing out. All this time, and I really thought I was feeding you by hand.

I grab my purse and pack a few belongings. Then, standing in front of the mirror, I smile and open my mouth. My grin expands. I've never felt my lips spread this way. Impossibly wide until my jaw unhinges and arcane light splashes over the walls of my apartment. I stick a hand inside my mouth and force it down my throat. Carefully, my fingers advance along my esophagus like inchworms, pulling my wrist and elbow behind them. I've nearly swallowed my entire bicep when Jackson, the facility's Health and Wellness Ambassador, knocks on my front door and pokes his head inside the apartment. He screams. I swallow my shoulder.

My fingers reach the gate inside my chest and plunge through. I can feel the cold of space beyond, and as my neck and face implode into themselves, I see you. Like two cars driving along the coast on a moonlit night, passing each other in opposite lanes. I smile and wave, and you return the gesture with one of your many megafaunal limbs. You. My little ceiling fan. Up and at 'em.

The void of space is all dark matter and unidentified colors.

Like a starfish in culottes, I cartwheel through darkness. My wrinkled skin is bathed in historic light, and what stars I can see here are not my own. The gateway is in a fixed position behind me. It's a muscular, pink oval, like ringworm on the flesh of space.

Slowly, I reach into my purse and pull a pair of Sony headphones over my ears. I press play on my phone and Japanese Lo-Fi scores this slow retreat from home. Within minutes, bits of detritus pour through the gate after me. Small objects at first: a quilt. Some sheetrock from the apartment wall. Then Jackson, the Health and Wellness Ambassador. He's been torn in half like gift wrap. More staff and residents follow. Then a park bench, some maple trees, a police cruiser. This goes on for twenty minutes or so before the national guard appears. There's dead bodies floating in each direction. A tank spills out followed by an explosion and one of those airplanes that Mr. Tom Cruise flew in *Top Gun.*

In that moment, something touches my elbow. I look down and find a piece of chocolate cake drifting alongside me, and my heart swells. You absolute darling, you. I drift there a while, nodding my chin to the celestial beat of our annihilation, enjoying German chocolate cake and this truly, *truly* delightful music.

⋈

Carrisa and Kevin
Gaze Into the Abyss

~ Rajiv Moté

JIMOTHY: We're back to our "Ghosted" segment on the *Jimothy and Abaddon Show*, 98.3 KISS FM! To recap, Kevin, you met Carissa on the dating apps, went out, had a good time, and even ended the night with a kiss. Now she's not returning your calls and you want to know why.

KEVIN: I'm grasping for meaning, Jimothy.

ABADDON: *[laughs]*

JIMOTHY: We'll get her on the phone. You know how this works, we'll talk with her, try to figure out what happened, and you're welcome to jump in after a while. If we clear things up, we'll pay to send you on a second date. Let's call . . .

CARISSA: Hello?

JIMOTHY: Could I speak to Carissa, please.

CARISSA: Speaking.

JIMOTHY: Carissa! I'm sorry to bother, but this is Jimothy from the *Jimothy and Abaddon Show* on 98.3 KISS FM. We're on the radio, so I need your permission to continue with this call. Could we chat for a minute?

CARISSA: *[laughs]* Did I win something?

ABADDON: *[exaggerated laughter]*

JIMOTHY: Maybe! I'll take that as a yes. We were contacted by a guy named Kevin, who met you on a dating app. He described a good first date, but now you're not answering his calls. He asked us to find out why. Do you remember Kevin?

CARISSA: I remember Kevin.

ABADDON: *[raucous laughter]*

JIMOTHY: When we hear that tone, there's usually a story.

CARISSA: No, I mean, it was fine, he was a gentleman. We even . . . But first dates are always the same, you know? The same questions, drinks, biographies . . . They all go the same way. Even if you think, like, *maybe* this time it'll be different. That's just hope. Treacherous hope . . .

ABADDON: First dates! Empty rituals on a loop! Lies in the hollow shape of human connection! *[wild laughter]*

CARISSA: Yeah! It's like a total waste of time, right?

JIMOTHY: Now hold on. Isn't that what a first date is—

KEVIN: What about our kiss?

ABADDON: *[air horn sound effect]*

JIMOTHY: I'm sorry, I always forget to mention, Kevin is on the line.

CARISSA: What?

KEVIN: The kiss at the end of our date. I mean, it didn't have to happen, but it did. There was something there.

CARISSA: *[nervous laughter]* It didn't mean anything. I know that now.

ABADDON: *[singing]* A kiss is just a kiss! A sigh is just a sigh!

JIMOTHY: Kevin, are you reading more into—

KEVIN: Your eyes are green, with flecks of gold. They looked into mine. I felt the connection. You put your hand on my shoulder and leaned in. There must have been something in that moment.

CARISSA: Kevin, listen. A kiss is just, like, the membrane separating me from not-me, brushing up against the membrane separating you from not-you. You know? Particles randomly colliding on their way to the heat death of the universe. Or something. Nothing matters against the background of Nothing.

ABADDON: She sees! She knows! *[mad laughter]*

KEVIN: Wait! There was intention behind that kiss. It was a choice to push what we were into what we could become. You extended your hand. I took it. We had a spark!

CARISSA: What are sparks, even? In my mind's eye, I've seen stars collide and annihilate each other. I've seen molecules carom into molecules, all bouncing their way into the void. My seeing-beyond-sight beheld the cold, dead center of the universe. The abyss is, like, inevitable.

ABADDON: The universe was exhaled from Nothingness and now Nothingness inhales! *[sound clip of Rob Zombie singing "Living Dead Girl"]*

KEVIN: I'll admit I was afraid when you leaned in. It yanked me out of the first-date routine, and suddenly everything felt real. Scary. But that's what I wanted, and I saw that you did too. Something real. Please don't retreat back into meaninglessness. Not now that we've broken through. The spark was real!

JIMOTHY: It does beckon the question, if everything is meaningless, why go on a dating app?

ABADDON: *[mad laughter]* Puppets on the strings of a clockwork puppeteer!

CARISSA: Have you ever looked into the dark heart of everything there is? The place that's blacker than black? The emptiness has teeth, guys. It has *arms*. It reaches out and it never lets go. I made a mistake. There's, like, no escape.

JIMOTHY: Well, I've looked at Abaddon's dating profile, which sounds about the same.

ABADDON: Oh no you did not look at my profile! *[laughter, so much laughter]*

KEVIN: Carissa, are you looking into the abyss right now?

CARISSA: I'm always looking into the abyss, Kevin. And, you know, vice-versa.

ABADDON: The abyss doesn't just look into you, it makes you one with it! *[toilet flush sound effect]*

KEVIN: I know what you're seeing. I've looked too. But Carissa, can you do me a favor? Find the edge. Find where the abyss gives way to stars.

CARISSA: I . . .

JIMOTHY: An out-of-body moment here on the show.

CARISSA: There's no edge. The more I look, the more I see the faintest lights in the darkness. It's not really empty.

ABADDON: Those stars have been dead a long time. A memory of light!

KEVIN: The void isn't devouring us. We're filling it. Slowly, maybe imperceptibly. But if you look hard enough, you can see the sparks throughout the dark. Those are people. People like us! The void is a lie. It can be banished with a kiss. I'll stand by you, Carissa. We can find the light together. We can *make* the light.

CARISSA: I could almost believe . . . Kevin, I'm so cold. Its arms are coiled around me. Its touch is ice. But . . . it wants me. That kind of feels like love.

KEVIN: Carissa, that thing holding on to you . . . It's literally *Nothing*. It has no power if you don't let it. Let's make sparks together. You reached out, I took your hand. Don't let go now. Let's fill the abyss with light and heat!

CARISSA: I miss being warm. I miss it so much.

JIMOTHY: I think that's my cue. Carissa, I have to ask, will you give Kevin another chance? We'll pay for a second date.

CARISSA: *[silence]*

ABADDON: Entropy is inevitable, kiddos! *[sad trombone sound effect]* It's the only thing that's real!

KEVIN: Your kiss was real for me, Carissa. What about you? Was it real?

CARISSA: *[quietly]* I think . . . Yes.

JIMOTHY: That sounds like a second date! Congratulations! Please stay on the line so we can get your information. We wish you all the best.

ABADDON: Good luck, you crazy kids! *[uncontrolled, echoing laughter]*

JIMOTHY: This never happens, Abaddon.

ABADDON: They'll never make it to a third date.

⌗

In Another Distant Land, in a Luminescent Land

~ Daniel David Froid

1.

"I think it's gonna rain, Clive. I really do think . . ."

Her voice trailed off. She looked back at her husband, where he sat on the couch, oblivious, and then at the window once more. Her fingertips touched the panes of glass and felt their cold surface. Cold as glass, she thought. That's good: no, it's not.

". . . it's gonna rain. If it rains I'll just die. It'll ruin everything. I'll just die."

She looked at her husband once more. His eyes remained fixed on the TV as on some distant lodestar. This ship set sail at dawn and has not yet ceased its voyage. This ship—

Yes, he was thinking about ships, and not just ships. His eyes were drawn to the sailors in the film he was watching, as they strode about a vast deck. One sailor caught his eye in particular, dark of hair and thickly muscled, with curls of hair atop his sun-browned head and just at the line of his collar. Those hairs seemed to wave hello at Clive, who would have waved back. The sailor turned, to look beyond the prow, toward the blue that carried them afloat, and Clive caught the thrilling glimpse of a firm buttock.

—this ship could sail forever.

He did the thing that drove her nuts. She repeated his name. His eyes remained fixed on the TV, but she could see in his face that he had heard her. Slowly, as if he wanted to let her know how little he cared to speak to her, he drew his eyes away from the screen and in her direction. "What," he said.

"My party, Clive!" she said and tutted. "Do you ever think about anything but that damn TV?"

Suddenly Clive burst into flame. Just where he sat, his soul—were it his soul—caught fire. The conflagration began in the center of him and spread out on both sides. The couch, where it sat on one end of the room, would soon dissolve to pungent ash. It would take with it the end table, first, then the curtains, then the stand on which the TV sat. The TV would fall. The fire would subsume the house. All would be destroyed by the flame of him, the soul of him.

He wished it would happen. To have combusted would have been easier in every way than the other thing: easier to explain, to rationalize, to bear. A fire would in fact explain the other thing. Perhaps. Did he know the melting point of flesh?

He was getting carried away. But here is the thing, nonetheless: he did not catch but fire, but little gobs of flesh plopped away from his arm. They landed on the couch. His flesh was melting at a leisurely pace. There was no other way to explain it. It had been going on for about a half an hour. It seemed that Jane had not yet noticed. It had taken him a while to notice himself, for he didn't feel any pain. Thirty or forty minutes into the movie, he sat up and stretched his arm and noticed a wetness and then, on the couch, a stain. The thought seemed clear as day: Oh, he thought. My arm is melting. But he didn't feel any pain. Neutrally, he observed and accepted it.

"Damn it!" she said. She screwed up her face and clicked her nails against the glass, hard, inconsequential outlet for her anger. "It's really coming down now. Well, we're gonna have to clean this place up. Just can't have the party the way I planned it." She raised her arms, as if toward God. "Oh well! What do you do! Clive. Come on."

Clive again spent some seconds looking away from his arm and toward his wife. "What?"

She rolled her eyes and then startled, flickering out of this world. She saw the endless desert for a moment that might have been years, and then she flickered back.

Clive, who may not have noticed at all, felt a warmth and wetness in his arm, which he lifted uneasily.

Now Jane stepped closer to Clive and saw a glob that rested on the sofa. Though she knew what it was, she yelped, pointing with her index finger, "What the hell is on that sofa? Clive, what is that? You better clean it up right now. We'll have guests coming at five!"

He stood up uneasily. He had to heave, holding his arms above his head. His stomach pushed against his thighs. He grunted. Another bit of flesh fell now on his stomach.

Clive cursed. His arm continued to melt, dripping a path behind him as he shuffled toward the bathroom. He looked back at his wife as he moved. Where she stood, a silhouette etched out her place in the world, a Jane-shaped outline within which he thought he saw stars, the light of a distant dark place that might yet engulf him. His head snapped back. He moved into the bathroom and shut the door.

Once there he sighed in relief: solitude again. No more visions of the place her silhouette sometimes showed him and the monstrous beings that lived there.

In the mirror he looked at his face, sallow and bloated. He thought, I look tired and old. He thought, I am. He clapped his hands on his stomach, feeling the flab that had come there to roost. It was funny: his own perception of his body was divorced from its appearance. To be in his body still felt and looked, in his mind's eye, the way it felt and looked twenty years ago. When he looked in the mirror, he felt always the discord between the two, ghost and reality. He wondered if a day might come when he was no longer haunted by his own body's ghost.

Now he raised his arm and looked at its reflection. The melting had deformed it: the underside of his arm looked almost blurred, its edges softened. Then again, it was not quite as severe as he had initially thought. Not so much flesh had melted after all. He did not know, to tell the truth, whether it was correct to say the flesh was melting. Yet he had no other way to describe it, the way the skin would heat and seem to loosen and then drip from his arm. It seemed to happen whenever she blinked out, as he thought of it, and showed him that landscape, those things within it.

Taking a washcloth from the closet, he moistened it and wiped his arm. His arm had a scent: sweet and bitter, as of cooking meat. He swiped his arm a few more times. He didn't know how he'd clean the couch. When his arm seemed clean enough, dripping no longer, he moved to the bedroom and changed his shirt, opting for a long-sleeved shirt that might disguise his unsightly arm. Then he got out the carpet cleaner.

When he returned to the living room, he could see Jane in the kitchen on the phone, muttering about her party and the rain as she moved things around on the counter. She pulled a box of crackers out of a cupboard and set it down, and then she picked it up and moved it somewhere else. He plugged in the carpet cleaner and uncoiled the cleaning brush. Then he swiped it on the couch and the carpet until both looked sufficiently clean.

By the time he was done, and the appliance back in its home on the floor of the bathroom closet, Jane was in the living room, picking things up: keys and a shopping bag from the side table, a cardigan draped on the back of the couch. "What a mess," she tutted.

"Everything all clean now?" she said.

"Sure is," Clive replied.

She smiled. "Good. Now please go work on the dining room. We're going to have to put all the food in there."

He moved away from her. He sighed and began to clean the room.

2.

She thought, *This is awful.* Her fingers were coated in cream cheese. She was spreading cream cheese on little strips of faux ham, trying her level best not to make a mess. The only reason she ever bothered with pickle rollups was because everyone else seemed to love them so much. She found them revolting. And it had been at least a decade since she'd last eaten meat. *Am I ethically compromised,* she had thought at the grocery store, *if I buy the ham anyway?* But she opted always for the fake stuff, and nobody ever noticed, or they never said a word.

She glanced up from the counter and craned her neck to see if Clive had finished cleaning up the dining room. *Dining room,* a term that felt grandiose for a space hardly more than an alcove, which housed a table and chairs and a tall, narrow cabinet in which she stored her china. He'd gone away again. *His arm,* she thought. She pulled another slice of imitation ham from the container and spread it out flat. She took her knife and spread the cream cheese on it, and then once more she used her finger to effect more even coverage. Once it was well and truly smeared, she stabbed a pickle with her fork and laid it on its cream cheese bed.

It was an interesting problem, an embarrassing problem. When she saw the stains on the couch, the drips on the floor, she knew immediately that his flesh was melting. And her body had flickered out of this world (she saw the desert, the sky) before returning here. She mused that he was so inattentive, so consistently foggy of brain and soul, it was likely he scarcely even noticed something wrong. And it was a situation she herself preferred not to confront.

At last the rollups were rolled and sliced: finished. She arranged them on a platter and put it in the fridge. When the phone began to ring, she was standing at the sink, scrubbing her hands, feeling her body flicker away once more.

She left the world. She was bathed in fluorescent color. A landscape of luminous purple, pink, and orange stretched before her. Oh god, she thought. And then she looked out on the sand, thick and sludgy beneath her feet. Though she did not move a muscle, she felt the landscape shift as if she were in motion; pulled closer to the sea, to that lonely shore's very edge, she looked into the endless waters. Sometimes, she thought she could espy a distant island—another one—in the far distance. She saw monstrous things cavorting, thrashing with all their might. Perhaps she was looking behind her. Sometimes it felt that she could see in all directions at once, which lent the island the illusion, the feeling, of endlessness, all things in all directions forever. She lingered in that place until it gave way once more to the sink with its water that ran into the drain. She breathed in, deep. The phone continued ringing. The caller, it seemed, was prepared to wait.

She snatched the phone and held it to her ear. "Hello," she barked.

"Jane—you okay? It's Lisa . . ."

"Yes, I'm sorry. I'm, um, a bit distracted."

"Sure. Well, sorry to interrupt. Just calling to ask if I can pick anything up before we head over."

"Oh, you know—I don't think we need anything. I think we're all ready. I assume you've seen the weather. It's raining. I hate it. It kills me."

She and Lisa continued to chatter while she tucked some dishes into the dishwasher. She heard the gentle roar of the carpet cleaner as Clive cleaned up his mess.

After Lisa hung up, Jane moved into the living room, noticing that he'd missed a spot. A little flesh-gob clung to the carpet right in front of the couch. She returned to the kitchen, retrieved and moistened a rag, and scrubbed the stain. It came away easily. Furtively, she sniffed the rag. It smelled like meat, which after all it was; her nose wrinkled as she sneered at it. A thought blew through her mind: *Has Clive ever tried to taste it?*

As she stood up, she saw Clive leaving the dining room. His hand clutched a sheaf of junk mail and receipts, which he dropped, unbidden, for no reason at all. Then he leaned over to pick them back up. Sometimes, near Clive, she would feel the sudden flush of hot shame: not hers, his. He was embarrassing; the thought would suddenly flicker in her head with an uncomfortable clarity, it would pierce her, and she would feel unsure what to do with it. She scowled.

She thought of a night two weeks ago now, maybe three. She had found him in the bathroom, sitting up in a tub of lukewarm water. "Oh Clive," she'd said when she opened the door. Had he thought she wasn't home? There he was, caught in the act, sawing his wrists with a dull knife and bleeding only lightly.

She'd told him, "Life is miserable for everybody. There's no need to make such a big deal out of it." He would not die, nor would he even need a trip to the hospital. She helped him out, coaxed him into his bathrobe, swabbed his wrists with cotton pads soaked in alcohol, wrapped them in gauze. The pads made him yelp.

"Well, it stings, doesn't it!" she said. "That's pain. Thought that's what you were looking for."

Now she said, starting to laugh, "Ha-ha-huh-remember the—remember the other day? Ha! When I found you in the tub? Ha ha."

His face flashed in anger: a broken grimace. He said, "Maybe you led me to do it in the first place."

She said, "Oh, sure. Ha ha. Clive, you're such a fool," she said. She began to laugh again. Then he, too, started to laugh and shook his head.

The doorbell rang. She sighed, wiping eyes wet with jovial tears, and said, "Someone's at the door. Oh Christ. It's early! What time is it?"

He glanced at the clock. "Four thirty," he said.

"Half an hour early? Really," she said. He shook his head in reply.

"Can you go get it, dear? Guess we'll have to let 'em in."

Clive strode to the door and pulled it open, revealing a short, scrawny child with his brown hair buzzed into a flattop. It was Garrett, the only child of their friends Lucas and Mel—Garrett, who resembled far too closely his good-looking father. Separately and simultaneously, Clive and Jane each felt a withering sadness inside. Neither wished to attend to this irritating child and wondered where his parents were.

Clive broke the silence. He said, "Hello, Garrett. How are you?"

He said, tilting his head downward with a shyness that felt performed, "I'm fine. How're you?"

Clive smiled and said, "Fine. Where are your parents?"

Garrett looked back and pointed at the driveway. "They're coming," he said.

Then he looked at Clive and said, "Don't you want me to come in? Or do you want me to disappear?"

Clive gave a nervous laugh. "No—uh—what? You can—"

He ran off. Clive poked his head out, following the boy's path across the lawn. He saw a dark-green minivan in the driveway with Lucas and Mel in the front seat. Immediately, with that first glimpse of Lucas, a hot flush of shame and desire bloomed within him. He smiled and waved and awkwardly stood in the doorway as Lucas and Mel left the car. Clive waved at them.

3.

A stranger in his own abode, Clive stood suspended near the entryway, hearing guests' speech but not taking it in. Where was this place with that old beige sofa, that TV that played reruns of old movies, and the cuckoo clock that stopped to chirp its horologic call once per hour, always two minutes late? It couldn't be his, but it was his. The dozen-odd guests who now loitered amid its shabby furniture served to distort it, estrange it. It seemed, for some few disorienting seconds, or were they minutes, that he did not know where he was. He looked at the plate that rested in one hand: deviled eggs with flecks of bright paprika, pickle rollups with spurts of cream cheese leaking out. Someone was speaking, but the words that they had spoken could not encroach the barrier of his disquiet. He listened and thought for a moment, struck by the awareness that he had no idea to whom he was speaking or what they might have said.

He looked up. He looked into the face of this someone. It was the handsome chiseled face of a man he knew well.

It was Lucas who spoke. He and Jane had endured the same social circle for decades, the friends with whom they'd gone through school, who, like them, had never left this town. It was hard, he thought, too hard to bear the weight of all those years. Whenever such a thought crossed his head, what he meant was that it was hard to bear the weight of his history with Lucas, Lucas his friend, Lucas Jane's half-brother, a man whom at one time he had wanted to be part of his life forever—whom he now wished would no longer be part of that life at all. Too many years. Now some images appeared in his mind, snapshots of twenty years ago that he savored and that never seemed to drift very far from his consciousness. Fooling around is what they called it then, an activity that, it seemed, bore little meaning to Lucas beyond some moments' pleasure, an activity of which, if it did penetrate deep in his soul, he had never breathed a word to Clive in all these years, never shown signs of disturbance, regret, or desire. Yet desire formed the substratum of every thought Clive had about this friend, whom he hated to see. And Lucas, too, had flickered out a couple of times, leaving a dark silhouette inside which Clive could see the desert and the creatures that lived there.

Clive's mind juggled those images as well as the thought that his arm had once again begun to melt. Scarcely any room remained for the Lucas of the present, who had made an uninteresting remark about his son. Clive laughed uneasily. He nodded. Then he clapped Lucas on the shoulder, an imitation of a jovial host (did it work?) and said that, soon, he would return.

In the kitchen Jane stood speaking to Lisa and Kathy, her closest friends. They stood as though guarding the food. Jane called out, "Hello dear!" as Clive came in. He noted her smile; she seemed to be enjoying herself despite the weather. He nodded back.

"After all that, the weather's clearing up!" she said. He laughed.

Then her face turned dark. "Honey," she said. "Your shirt's wet."

"It's—" he began. He put his plate on the counter and moved away quickly, heading for the master bath hidden in the back of the house.

There in the bathroom he looked once more in the mirror, rotating his arm to inspect both sides. It was true: his sleeve was wet. He unbuttoned the shirt and hung it on the doorknob then came face-to-face once more with his skin. The arm was looking oddly distorted, not thinner but flattened somehow, stretched. His shirt was ruined, covered in gobs of flesh. But, strangely enough, it didn't hurt. He balled up the sodden shirt and tossed it on the floor, in the corner, onto a small pile of other discarded clothing. Then he used a wash-cloth to wipe off the back of his arm, swiping several times across its surface in succession until at last he seemed clean. And then he sighed and changed his shirt.

He returned to the party.

4.

Jane and Lisa and Kathy were standing in the kitchen. Clive had just ducked in and she'd told him, before she could help herself, that his shirt was wet. His face looked flushed. He must have been talking to Lucas. A dark thought about her half-brother flitted across her con-sciousness. She put it away.

"Poor guy," Kathy said. What was that on his shirt?"

Jane rolled her eyes and shrugged. "It's hard saying. Probably spilled something. You know how clumsy he is." Her eyes met Kathy's—close-set, a grubby hazel—and she thought about how homely her friend was. With devotion and resentment, sometimes more of one than the other and sometimes less, she had peered into this face for too long. Kathy laughed. Jane smiled.

The party had, after all that—the anxiety and rumination and plan-ning and preparing—been a success. She thought it was a success. It had rained only a little, but everybody stayed inside. There were just enough people, and they seemed to be enjoying themselves. Despite her role as hostess, she enjoyed remaining here in the kitchen, where she could just see into the living and dining rooms—where she felt as though she were surveying her kingdom. And, after all, her guests would eventually find their way here to get snacks and drinks and pay their respects to her and her house and her food and good taste.

But of course, she thought, Clive barged in and threatened to ruin things with his disgusting arm.

As she stood here in the kitchen next to her friends, her mind on Clive's arm, Jane felt again the shift or flicker within her. As she stood, she closed her eyes, opening them to see again the desert at night. The sand was bright pink and so heavy. She could feel its chill beneath her feet. Above, a bright moon hung against a backdrop of sky, which had shaded now into a deep rose color that she loved. Somewhere, not near, the dark sea's waves lapped against an unseen shore. She could hear it. As she gazed out on the landscape, she wondered for a moment what Kathy and Lisa saw. She walked forward on the sand and, as she walked, she saw one of those enormous creatures. Its roaring grew louder and louder. She knew their work would come to fruition one day soon. They wouldn't need her anymore.

She'd been going here since she was a child, as far back as her memory stretched. The first time she'd gone there—and "gone there" is how she always tended to regard it, in all the simplicity and vagueness that phrase implied—she was in the bathtub, and when she came to she found that most of the water had drained away somewhere. Her perceptions of the place engulfed her. In some ways, she felt she knew as little now as then, though she knew that was categorically untrue.

Now, she gazed at the creature before her, wondering what she would see when they infiltrated the other world at last.

Suddenly, her arm was shaking; a hand was pulling on it. "Whoa!" she heard Lisa say. "Lost you there for a second." Jane looked at her and smiled.

"Sorry," she said. "I was just. I spaced out." She paused. Lisa's face indicated concern.

Then Jane began to speak, an effort at diversion: "Hey, did I tell you who I saw at the store this morning? It was"—her voice fell— "Teresa." As her friends' eyes widened, the satisfaction of delivering a piece of gossip overtook them as well as her. "She looked like a disaster. And she had that man with her. What's his name." "Ricky?" Lisa whispered. Jane nodded. For a few minutes, they mocked Teresa, though they soon exhausted the subject. Jane yawned, took a step away from her friends, and stretched her arms behind her back. She said, "Why don't we get out the dessert." Then she moved toward the far counter, where the chocolate cake she'd made sat in its covered dish. Lisa moved to a nearby drawer and found a butterknife, which she handed to Jane. Kathy got the plates. They moved in synchrony. When they were done, Jane poked her head into the living room and called out, "We have cake!"

○

5.

Later now, in dusk's soft descent, Clive stood in the kitchen all alone. He saw Jane in the living room, perched on the couch next to Lisa. Lucas and Mel stood near Kathy, by the door. He had heard her say she had to leave. Nonetheless, she had been standing at the door with her coat on for almost twenty minutes now, chattering away. She was talking about her plans for tomorrow, errands she intended to run. Clive was sipping a beer and shifting his glance from guest to guest. He liked being alone here, feeling more natural as a voyeur in his own home than he ever did mingling among his guests. From his vantage point near the refrigerator, nobody could see him, but he could see almost everybody. Only Jane, on the couch's nearest corner, escaped his sight. He took a sip.

Jane sat on the couch. She and Lisa spoke about how their lives would unfold in the next week or two. Jane was going to take a trip soon to visit some family, she said. She apprised Lisa of the route she would take and spoke of what her aunt was like. Lisa was describing her new job at the medical center. Jane nodded, paying less attention to her friend as she spoke. She knew Clive was hiding. Strange man, she thought, what do our guests think?

"Hey," Clive heard. Jane projected her voice so it would sail into the kitchen. "Where's Clive gone off to . . .?"

Taking a deep breath and slowly expelling it, Clive waited. He let several moments pass so as not to appear in an instant, which would seem to suggest that he really was hiding, listening in. Then he took another deep breath and shuffled into view in the doorway to the kitchen. He gave a terse smile. "Just getting a beer," he said, holding it up as proof.

"You're missing out on all the fun!" Lucas called out. He seemed so at ease, as if he were the host. Lord of all he surveyed. He was, thought Clive. He Resenting it, resenting him, Clive nodded and shuffled toward an armchair, settling in.

Kathy said, "Okay! I really should get going." She placed her hand on the doorknob and then said, "Oh, Jane, first I wanted to ask you . . ."

Jane listened to her friend's question but glanced again at Clive. He seemed fidgety.

And in truth he felt near to bursting. What sort of pressure can build in a body, hurtle it close to explosion. He wondered whether he would explode. He wondered whether that was possible. It's not, he thought. It isn't possible. It wasn't possible, but nor was the melting of flesh from an arm, and he could feel it dripping, could feel the slimy wetness of flesh as it slid from bone.

At last Kathy left, saying her final—"I mean it this time!"—good-byes. Lucas and Mel moved into the living room proper. Jane and Lucas made eye contact. Lisa murmured to Jane and then stood up.

"Well," she said. "I need to get going, too. I've got work in the morning." Jane walked her to the door; they exchanged brief hugs. By the time she returned to the couch, Lucas was back, now sitting next to his wife.

Something was different. Clive could tell. His arm continued to melt. The other arm was melting too. He felt the flush of heat on his face. And he believed that his vision was beginning to blur. He looked across the room at Mel and Lucas, and they appeared to him as though through a thin layer of water. Everything before him seemed runny at the edges. He squinted, opened his mouth to breathe, and shut it once again.

"Are you okay?" Mel asked him. It seemed that blood was rushing in his ears. He couldn't hear anything she said, nor could he see the worry that now crossed her face: furrowed brow, a frown. With both hands, he gripped the arms of the chair. He tried, and failed, to stand up. Then he tried again and succeeded. He was on his feet and facing the rest of them.

"Uh—I—" he began to sputter.

"Clive!" Jane called. All three on the couch stood up when he did. But, as they did, he noticed not only Jane but Lucas, too. He could see it through his blurred vision: both of them gone, in their places outlines that revealed, piecemeal, glimpses of another distant land, a luminescent land. He pointed, futilely, at nothing. It seemed to him an eternity that he stood there, watching them and the creatures he saw within their outlines. Standing, waiting, struggling to breathe—or was it to stay alive—summoning up the courage to move, he remained in suspension. His arm felt funny.

He considered running headlong into one of their silhouettes, wondering whether he would vanish. Instead, he fainted.

○

6.

He woke up in bed. His arm felt considerably lighter. Jane was sitting next to him, reading a book. She put it down when she noticed his stirring.

"You're awake," she said.

"I have a headache."

"You fainted again," she said and sighed. "And your arm . . ."

"I feel like an idiot," he said. "Fainting. At your party."

"That's probably because you are."

"Yeah," he said and began to chuckle. They both had a good laugh.

⌗

Shine

~ Kate Ristau

You pull back the creaky front gate. Paint comes off in your hands, black and crusty. This place is old—like Civil-War-old. It's ancient.

The trees droop down around you, ancient willow branches sinking toward the ground, dark and gray. The path is worn out; bricks covered by dying moss, dry and dusty.

Chad made you come here.

You wanted to be done for the day. You were so over the endless solicitations—that is Chad's fancy word for knocking on people's doors and selling them stuff.

This job sucks.

You used to work at Tiny's, down the road, but Tara called you out one night in front of everybody, and you called Tara's bluff. But then Jason sided with Tara, and then she brought Mark in, and oh my gosh that whole story is so boring.

So, Chad.

Chad with the solar panels. Chad with the green dream. Chad with the up-selling.

"Come on, Sarah," he said. "It's not that hard. You just knock on their door. Use the talking points."

"Chad. People hate this stuff. *I* hate this stuff."

"Solar is the next generation of—"

"I know. I watched the training video. I learned all about the breakthroughs in scientific technology that have led me to knocking on some weirdo's front door, trying to convince them to let me in, so I can walk them through a complicated solar test that really just gets me into the door and directly into their hearts."

"Exactly."

Chad missed the sarcasm. You can rely on Chad for many things, but subtlety is not one of them.

Now, you are walking through the front gate of Miss Havisham's decrepit old mansion, looking to sell her solar panels on what has suddenly become a very foggy, very gray day.

Where did the sun go?

Focus. The sun doesn't matter. Who cares if you are hurtling through the universe on a gigantic pile of rock? You are selling the dream, not selling a burning ball of eternal fire.

You knock on the front door.

She opens it before you can back away screaming. Wait, why would you scream?

"Oh, hello honey. It's so good to see you."

"Um, you too? I guess?"

Oops. Chad told you to be affirming. Confident. To stop ending your sentences with questions?

"Yes," you say, affirmatively. "Yes. I am happy to see you on this sunny day."

"Sunday is my favorite day."

Your favorite day is Thursday. But this is what you've got, so you nod your head.

Her gray hair falls down her forehead, swirling into her veil. You can't tell where she ends and the darkness behind her begins. Wait a minute. Is she seriously wearing a veil? It's like, August.

Talking points.

"Have you noticed how expensive your electricity bill is?"

"Oh, the cost of living is just atrocious, isn't it?"

"It really is."

You glance into the darkness behind Miss Havisham and the flame of one candle takes shape. You remember the training, though. The electricity isn't actually the point.

Compliments.

"I love your candles! They are so bright. And shiny. Do they smell? My mom has candles that smell."

Not true. Your mom is dead. She did not like candles. She said that if she wanted things to smell like a Pottery Barn, she would move back to Connecticut.

Compliments first, then connections.

"Listen, I know this might be a little uncomfortable. Not everyone likes standing in their doorway talking to random—"

"Oh, I do! I just love visitors. I don't get enough of them. They're are always scared off by the dead sunflowers. I desperately need a new gardener. Would you like to come in?"

You stare into the fathomless depths of her veil, and slide your eyes toward the wooden planks on the floor, where her dress shifts in the dying light of the sun.

It's noon.

"Sure!" Confident. Like page 42 of the manual. "I would love to." You step in immediately. If there is one thing you learned in training, it is that an opening in a conversation is your chance to shine.

You look around the entryway, searching. Compliments. "I just love the—" You don't know what you love. Dust? Sure. You could love that. But that's not a compliment. Architecture. Yes. "Balustrades!"

You maybe yelled that too loud.

But Miss Havisham does not care. She is heading down the hall-way, gesturing at you with a claw-like hand. You follow.

Should you go back to the balustrades? Or focus on those weird tables with the octopus legs?

"I like your tables!" you yell.

"Mmm-hmm."

You should probably stop yelling. It didn't say anything about yelling in the manual.

What's the next talking point? No question marks. Stop that. Compliments. Connections.

Clinching.

Is it time to clinch yet?

No. That's wrong. Components! Components first, clinching second, money third.

You need money. Thanks to Tara and Jason. It's been a dry month.

"Would you like some tea?"

She's asking a question. You sit down in a chair. The dust puffs up around you.

"Yes. That sounds lovely. Thank you. I was hoping, if you have some time, to talk with you more about," you take a deep breath, "the wonders of solar."

Miss Havisham toddles toward the tea cart in the corner, quietly bustling. "Oh, is that the sun? I love the sun. Tell me more. I've been trying to capture the sun for years. Decades. Millenia beyond mea-suring."

"Well, if you don't have TRITECH solar panels, you're not capturing it the right way."

Miss Havisham floats over to you, tea cup rattling, and sets it down on the table beside you. The dust scatters beneath your saucer.

You pick up the cup hesitantly.

She stares at you intently.

So many adverbs. It's like, a whole thing.

"Did you know," she says, "in ancient times, the Sumerians worshiped the sun? The Egyptians did too. And the Indo-Europeans just cannot seem to get enough of that divine power. In truth, many cultures throughout time have fallen down prostrate before those flaxen amber rays. We worship what we think we cannot consume, don't we?"

The conversation is getting a little meta, but you think you can still save it. "Yes! The sun. I know exactly what you mean. Energy consumption is the real problem here. And we can solve it for you. Not only that, but if you save up enough energy, you can even sell the electricity back to the electric company."

"I did not know that."

Your fingers wind around the handle of your cup. You open your mouth, unsure what to say next, but thank the gods, she's not done yet. You need time to think.

"All those new, fancy words do not really matter, do they?" Miss Havisham says. "I have worshiped the sun myself, without telescopes and science and all that balderdash for time out of mind."

Clinching. Screw the components. She's on board. She wants in. Get to the good part. Seal the deal.

"Would you like me to do a full solar outlay for you? I can measure, examine, and design a complete solar package to make sure your house is suitable for capturing sunlight on a regular, consistent basis, thereby saving you untold amounts of money throughout any season. You won't have to worship the sun. You'll have it right in the palm of your hand."

Chad says to always echo back what the customer says. Capturing sunlight? *Check.* Worshiping the sun? *Check.*

Miss Havisham gestures toward your teacup. "Please. Don't wait on me. I'll pour my own in just a moment."

Maybe she's not sold. Maybe she needs a little more convincing. You lift the teacup hesitantly to your lips. The moment the steam hits your nose, you sigh. You pull in a sip. The taste is like liquid gold, the flavor like ambrosia. Like honey.

"It tastes like the sun, doesn't it?"

You pause, looking over your teacup at the old woman. Her bones crackle beneath her, the weight of a thousand years pushing against the frail carbon cage that holds her soul in check.

You look around the room, and realize for the first time that daylight is gone. The windows are black, and the flames of the candles bend toward her open maw.

Holy shit.

Her eyes are the death of the universe. Her teeth tear into your soul. She will eat the sun like an apple and crunch on the seeds and never, ever stop until all life is gone and nothing remains but shadow and death. She is endless.

You nearly drop your teacup, but instead, you shake your head.

"Sorry, I clearly got too much sun today."

You need some more water, some less fancy tea, and a really long nap. Or maybe just a two-liter of Coke.

Stop messing around. It's time to bring it home.

You set the teacup down and lean in.

"With our TRITECH 1400 panels, you can capture the sun. You won't just light up this room, you'll light up the entire city. With the flick of a switch, the power of the sun will be yours. Don't you want to shine?"

That was a question, Chad doesn't like questions. But Chad didn't miss his last rent payment, and Chad's dad pays for his Honda. Chad can suck it.

For one long moment, the world is still. The air is heavy with anticipation and dread and just a little too much dust.

Then, her veil falls back down around her open maw, and she picks up her own teacup.

"Tell me more."

And you know this is going to be your biggest sale. The company's biggest sale. Enough solar panels to cover this side of the river. You'll have Chad's job. Tara's too. You tell her about TRITECH—*always the sunniest side of the street!*—but the words sound distant, caught up in some shadows. Slippery, sliding away. Not that they matter. The words, that is. You've made the deal. It's all teacups and sunlight now. Brilliant and bright, light unending.

⊐

Fuzzy Fuzzy Kitty Kitties

~ Erik Grove

That Professor Armitage thought of me for this job was a little surprising. When I took her class, she'd told me I "lacked rigor," had "insufficient intellectual curiosity," and "never did the reading." Which, fair. Whatever. I got a good old reliable C+ so she must have come around. I was also surprised that campus was open considering the pandemic and all but when I got to the staff entrance of the Miskatonic U Library, the lights were on and the door was unlocked.

"Hello?" My voice was muffled by a cloth mask I got at the grocery store in a six pack.

Armitage's office was down here tucked between the coffee shop and long term storage.

I used to spend a lot of time here when I dated a barista at Jittery Joe's. Didn't work out. She got a job at Starbucks off campus.

"Through here, Mr. Keating."

I knew her voice when I heard it. Professor Henrietta Armitage still called people Mr. or Mrs. So-and-So because she probably learned it listening to people from the 19th Century back when she was an undergrad.

When I got to the doorway of her office, Armitage held up her "wait a minute" finger before I crossed the threshold. She hurriedly made a notation with an actual pen on actual paper. Armitage was the kind of old and thin that looked like someone messed up and didn't give her enough skin. She wasn't wrinkled. She was taut. Her lips pulled back into a leathered rictus. Maybe she did botox. She took off her reading glasses and put on a mask.

"This way."

The library was closed to patrons and had a vibe like a haunted garage sale. After months of social distancing, watching my roommate's sourdough starter grow, and Quarantine Cat lick his litter box hole, I'd have taken any job I could get.

Armitage stopped at an elevator and pressed the button.

Foot tap. Foot tap. Love that imaginary muzak. "You watching a lot of Netflix?"

"We don't need to talk casually."

I almost said, "Thank God."

We took the elevator down to a windowless expanse of over-crowded bookshelves.

"There are certain guidelines you must abide by during your time here, Mr. Keating," Armitage said. She fished out a set of keys from her pocket with her weirdo tight-skinned hand and walked briskly into the stacks.

"You can call me Andy," I said.

The look she gave me emphatically informed me that she absolutely could not.

At the end of a row of shelves Armitage stopped at a door with multiple padlocks. She unlocked two of them and the knob, then started on the first of two combination locks. "The books we will be working with are sensitive."

"Like . . . emotionally?"

She popped the first combination lock off and gave me a Sad Teacher with a Slow Student look.

"To sunlight and stuff obviously," I fake-laughed.

Armitage detached the second lock and picked up a cardboard box from the floor. "Deposit your phone please, Andrew."

I took the phone from my pocket. "Do you have music in there?"

"Music?"

"Spotify," I said. "Makes the hours—" I snapped my fingers.

She pushed the cardboard at me. "I will bring you a radio."

Which—not going to lie—was how I found out radios were still a thing. I put my phone in the box because arguing about it seemed like it could cost me the job and I swear to god if I had to go back to my apartment and watch Lester play Critter Carnival until they made a vaccine, I'd lose my god damn mind.

Armitage opened the door to a small office with old books and papers stacked from floor to ceiling with a cramped desk under a single swaying light bulb at the far end.

"What is this place?" I reached for one of the books and Armitage slapped the back of my hand. "Ow!"

"Gloves." She prodded me with a box of latex gloves. "You will not handle these items without gloves."

I pulled out a couple gloves from the box. I thought about telling her we were supposed to be giving all these sorts of supplies to hospitals and stuff like that TV show about the fake autistic doctor, but I was pretty sure she hadn't seen that show.

"This is the special archive," Armitage explained. "These books are very old, very delicate, and . . ."

"*Sensitive.*"

Armitage nodded. "Your task is using the scanner to digitize the pages."

With my gloved hands I went back for the book I wanted to look at. Armitage didn't hit me again and I almost didn't flinch worrying about that. "These aren't in English?"

The pages were all hand-written in tight, neat script that didn't use any sort of alphabet I'd ever seen. Triangles with dots in the middle. Like eyes. Crescents and squiggly lines. The pages were rough, thick old parchment, and the cover some sort of leather.

"Pigskin," Armitage said, answering a question I hadn't asked. Weird, right? What other sort of skin would you use to bind a book. She took the book from me. "These tomes are written in different forms of . . . code," she said.

She looked like a straight up skeleton under that single light bulb. A gentle breeze ran across the back of my neck followed by a creaking moan. Probably the HVAC. Old buildings, you know.

"So I just put the pages in the thing?" I pointed at the scanner.

"*Do not* read read them, Mr. Keating. Do not read *anything* in this room. Some things are safer untranslated." The professor and her whisper inched closer. "I can't have you breaking before the task is complete."

I nodded. "Sure. They're not for reading. Got it." Maybe I'd have done better in her class if she had more material. "So, when do I get paid? Is this a biweekly or monthly sorta deal?"

Armitage told me to email someone in university HR for answers to my payroll questions, demonstrated how to use the scanner, and told me that she'd be upstairs.

I sat down at the desk and moved around to get comfortable in the chair. Hundred-year-old asses wore it in real nice. Supple. Like pigskin.

"Do be mindful of various . . . stresses," Armitage said.

"Carpal tunnel," I said. "Totally."

She backed out of the room and closed the door. Moments later multiple locks clicked into place.

"Hey!" I called out. The room moaned and sounded like a dozen overlapping whispers filled the room. "What if I need to go to the bathroom?"

That first day, time flew by. I scanned pages from the first book, and I must have zoned out because the next thing I knew, Armitage shook my shoulder.

"Lunch time?"

"You're done for the day, Mr. Keating," she said.

On the desk a small radio played greatest hits from the naughty oughties. Puddle of Mudd y'all. There were six books in my finished pile. Wild. I'm *crushing* this job.

After we left, Armitage locked up the special archives. She handed me my phone. It was after 6 o'clock.

"Didn't seem like nine hours." I winked at the professor. "It's the music."

She nodded solemnly. "Indeed."

Outside of the library, all the movie theaters and bars were still closed, and the dumb virus was still everywhere. Back at our apartment, Lester was selling radishes or something in his game, Quarantine Cat was licking his paws, and I could smell fresh bread. At some point the smell of fresh bread stopped being a comfort and started haunting me.

"So are you a librarian now?" Lester asked me while I cut off a hunk of sourdough.

With my mouth full of carbs, I said, "Archivist."

"How is it?"

I swallowed and chased the bread with tap water. "It's nice to leave the house," I said.

Lester nodded. "Self-care, man." He paused his game. "I'm thinking about making my own tea blend."

"In the game?"

He shook his head slowly. "No, dude. No . . ."

We sat in the living room lit by our screens until almost midnight. I got up and told Lester, "I've got an alarm tomorrow morning."

He nodded. "I remember those."

In my room, Quarantine Cat nested in the dead center of my bed. I curled around him, with my ass hanging over the edge and fur up my nose.

I dreamt voices and symbols. I dreamt slimy-skinned ocean walkers rising and teeth in the sky. Quarantine Cat perched on a throne of bones and madness with a cult of robed chanters bowing and praising. Quarantine Cat's eyes burned with a cold infinite dark and his voice sounded in my thoughts.

Ph'nglui mglw'nafh Cthulu R'lyeh wgah'nagl fhtagn.

Too much bread and Critter Carnival before bed.

When I got back to the library the next day, the first thing Armitage asked me was, "How was your night?"

"Can't complain," I said. "Sweet of you to ask."

I scanned another seven books on day two and when I was leaving, I patted my gut. "Worked through lunch again," I told Armitage. "This is going to be good for the old Covid-19 pounds, if you know what I mean."

"Yes," she said. "Oh, yes."

I think if Armitage lost 19 pounds she'd turn to dust.

Quarantine Cat was extra frisky when I got home. I tossed him the mouse with the bell thing, and he went HAM all over the living room.

"Dead bird." Lester pointed with his video game controller. "Over there somewhere."

I found the dead bird nestled in one of my sweatshirts. "I don't even know how he's getting out of the house," I said.

"I made croissants," Lester told me. "The lamination isn't great but they're edible. Try one with Nutella."

Well, that was dinner sorted.

"You were talking in your sleep last night, dude," Lester said. "Couldn't make out the words. Like, I dunno, song lyrics maybe. Sounded German."

"Wild." I tossed Quarantine Cat a hot dog.

Lester walked to the window and looked out at the reddening sky. "Do you wonder if we're living in the end times right now? This plague is only the beginning. Soon the stars will fall, and mankind will scream and scream and scream."

With my mouth full of croissant, I asked him, "What?"

Lester went back to the couch. "Never mind."

Late that night Lester shook me awake. I was standing in the kitchen writing on the refrigerator door with a dry erase marker. Triangles and eyes looking through me.

"Bro, I'm watching Tiger King," Lester said. "You were doing Rammstein again."

Quarantine Cat perched on the counter and licked his hungry jaws. *Cthulhu fhtagn.*

I pointed the dry erase marker at the TV. "That lady 100% killed her husband."

Lester punched my shoulder. "Spoilers."

I mentioned to Armitage at the library that I was having really vivid dreams.

She leaned toward me like a plant growing toward the sun. "What do you see in the dreams?"

"I think the end of the world?"

"Good," she said. "Very good."

She gave me a notebook and pen to keep a dream journal.

On his island, Lester's squirrel sold bones and lies harvested from the dead.

"Is this DLC?" I asked him.

"Shh," he said.

I found more dead birds.

"I don't get it," I told Lester. "He's not eating them. He just . . . likes killing."

Lester nodded. 'That's what they do," he said. "They don't like being cooped up, y'know? This flesh, it's a heavy cage that must be rent and broken to set the whispers free."

"For sure," I said. "But do you think I should get a second cat though? To keep him company?"

"I'm not cleaning that litter box," Lester said.

Listening to Spotify on the walk to the library all my playlists were scrambled up. Instead of Doja Cat I got a lot of whispering and screaming. Experimental indie, I guess.

While she reviewed my dream journal, I said to Armitage, "I think my cat might be evil now."

She looked up from the symbols. "We are all under significant strain during this unprecedented year, Andrew," she said.

"I haven't been paid yet," I said.

She quirked an eyebrow behind her reading glasses. "Did you email the HR department?"

I nodded. "Carol said she had no record of this position."

"You need to email *Emily*," Armitage said.

"Oh. Shit. Right. Sorry."

I translated more books.

Lester's sourdough grew. It breached containment and oozed through the kitchen.

"Let it go," Lester said. He'd taken to wearing a robe around the apartment. Crushed velvet. "All our walls, break against the waves of his unstoppable hunger."

"So, we're not doing the chore wheel then?" I pointed at the dishwasher with sourdough starter dropping down the front. "Because I washed those dishes. And I don't want to do them again."

Lester got a sponge and got to work cleaning up the counter.

In the year of our long plague 2020, roommates were harder than ever.

Emily emailed me back. "You're not safe," she wrote, and I asked her if she had my W-2 and everything.

Days and nights and days and nights. When I slept, I didn't sleep. I walked along a bloody shore and when there were one set of cat paw prints, that was when Quarantine Cat carried me. I filled the dream journal and then the walls of my bedroom and then my arms, crisscrossed with ink and scratches.

You will call me Imliogdu the Harbinger, Quarantine Cat told me on a Thursday. I think it was a Thursday.

I gave him pets and Imliogdu the Harbinger nibbled on my finger.

"People have been coming to see him," Lester said.

"The cat?"

He nodded. "Real creepy. I think they're Mormons."

"Wild." I bit into a calzone and pulled out a bird feather with my teeth.

○

I asked Armitage how the project was going.

She put her hand on my cheek and smiled. She had so many yellow teeth. "You are a perfect conduit, Andrew. The word passes through you with little resistance."

"Nice," I said. Take that, C+. "So where are the scans going?"

"Everywhere," Armitage said. "Facebook. Twitter. JSTOR. The dreams are untethered from these pages. This is the year he wakes. *Cthulhu fhtagn.*"

I had no idea Armitage was political but the election was a fucking nightmare already, so I didn't say anything about it.

Before I left the library that evening, I nicked a German to English dictionary from the general collection, but I couldn't find the right words. Maybe Russian?

When I got home three new people in robes sat around the television watching Lester's Critter Carnival panda bear preaching to a thrall of radicalized forest creatures.

"What the fuck?!" I called out from the doorway. They all turned to me in unison, their faces emotionless and eyes empty, each wearing crushed velvet.

On a pile of cushions, Imliogdu the Harbinger, ran his sandpaper tongue along his barbed cat penis.

They are my voice and my tendrils. They are the beginning of the end of all. Klaatu barada nikto.

"Guests need to wear masks in the house, dude," I told Lester and opened the windows. "I'm not catching covid."

Cover your breath and swallow the disease.

Everyone put masks on. I took one from my pocket and sat by the window. I searched on my phone for "triangles with eyes" and sure enough, I found scanned pages from the archive all over. Friends shared them on social media with different emojis. Eyeballs and octopuses and knives. On news websites the stories were all *Trump this* and *Trump that* and *Cthulhu fhtagn*. Swirling symbols flashed and pulsed in the margins of CNN dot com.

"Does it seem like the internet is—I dunno—different?" I asked Lester.

Lester and his three buddies all answered, "No. It's fine. Everything is fine."

I shook my head. "2020, man," I said. "This fucking year, I swear. Is there fresh bread?"

"There's always fresh bread," they said.

Waiting for me in my bedroom, a crushed velvet robe.

Imliogdu the Harbinger sauntered in after me.

When you are ready you will be the sword in my right hand. You will bleed the world.

He flopped onto his side and rolled around.

I would like the mouse with the bell thing now.

I tossed the mouse with the bell thing into the corner of my room and Imliogdu the Harbinger pounced.

"Hey," I interrupted the group in the living room again. I held up the robe. "Are you people free balling on the furniture? Two layers minimum, guys. That's not optional."

I got a text from Emily in HR. "Have you lost your mind yet?"

"Hahahaha," I replied.

She sent back a video of shifting black with muffled sounds that could have been crying in the background.

"I think this HR person might be flirting with me," I told Lester.

He clacked his jaws and his eyes rolled back. On the screen a little video game fox with a bow on her head bounced up and down hypnotically and text read, "Apocalypse? Yes/No."

I thought about asking Lester to send his friends home before it got too late but they were quiet so I left them to it.

While I brushed my teeth Emily texted again. "They will try to stop this please stop this please they can't they can't oh no it's too late."

I reacted with a heart. "You want to meet in the park or something sometime?"

I gave Imliogdu the Harbinger pets until I fell asleep. With everything happening since the lockdown and everything, I'm glad I had him and Lester. I can't even imagine how crazy I'd have gone all alone.

I dreamt of ashes and monsters climbing out of my eyes. Imliogdu the Harbinger purred, and the heavens wept.

The library was locked when I got there in the morning. I pounded on the door, but Professor Armitage never came. She probably had an appointment she forgot to tell me about.

I texted Emily. "Guess I have the day off!"

She replied right away. "The professor is gone. She is lost now."

I frowned. "Does this mean I'm getting a new boss?"

"Run," Emily texted.

Lester had more people over. The living room was full of them and they loitered around outside the apartment. Dozens of people in robes. My bedroom was full of cats.

I required consorts, Imliogdu the Harbinger purred. *And we require more mice with bell things. And hotdogs.*

I took Lester into the kitchen. "Roommate meeting," I said. "What is happening here? You should ask me before you invite people over for a party. I could have invited someone."

Emily from HR. We had a real connection going.

Lester wet his fingers with his tongue and ran them through my hair. "The pieces separate at the seams," he said. "Annihilation comes from a place beyond light and dark. Cthulhu rises. Cthulhu hungers."

"I get that," I said. "But I don't want them eating all of our snacks, dude. I'm sure Emily will get it sorted but I still haven't gotten paid and then there's the supply chain. I'm not even sure we can get more barbecue potato chips right now. And don't get me started on the toilet paper."

"Do you see, Andy?" Lester asked me all hush hush. "Do you see that we are hurtling toward oblivion? That the hourglass of time is shattered? What has been started cannot cease. The age of man ends in the wet crunch of an alien maw. Our fate is to digest in the gullet of a tremendous horror."

"Fuck 2020," I said.

Lester pointed at one of robed people in our living room. "Frank brought more chips. Sour cream and onion."

I spotted the bag on the counter and took it. "If you order pizza, let me know."

"I will miss you in our meaningless end," Lester said.

"Same," I said.

I took the last of the hotdogs with me for Imliogdu the Harbinger. Cats crawled over me meowing and kneading with their little toe beans.

On social media and news websites everything was Cthulhu and the eldritch script from the archives that I scanned for Professor Armitage.

"Thank God," I told a purring Imliogdu the Harbinger. "No more election bullshit."

Would you like to know? Imliogdu the Harbinger asked. *I can give you everything.*

I scritched between his ears. "Knowledge is madness, isn't it?"

Life is madness.

"You're not wrong." I shrugged. "Why not?"

I lobbed the mouse with the bell thing and so many cats ran for it.

⊐

Poe's Guys Respond to Their Significant Others

~ William J. Connell

(Narrator, at a podium before a group of men in a deep, dark, and dank catacomb)

Ok, ok, ok, we all agree to disagree on what happened with Ligeia and Rowena.

Now let's take it from the top. One—two—three.

(Chorus)

We're Poe's guys, and we're not fey

We're scientific sorts who work all day,

We study hard, we walk our yard,

We seek the powers of strange things like mycelium,

So what if we wander at night into a mausoleum?

(Narrator)

Take it Rod.

(Rod)

I'm Rod Usher, and I got a house built like a rock,

Loaded with art, its full of stock,

(Were those footsteps?)

Own it outright, no conditions,

(Did you hear that?)

Full of life and lots of provisions,

It's—she's near.

(Narrator)

Come on, Rod, you can do it!

(Rod)

It's a ma–ma–mansion with—SHE'S HERE!"

(*Narrator*)

Ok—Ok—Ok! Cut!

[*Pause for technical difficulties*]

(*Narrator*)

Somebody check Rod, did he hit his head?

Doctor Ponnonner, can you look at him? Make sure he's not dead.

(*Chorus*)

What's she doing here?

(*Emaciated figure wrapped in a bloodied robe*)

Oh it is just too easy.

You guys make me queasy.

You're not fey?

You sleep all day,

Then go in a trance.

Look at this, my brother loses his balance,

Just at the sight of my entrance.

(*Narrator*)

Come on Maddie, we're trying to respond with some elegance.

We've got this poem to put together.

How's he doing, Dr. Ponnoner?

(*Dr. P.*)

He'll live for now, and I'd say a while longer.

(*Narrator*)

Ok good. Now please Maddie,

I get your point, Rod buried you alive, he made a blunder,

But just for today, please, end this encounter,

Can't you just find a nice vault where you can meander?

(*Emaciated figure wrapped in bloodied robe*)

For you—sure.

Guys, to the hereinafter, I am off.

Ha! Don't scoff!

    [Emaciated figure wrapped in bloodied robe exits]

    (Narrator)

Ok, ok, let's try this again. This time we'll go one from the top.

    (Chorus)

We're Poe's gents, and we're okay,

We ain't nothing like what our gals say,

    (Narrator)

Alleo, take it.

                    [Crickets chirping.]

    (Narrator)

Uh, Alleo, take it away!

                    [Crickets chirping.]

    (Dr. P.)

O come on Alli.

    (The Count)

Oh, come on yourself, doctor. And It's Allamistakeo. Count Allamistakeo to you.

    (Narrator)

Can't you just get in the spirit of things?

    (The Count)

I'm sorry, but as a group, you have your failings,

    (Narrator)

You know—Do you always have to be so mean?

    (The Count)

This is the most idiotic thing I have ever seen.

    (Dr. P.)

We have to do our best, even though we have some challenges.

    (The Count)

Sorry, but this is more ridiculous than Ponnonner's lozenges.

(Dr. P., others)

Get him out of here!

(Narrator, under his breath)

For the life of him, that mummy hears no rhythm in his ear.

[Pause for technical difficulties as the Count is ushered outside the tomb]

(Narrator)

Ok. This time let's start with the third stanza.

(Grumbling from Chorus)

(Narrator)

Come on, the girls beat us like a drum!

We need to show 'em we have more aplomb!

(Chorus)

We're Poe's guys,

And our minds we exercise,

Knowledge is king, that's our prize,

Though sometimes it leads to our gals' demise,

(Narrator)

Take it Egae!

(Egaeus)

I live to study, the little minutia,

Some might say tis too much monomania,

The look of a book,

The perfume of a flower,

For me, that's no source of horror,

It's what really gives me power.

(Chorus)

Yeah!

(Egaeus)

I had a girl, such a lovely creature,

She was so delightful, a child of nature,

My cousin, my love, and also my teacher.
One day she passed, and I could not retrieve her.

(Narrator)

Uh, careful Egaeus—look behind you, there's a figure.

*[Egaeus turns to see an enshrouded figure, which drops the
shroud to expose her face]*

(Egaeus)

Berenice! My love?
What can I compare thee to?
The shine of a—

(Chorus)

OOOOOOOOOHHHHH!
That was one heck of a punch!
He is out cold—you could feel that crunch.
That toothless girl has got some brass!

(Toothless gal)

Monomania, my ass.

(Man with raven on shoulder)

She hit Egaeus! Guys, let's get her,
We need to toss her out in a blur.
Grab on hold and throw her out of here!

(Narrator)

I'd tread lightly, if I were you, Mr. De Vere.

(Man with raven who just flew off his shoulder)

Don't worry, Mr. Narrator, of this lass I've no fear,
Listen you, you should know, I'm Guy De Vere,
And you can't punch my friend in the ear,
You had better make light and get out of here,
These are my—

(Chorus)

OUCH! AGAIN! Wow. That had to hurt,

(Rod)

There's our Guy De Vere, sleeping in the dirt.

(Raven, circling in the air above Guy)

Nevermore.

He'll walk. Ha.

Nevermore.

(Narrator)

Doctor Ponnonner, please take care their ills.

(Dr. P.)

I'll try. I'm guessing they'll both live,

But I'm going to need more than Brandreth's pills.

(Narrator)

Berenice, we know you're mad, we get it, we do,

So, I am very apologetically asking of you,

This group can only handle so many adventures,

So please go – I'm making my sincerest overtures.

(Recently unshrouded figure)

You folks are weird, but I'll give you a break,

And leave you with one of my new favorite gestures.

[Recently unshrouded figure who knocked out two gents, reaches into robe, pulls something out and inserts it into mouth]

My favorite new toy: ivory dentures.

How do you like my new pearly whites?

(Chorus)

We're blinded—Blinded—They're just too bright!

(Recently shrouded figure who pulled down shroud, knocked out two gents, and then inserted her dentures)

Then I'll be off, but don't you forgets,

With my new teeth – now I bites!

[Pause for technical difficulties as partially enshrouded figure exits.]

[Several members in the chorus swoon and are escorted into fresher air.]

(*Narrator*)

Ok. Ok. Ok. Let's try it from –

(*Voice from Chorus*)

Hey who are you anyway?

(*Narrator*)

What do you mean? I'm—the narrator.

(*Voice from Chorus*)

Yeah? Well from where?

(*Narrator*)

Why I—well—

(*Rest of Chorus*)

Yeah, who are you? Where are you from?

(*Narrator*)

Me? You want to know where I've been!

I was at the House of Usher,

I saw it fall into that tarn gutter,

At the haunted palace, I went through that door,

I'm the one who got rid of that odor,

You all think that I'm tolerant, patient, and humdrum?

Well, I'm the one who escaped from that pit AND the pendulum.

I've seen Cthulhu—

(*Voices from the Chorus*)

Ca-tha-who?

(*Narrator*)

Uh, of course, I meant El Dorodo,

With instructions from my copy of the *Necronomicon*.

(*Chorus*)

He's putting us on!

What's your name?

(Female voice from the crowd)

It's really quite tame.

Come on honey, don't be so doom and gloom.

(Narrator)

Aww heck. Why now, Ulalume?

(Ulalume)

Honestly, hon, you think your guys can top my gals? You're as smart as a brick.

And just as thick.

You are a good artist, a great painter, you betcha,

But you really do miss what's right in front of ya.

Think about it honey, you know why I came,

Come on, go on, tell 'em, your name!

[Pause]

(Narrator, after taking a deep breath)

It's Pickwick. Richard Upton Pickwick.

[Longer pause]

(Voices from the Chorus)

He's a LOVECRAFT CHARACTER!

[Extended pause for mayhem, disarray, men exiting the crypt]
[Ulalume gives gentle hug to narrator and speaks as she is exiting]

(Ulalume)

I'm going back to my tomb, catch some moon rays on Lake Auber.

Then me and the girls are getting together,

Some fishy-looking person, came over,

Kind of weird, Called himself, Howard Lover?

Anyway he kept saying trouble's coming from a bad-ass invader.

Some cat named Azathoth, and his lackey, Yog-Sothoth,

But don't worry. Me and the gals, we'll take care of 'em both.

Sorry honey, but stick to painting, of that, you're so capable.

Oh, and I did leave you a roast duck out on the table.

—Love ya.

[Ulalume exits, stage right]

[Rod and Narrator, sitting near the podium, alone in the crypt]

(Rod)

Mr. Pickwick, it has been very long day,

Maybe the truth is we really are fey.

You tried, you made, a truly noble effort.

In that I hope you take some comfort.

You sought to get us to drink from that silver cup.

And—

(Narrator)

Hey, Rod?

(Rod)

Yes?

(Narrator)

Just shut the @!#* up.

⊐

The Museum of Endless Summer

~ Paul Jessup

Daria loved the feel of mermaid skin, pinched between her fingertips. Rustle, rustle, the soft music of dead leaves on an October path.
Not too hard, though, she didn't want to break the skin, or crack the
bones in half. It could be bad luck, you know, to defile a mermaid
corpse like that. Even though her mom always said that eating a bit
of the flesh would be good for you, she did not want to try it. It just
all felt wrong.

The Museum of Endless Summer held over thirty-eight mermaid
mummies in total, their dusty old bones propped up on taxidermy
display throughout the building. It was crouched in an old lighthouse, no longer functional, near the edges of the great lakes.

She'd been surprised when they first came here, about twelve
years ago, when she was only five. She thought the lake was the sea,
the gray towering waves, the beaches coated in the skeletons of fish.
Seagulls danced about on the air, and in the winter the waves froze
like ice giants guarding the world from the oncoming storm. Lighthouses like theirs crowned the edges of the lake on the state side,
barely working anymore. There was no room for lighthouses in the
modern world near the end of time. No room for mermaids, either.

They'd all died long ago, before Daria was even born. Every once
in a great while their corpses washed up on the beach for scavengers
to find. Some would bring them here, and dad would try his best to
taxidermy them up and get them looking nice once again. He never
enclosed them in glass, he didn't like that idea at all. Let the ghosts
breathe, he said. They need every bit of freedom they could get.

Her parents had been worried that she would be scared of the
mummies when they first moved in and started work as caretakers
of the museum. But oh contrare, Daria was a strange girl, wasn't she?
She loved the mermaids, and set about naming them and becoming
their very best friends. At night, she dreamt of playing games with

their mermaid ghosts. Dad never understood, but mom completely got it. She seemed proud of her little mermaid girl.

If only, if only. She wished she were braver, then she could join them beneath the sea without fear of drowning. Maybe then she could figure out where mom went, all those years ago.

Mom's bedtime stories hung around in Daria's mind long after she left them both behind. Stories of cities beneath the waves, calling out to her, telling her to come and find them. These stories always scared Daria a little, unnerved her, the way her mom's face would light up with a manic glow, her eyes wide, her teeth chattering. "They would sing to me, in dreams and waking hours, sing so sweetly and so light."

And then her mom would sing that drowned song, and Daria would hide under the covers, trying to muffle the half-whispered words. *A la, a la, to love beneath the waves, a la, a la, to feel the lake in the heart, a la, a la, to give back to the blade, a la, a la, to drink the stars and the dark . . .*

Chills even now, thinking about it in odd moments in the middle of the night. Hours when she couldn't dream, and she swore she heard the soft haunting whisper of the same song. Though not her mother's voice this time, no, a chorus of voices, all raspy and ragged. It came from the edges of the museum, followed by the sound of creaky boards and old footsteps.

The first time she heard this at night she thought mom had come back, maybe. That maybe everything would be all right and normal once again?

But no. She went and explored the whole museum, with shaky cell-phone in hand scattering artificial light across the mummies and the plush mermaids and t-shirts they had for sale, and found nothing. No source of the song, no bodies moving about, creaking the floor-boards, no mother, nothing. Save for some small water-logged foot-prints that might've been there before, she wasn't sure. They didn't seem fresh? They probably weren't.

Ever since then she just laid there at night, listening to the ghosts sing her mom's old song, and let the sense of melancholy and loss wash over her until she slept.

○

"New bodies, new bodies, look at all these new bodies! Quite the haul we have here, wouldn't you say, Dar my dear?"

She woke up all groggy eyed to see her dad with iron hooks in hand, dragging large rotting corpses of mermaids. So many! She wasn't even sure they would have anywhere to put them right now. Seagulls cawed over the sound of the lake waves behind him, as he pulled yet another one up and slapped it on the same pile of corpses as the others. The air smelled damp with lakewater, a bright fishy scent that clung to the beaches in spring.

"How long they been out there, you think? These seem older than the others, less fresh."

Dad nodded and brought in the last one. "You got me. The lake gives up the dead on its own terms and timeline, the waves doling them out bit by bit. We always get a few new ones when it thaws out after winter, but this is a bit more than usual."

"I'd say."

"Still, got my work cut out for me now. A few of these are pretty far gone and will require a bit of creative reconstructing. A little bit of toothpaste here and there, some wire and some paper mache would do wonders."

"Yeah, but where are we going to put them? I don't think we have much room anymore, do we?"

Dad laughed. "Naw, we don't, we don't. But we do have a few buyers who've been sniffing around, looking for the odd curio or another. Something they can brag about to their rich friends, *oh look I've got an honest to goodness mermaid!* That kind of thing."

"I thought you were against selling them."

"I was, I was. But Dar my dear, my love, my heart, times are tough. Not as many tourists coming through like they used to, and money's a bit tight."

"Oh."

"I know, I should've told you sooner, but, hey. Things are better now, aren't they? Look at this brilliant haul, I'm going to make some phone calls in a bit and get the ball rolling. You all right watching the front desk for a bit by yourself?"

She nodded. Of course she would be all right. Of course.

○

The front desk was a usually such a boring affair, and today was no different, it seemed. It was the wrong time of day for this kind of work, the wrong time of year. The tourist season had been over for awhile, and already the promise of winter stretched across the skies in long gray clouds. So, you could imagine her surprise when the bells chimed and front door opened, and a boy appeared there, framed in the archway. His skin was pale and almost blue, and he shivered as he walked. His eyes had a transparent gray look to them, like soft mist or stormclouds. His hair had a similar color to his eyes, and his hands were steepled as he walked, like he was praying. As he moved water dripped from his body, every bit of him soaked, leaving soggy footprints behind.

She was mesmerized by this strange boy. He was ten, maybe eleven years old? Each footstep painful, the way his face grimaced and his body trembled. His hands never changed position, not even once. As he walked, she heard him muttering something under his breath over and over again.

"They're still singing, and they're getting close . . . too close . . ."

And she couldn't help herself. "Who's singing?"

"The mermaids. A song for their red king, who dreams under the lake."

Did he say dead king, or red king? She couldn't tell, and part of her knew better than to ask. Mostly because she did not want to know the answer. Instead, she moved out from behind the register, and walked slowly forward. The soggy footprints looked familiar. She felt a chill run up and down her spine.

"Who are you?"

"I am Nothing. Who are you?"

And then he collapsed.

Dad was busy in his workroom the entire time, so Daria had to move his body all by her own lonesome self. It was easier than she thought it would be. He was very light, as if he had no bones or muscle tissue in his body at all, and it was just a hollow cavity filled with sawdust. She knew leaving him there would be wrong. What if they had other customers? But also . . .

He freaked her out more than a little bit. Which she knew was not a nice thing to say. If mom'd been here, she would've yelled at her for even thinking such a thing. Still, she didn't want him there, moaning, eyes fluttering, crawling half conscious on the floor. Touching him was weird and gross and somehow sticky. Like flypaper. And lifting him up eerily painless. Later on, after she placed him in the bathroom tub, she quickly changed out of her clothes and threw them in the washing machine. She then cleaned herself as best as she could with a loose towel, some soap, and water from the sink.

She wasn't going to go in the tub to shower off. Not with him in there. He smelled like the lake, all seagull and fishbones.

She tried to go and see Dad, to let him know about their new visitor. After all, what if he goes to take a piss or something, and sees him? Wouldn't he be surprised? But his work room door was locked, and when she knocked, she didn't get a response. Not even a solo grunt telling her to go away, nothing. That was odd. Very unlike dad! He was always open to her coming into the work room. Some days, she would just wander in and watch the mummification process. It was disgusting and fascinating at the same time.

A lot of the mermaids they'd found on the beach have been dead for awhile, and fairly well preserved. Most of what he did involved reconstruction with toilet paper and putty, and cutting away the rotting bits or decaying bits. There was something pleasing to this, watching him rebuild the corpse from scratch using base materials.

But no. The work room, which was further down the beach and a little to the left in the woods, was padlocked. The windows were locked, too. And he'd placed blankets over them, so no one could see inside. She knocked on the door, knocked on the windows, no response.

She was worried about him, but decided not to think about it. Thinking about it was a painful thing. What if he was dead? A heart attack in the middle of work? What if?

No. She did not want to break into the work room just to find his body flat on the floor, attracting flies and the scent of death. No.

○

Later on in the evening hours, when the sun bruised the sky with deep purple reds and oranges, she went back up into the bathroom to check on their visitor. He was sitting up in the tub now, dripping water from his body. He looked like he was still submerged somehow, as if the lake had seeped into his pores and under his skin. His eyes were wide, and it looked like the face of someone drowning.

"Don't trust the one with your mother's face."

She had to stop mid-stride and say, "Huh?"

"She's not who you think she is. She is the daughter of the dead king dreaming."

Dead king, or red king? He must've said Red King Dreaming, how could a dead king dream? Dead things are just dead things, inert, unable to move or dream. If they could dream . . .

Oh no. Then all the mermaids here were dreaming and for some reason that scared her more than anything else.

She ran out of there, she couldn't talk to him anymore. Not after hearing that, and thinking that unsettling thought, that all the mermaid corpses were dreaming here at the Museum of Endless Summer. What could they be dreaming of? Did they dream of her? Did they dream of dad? Were they good dreams?

No. She knew for a fact that the dead did not dream good dreams. They were always nightmares. After all, it only made sense. How could you dream anything else when you're dead? She ran and kept on running, back down to dad's workroom, hoping against hope that the door was open, and he could hug her and comfort her.

She needed that more than anything else right now. To hell with bills and stress and money. To hell with the end of the world, to the lake, to the mermaids, to everything. She just wanted to be anywhere else with him. Just the two of them against the world. But, no. He was gone, lost in his work, and not letting her inside.

Please don't be dead. Please still be alive.

When she came back inside, and tiptoed up the stairs, and went past the open bathroom door, she held her breath. The sunset colors painted the room the color of blood through the open windows, and carried with it the distant cries of seagulls over the lake. She didn't want to look inside, see that creepy boy telling her terrible things. And yet . . .

She had to look. She peered around the corner, moving her head in, just a brief moment. So subtle her movements, she could dart away if he saw her. She couldn't see the tub just yet, so she moved her head in closer, closer. Still nothing, no sounds from the bathroom at all except the steady drip drip of a leaky faucet. She leaned in closer, and what if he saw her first? No. Closer. Come on. He can't hurt you, he just a little drowned boy, a thing from the lake. No more a threat than the mermaids, and the mermaids never scared you before today. And yet . . .

The thought of them dead and dreaming? Now she was scared of them. Closer, closer, her heart was in her throat. That boy, that drowned boy, what terrible things would he tell her next? That her dad was dead and dreaming in the workroom? No, please, no . . .

Closer, closer. Now she was in the bathroom, pulling back the shower curtain from the tub in one fast yank.

And saw nothing.

Nothing.

She searched all over the Museum of Endless Summer, looking for the little drowned boy. As she moved she heard the mermaid mummies whisper around her. The words were half hidden things, their words barely audible, like the sound of waves on the lake. She leaned in, strained, tried to understand them. Were they warning her? Telling her horrible things to come? She didn't know.

So she kept on searching, going up into the attic, down into the basement. No sign of the boy, not even the water logged footprints he left before. It was as if he completely up and vanished. Maybe, maybe he slid down into the darkness beyond the drain? She didn't want to think about that, though. The drain looked like an empty eye socket, staring out from the void beyond.

It was getting later and later still. A sliver past the outstretched arms of twilight. She made her way down the beach, new mermaid corpses floating in on the waves. She'd never seen so many before, there was usually one or two at the most. But now? Almost every other step she was walking around another tailfin, another arm, another corpse. The water moved them about gently, like they were crawling across the sand in strange formations.

Did the boy go this way? She wasn't sure. Up ahead, she saw her father, now with hook in hand, gathering more bodies back to his workroom. She wanted to call out to him, but stopped, and stared instead. He seemed obsessed, manic. His eyes wild with despair. He turned over another one, and another one, and another one. As if he was searching for a specific mermaid. This all felt so wrong, and obscene, like she caught him in a terrible act. But what act was this? A job he performed daily, constantly.

And yet, she could not deny the fact that something was different. He had changed.

"I know she's in here, somewhere! Show yourself to me! Come on! I've dreamt this night every single time I fall asleep, and I've been waiting for it since forever. This has to be it! This has to be right! Show yourself to me!"

And then he leaned down, head in his hands, and began to sob. His whole body shaking with tears. If she had been stronger, she would have gone down there, put an arm around him, and comforted him. But she was not strong enough for that. She was young, and small, and needing the comfort of her father herself. But he was gone, and here was this shipwreck in the shape of a man instead.

She woke to the drowned boy, sitting in a puddle in front of her bed. His eyes vacant, like two blue coins, reflecting an empty stillness outside of time. "We must go outside and burn the bodies."

Groggy, she rubbed her eyes and said, "No."

He did not move when she said this, did not flinch or scoot back on the floor. He did not even raise an eyebrow, nor twitch a muscle, nothing. He was stillness itself. Like a stone in water. "Your mom's not out there, and we have to do it. We should probably burn all the mermaids here as well . . ."

And so she said it again. "No. I'm not going to do that."

"Please, you don't understand what's going on. It was so hard for me to get out . . . so hard for me to come here and speak to you. We must do it, before they finish their song."

"You do it."

"I can't do it, the fire would burn me up, you have to do it, please . . . "

His lip quivered and his whole body shook. But she wasn't buying it, something about this request felt all wrong. "No." She said again.

"The one with your mother's face got to you, didn't she? I told you not to trust her."

But Daria simply turned her head, and said nothing in response. She was done talking to the little drowned boy. There was no way she was going to go out there and set all those mermaids on fire, no way she was going to burn up the ones in the museum, either. She wouldn't even know how to do that! It couldn't just be with a lighter or a candle, could it? No. That wouldn't be enough fire.

"Don't leave the house, then, especially not tonight. Please, promise me that, at least."

But she didn't trust him enough to promise him that.

Eventually, he left her room and wandered away. Where he went she didn't care. She waited for a bit longer, and counted under her breath to one thousand, hoping that would give him enough time to be completely gone from her life. And then she went, crawled out of bed, and tip toed down the stairs into the museum on the first floor. Mermaids everywhere. They seemed to have moved in the night, and now they point towards all of the windows, as if they looked towards the lake beyond, watching.

As she walked passed them, she heard them singing in their uncanny, wave like voices. Their skin rustled as their lips barely moved, the sound wafting around her, hypnotic. She thought of her dad, out there, amongst all of those corpses, and all of a sudden felt terrified for him. She had to get him inside, and they had to stay inside until way after their song was finished. It might take all day, it might take all night. She had to do it. They had to stay there, unmoving, while this all played out.

She ran along the beach, past the piles and piles of mermaid corpses. Some of them crawled, still containing the vague memories of life in their muscles. Some just laid on their back and twitched. Each of them sang in their own haunting way, and she wondered if the drowned boy was right. Should she have set them on fire? She had no idea.

Eventually, she came to her father's work room. The large stone edifice cut into the forest by the lake. She saw new mermaids slung against the pillars by the front door, their bodies leathering in the sun. She watched as his shadow moved in the darkness beyond the windows, dancing with something. Was it a person? A corpse? She had no idea.

Part of her wanted to run again. Another part of her told her no, she must go forward. She must stop this all and save him. Save them both. Hide while they finish their song, and the Dead (Red?) King wakes from the wave tossed heart of the lake. And so she went inside, and her heart stopped. Her dad was dancing with a mermaid, whose water corpse sloshed back and forth in his arms. He hadn't even prepared her yet, didn't even do the most basic acts of mummification or embalming.

And as he spun around, she realized that the mermaid . . .

Had her mother's

face

And yet, it wasn't her face. The smile was all wrong, the teeth too big for her mouth, all angular and triangle sharp. The eyes were all wrong, they looked like the eyes of the drowned boy, all blue and dead and cataract coated. And her body was all wrong, with scales and fish tails and webbed fingers and gills. She gurgled and spoke, her eyes meeting Daria's eyes.

A candle sparked inside Daria's heart. She missed her mom. *This was not her mom.*

"Sing with me, my lovely dovely girl. Sing! Sing with all your heart."

But she could not sing. She could only step backwards, slowly, one foot at a time, trying hard not to trip over the other mermaid corpses. She wanted that to be her mom so badly. That somehow, maybe, when her mom escaped she went beneath the lake and became a mermaid, and lived happily ever after. But that was not her mom, it just looked like her mom, and she had to go away. She had to go away and never ever come back. Dad was gone now, with her mom and the mermaids beneath the sea. There was no helping him, no helping anyone. It was just her.

And outside, waiting for her to run, the drowning boy stood. And smiled. His mouth wet and dripping with the promise of waves.

⊐

Through Life and Death, Forevermore

~ Ngô Bình Anh Khoa

Much like all novelties that one may see,
Whose strange, exotic gleam lasts but a while
Before it dulls into mere normalcy,
A flash trend that is quickly out of style,
Such is the horror that once tortured me,
Which, after I had managed to survive
The first shock with my fractured sanity,
Is now an ingrained part of daily life.
Thus, I'm no longer startled when I spot
My wife's wan face protruding from my cheek
When my reflection's in a mirror caught;
The distant gaze, the gaping mouth, the reek
Of rot from that familiar visage form
A comforting sight in my long altered norm.

This is the punishment for my dark sin,
For daring to oppose the Natural Law
And steal from Death's dominion, wherein
My love was taken, bound to Life no more.
So strong was my desire to bring her back
That I used my position to get to
The *Necronomicon*, the tome of black
And terrible eldritch secrets known to few,

Among which is a spell that grants my wish
If one should yield to Yog-Sothoth and pray,
And if done right, the Heaven and Abyss
Shall open to the caster, where they may
Witness one mystery of the Universe—
A boundless blessing or a gruesome curse.

Desire and doubt waged war in my mind when
The tome was open right in front of me.
The borrowed time was ticking; soon it'd end;
I thus invoked the cosmic entity.
I managed to preserve a functional mind,
Whose threads were frayed but not yet snapped, before
The Outer God, both blasphemous and divine,
An audience that still shakes me to the core.
His monstrous eyeballs peered into my soul
As waves of knowledge crashed against my head,
Submerging my thoughts as they overflowed,
Which made me at that time wish I were dead.
Then, slowly, painfully, the great flood ceased,
And I was back in my room, whole at least.

The knowledge I'd acquired was quick to fade
Like grains of sand that slipped out of one's hand.
Posthaste, a circle drawn with runes was made,
Within which I would crawl and clumsily stand.
An alien incantation left my tongue
And floated round the room's dark, freezing air
That spread like poison in my heaving lungs.

Then, agony! Maddening agony everywhere!
A loud, unearthly scream tore through the space,
Composed of my own and another voice,
A female's shriek resounding near my face,
Which burned and bled amid the piercing noise.
I knew not how much time had passed while caught
Within the clutch of pain and smell of rot.

When consciousness returned, dark was the sky
Bathed in the corpse-pale essence of the moon,
Collecting my breath and my bearings, I
Then struggled to my feet, but very soon,
I heard a moan right next to me and turned,
But there was no-one, not a soul in sight;
The stench of rot remained. My cheek still burned,
And when I touched it, I was stunned by fright.
The texture was all wrong, and there were holes
That when I touched, sheer anguish stabbed me, and
Inhuman wails rang, wrecked with utter woes;
The shifting of flesh grazed my trembling hand.
I ran towards the nearest mirror, where
I saw my wife's distorted visage there.

Her mouth was moving, but no word I'd hear;
Her lidless eyes looked straight into my own,
Unblinking in a silent pleading. Fear
Of an intensity I'd never known
Consumed me, but a miracle (or a curse)
Kept my mind from collapsing then and there.

The face, a foetid parasite at first,
Grew more familiar the more I'd stare
And try to find old traces of my wife
Amid the twisted features of her ghost
Released from Death's shroud, once more given Life,
Fused my own, two souls within one host.
The fear and agony died, then came the birth
Of hope for brighter days full of shared mirth.

With such thoughts ricocheting in my head,
I thus caressed her face as laughter broke
Out of my dry and sweltering throat and spread
Throughout the moonlit room until I'd choke.
I've not stopped laughing since my ever fair
Wife was returned to me through the pain,
And now, I strive to take much better care
Of my love, whom I shall not lose again.
Her scent and presence can be hidden when
At work with bandages and some cologne;
I hold my lectures knowing at the end
Of each class, I can see the face I've grown
To love once more, true to our age-old vow
That we will be together, ever bound.

My peers and students view my bandaged head
As weird, but I care not about their thought
And state my face was scarred when fire spread
From my old kitchen's stoves that I forgot
To switch off as I worked on grading. Hence,

I'm left alone with my beloved within
My office and my home, where no pretense
Is needed as I feed her, whispering
Sweet nothings to appease her moans and cries;
Caressing her as she grows larger on
My face till half of it is hers. The eyes,
Once hollow, show a singular glow upon
Our rotting vessel where our souls are stored,
Entwined through life and death, forevermore.

◻

Javapocalypse

~ Jonathan Wood

It was Monday, and Deon joined the scrum shoving their way onto the Southwark Underground platform. Behind him, the train rattled away, creaky as a pensioner's joints. Spotting an opening in the crowd, he lunged for it, but took an elbow in the solar plexus for his trouble. He doubled over, wheezing.

It had been two weeks since Deon had moved into the attic room in East Ham. His dad had said it wasn't too bad if you didn't mind the smell of cat piss. His landlady, Mrs Murphy owned seven cats. They always looked like they were plotting a murder. Probably Mrs Murphy's—she was small and mouse-like enough that the cats could conceivably find it confusing.

"Deon?"

Deon, focused on recovering the power of inhalation, took a moment to register his own name.

"Hey." Small fingers closed on his bicep, and Deon whirled round as best as he was able, hands coming up in what he hoped looked like a serviceable kung fu stance.

He stared into the small, cherubic face of a girl about his age. She wore heavy eye make-up, and her lips were painted the color of Halloween. Black hair curled around her cheeks.

"Chloe?" he said.

Chloe had moved to his village when they were both sixteen. The Cambridgeshire natives had never seen a top hat and tails worn over ripped black jeans and treated her with a mixture of fright and tentative derision. The local pharmacy had needed to order black nail polish just for her. Deon, who worked a weekend shift there, once asked her why she didn't just order the stuff off Amazon.

"Good scenery in here," she'd told him, and that was all the explanation he got.

"I thought that was you," Chloe said to him now.

"What are you doing here?" Deon asked. Then he thought it would probably be a good idea to lower his hands.

"On my way to a meeting." Chloe was smiling very brightly. He couldn't remember Chloe smiling when they were at school together. There again, she'd taken A-Level history, and none of those kids seemed to smile much.

"I'm heading to work," he said.

He wondered what meeting she was going to. A business thing? Except she was wearing a black hoodie and ripped jeans. An Alcoholics Anonymous meeting? She didn't look like an alcoholic. Though surely not all alcoholics could be overweight men in their fifties like his uncle Michael.

"You graduated uni then?" Chloe asked.

"Yeah," Deon said. "I'm in advertising now."

"Oh brilliant," Chloe said. She was still smiling. "Which way are you heading?"

"Towards the Thames."

"Brilliant," she said again. "Let's walk together."

They wedged their way through the crowds to the escalator. "What you doing in advertising?" she asked as they headed up.

"Mostly admin so far. Everyone says my boss is a genius though." He shrugged.

"You disagree?"

For a moment, Deon felt like he was being peeled, layers of obfuscation and self-deception stripped away. But he hesitated before answering. Saying the truth out loud . . . well, it was dangerously close to admitting that he'd spent twenty-one years moving in the wrong direction, and that somehow, right on the cusp of life, it already felt too late to course correct.

"He seems very good at selling sneakers to kids," he said, hedging.

"Noble," Chloe said, in a way that sounded exactly like all of Deon's doubts summed up into one word.

"How about you?" he said to change the subject as they emerged onto the narrow Southwark pavement. "You said something about . . ." He hesitated. What if it really was Alcoholics Anonymous?

"Yeah. My meeting." Chloe looked skywards. The clouds curled low over London like clutching fingers. "We're like . . . a club," she said.

Deon felt vaguely relieved.

"Maybe a religious group," Chloe said.

Deon felt less relieved.

"You graduated uni too?" he said to change the subject again.

"Nah. Dropped out after my first year," Chloe said. "It all felt a bit pointless, you know? Like, what use is calculating the distance between two ancient stars if the world you're currently on is on fire?"

And Deon felt a little like she was really seeing him again.

"Yeah," he said. "I know what you mean." He swept a hand at London. "All of this, right? This is the great apex of society. And it's a whole city built on people selling sneakers to kids. Kids who don't even need sneakers."

Chloe's eyes were bright. She had quite pretty eyes, he realized.

"Exactly!" she said. "That's exactly the sort of thing we talk about at my meetings."

Deon felt anxious again. He really didn't want to talk about his immortal soul. He got enough of that from Uncle Michael.

"You want to go grab a coffee?" Chloe asked.

In Deon's pocket, his phone chimed. He took the opportunity for an exit. "Sorry," he said. "Running late to work."

"Hey Eddie," Deon said, poking his head into his boss's office. His boss was actually called Edward Winston Chamberlain III, but he'd stuck three skateboards on his wall and told people who used his full name, "That's not me, man."

"Yo," Eddie said in accent that sounded like Californian by way of Oxford University.

"Need any help with the pitch?" Deon asked hopefully. "Taglines? Research?"

"Hell yeah, buddy!" Edward Winston Chamberlain III said waving a piece of paper at Deon. "Got the group coffee order right here."

"What you got there?"

Deon, holding the coffee order and waiting by the elevators, was again possessed by the urge to unleash faux kung fu on somebody.

"Just a coffee order, Bryce."

Bryce was the other admin. The one who had been to a significantly better university than Deon, and who kept dropping hints that his father played golf with potential clients, and who had a sub-let in fashionable Soho.

"Eddie asked you to do that?"

"No," Deon said. "I psychically determined everyone's coffee order and later I'll hand them out at the exact moment they're needed in a protracted low-key magic trick."

"Oh," Bryce said, and then after slightly too long a pause, and with slightly too much uncertainty, "Ha."

"Yeah," Deon said. "Eddie asked me to do it."

"He didn't ask where I was?" Bryce asked.

"When he was asking me to get coffee?"

"Didn't ask to see if maybe I was free to do it?"

"I'm afraid you didn't come up in between me saying 'hi,' and him handing me the group coffee order."

"Oh," Bryce said. "OK." There was another slightly too-protracted pause. "You want me to get the coffees instead?"

"I'm good, Bryce."

Twenty minutes later, twelve coffees dispensed, Deon took the final cup to Eddie's office: a grande caramel macchiato in a venti cup with almond milk, a shot of decaf espresso and two Splendas. When he entered, though, Eddie was already holding a coffee cup.

"Oh," Eddie said. "Why don't you put that out in the kitchen?"

Deon stared at the coffee cup. "Where did you-?"

"Bryce grabbed it for me."

On Tuesday, the Underground train once more rattled into Southwark station. The place smelled sulfurous and made Deon think of something he'd seen on the news last night about a creature crawling up out of an abandoned coal mine in Yorkshire. The newsreader had sounded panicked, and Deon half-remembered images of tarry tentacles jutting from a cliff-side. There might have been police cars. He wasn't sure. He'd been playing Wordle at the time.

"Hey, you."

The words snapped him back to the present. Chloe was on the platform again. Same heavy make-up. Same bright eyes.

"Two days in a row," she said.

"Yeah." Deon looked back at the train. It didn't seem like she'd just shoved her way off it. Had she been waiting here? But . . . what for?

"Another meeting?" he said instead of any of that.

"Yeah!" Her grin spread. "I was telling them all what you said yesterday about London and sneakers. They thought you had it exactly."

That was a bit of a surprise to Deon. "Really?"

"Yeah," she said, falling into step with him. "We were all having some biscuits after the sacrifices, and I mentioned it, and Serge said, 'that guy really gets it.'"

Deon held up a finger. "Did you say sacrifices?"

"Yeah." Chloe let out a small chuff of laughter. "Blood for the blood god and all that, you know?" She grinned broadly. She really did have a pretty smile.

Deon decided she must mean some sort of symbolic sacrifice. Like giving up hard-boiled sweets for Lent.

"Meeting two days in a row?" he said rather than be weird about it.

"Yeah," Chloe nodded. "Bit intense, but a lot of people in the movement are making a collective push right now, you know?"

Deon did not. "The movement?"

"Oh, right!" Chloe rolled her eyes. "Sorry. I didn't really get into it yesterday. Maybe you've got time to grab a coffee, today? Catch up properly?"

Her big eyes bored into Deon. Something happened in his chest. Probably, he decided, some serious nerves about this being a big-time recruitment attempt. "Oh," he said. "Erm . . . "

"It's not a recruitment thing or anything," she said.

"Erm . . . " Somehow that made Deon feel more nervous.

"Just two friends catching up," she said.

"Erm . . . "

She sighed. "How's work?" she said.

This felt like safer ground. "Now, they're trying to come up with something for a new type of mortgage. Apparently, it's much worse than the usual type, but they want it to seem better."

"You don't really like your job do you?"

Deon wondered if he was this transparent to everyone.

"It's just . . . all the people there were making fun of mortgages, and talking about how terrible bankers were, and rolling their eyes at everything. But then my boss suggested we call them GLAM Mortgages, and do a *Sex In The City*-themed campaign and everybody said he was brilliant."

"And you wanted to summon dark gods to tear the place to the ground," finished Chloe.

"Well . . . not exactly." Deon had more been thinking it would've been nice if there'd at least been something good on Netflix when he got home.

"But what if you could?" Chloe said. She seemed quite intense.

Deon shrugged. "I mean, I'd probably start with the banks first."

Deon walked several steps before realizing Chloe wasn't still beside him. She was standing still, biting her bottom lip. "You OK?"

"Are you absolutely sure you don't want to stop for a coffee?" she said.

He looked at his watch.

"I'd love to get a coffee with you," she said.

It all seemed a bit too intense for Deon. "I should probably . . . " he said.

A look of surprisingly pure frustration crossed Chloe's face, and she raised a hand toward him and he saw that she had a tattoo in her palm, something very complicated, a tunnel that seemed to bore down into eternity, and then Chloe said something strange and guttural that he didn't really understand, but he wasn't paying much attention because there was something in that tattoo, something crawling across eons, something reaching across the stars and out of the depth of the oceans, and—

He blinked. He was outside a coffee shop. He didn't remember walking there. He looked at his watch. Where had the last five minutes gone?

Chloe stood next to him. "I'm sorry," she said. She seemed on the verge of tears.

"What?" he said.

"I shouldn't have," she said. "It was wrong."

"What?" he said.

But Chloe ran away.

At work, Deon was summoned to watch Eddie review the new mortgage concepts in the main conference room. The other creatives all huddled at the back like cool kids on a school bus, so Deon grabbed a remaining seat at the front of the room.

Bryce entered holding two coffees. Deon had no doubt that one was a grande caramel macchiato in a venti cup with almond milk, a shot of decaf espresso, and a two Splendas. Bryce sat opposite Deon, and then very clearly nudged his chair slightly closer to the front of the room.

It was small, and petty, and Deon knew he should be the bigger person and let it go. But Deon also knew that Bryce genuinely thought GLAM mortgages were a good idea, and that more people should buy sneakers they couldn't afford. So, Deon nudged his chair a little closer to the front of the room too.

Bryce narrowed his eyes. He nudged his chair forward.

So, Deon did.

So, Bryce did.

So, Deon did.

So, Bryce did.

They were both clear of the end of the table now.

Deon nudged his chair closer to front of the room.

Eddie entered. He looked at Deon and Bryce. "Come on guys," he said, "give a dude some room."

Deon's cheeks burned. Bryce handed Eddie one of the coffees.

"Life saver," Eddie said.

The next day, Chloe wasn't waiting on the platform. Deon's walk to work felt far lonelier than usual.

At the office, everyone was talking about Sheffield.

"Did you see them screaming?" said Jerry, one of the guys from the Studio.

"Looked like fish monsters with bat wings," said Cynthia from Production.

"It made my husband come over all funny," said Andrea also from Production. "He started yelling gibberish, and I had to make him sit in the corner with a rum and coke until he calmed down."

"Trashed half of downtown is what I heard," said Oscar, one of the associate creative directors. "Every bank was destroyed. Every single one."

"And those bloody lunatics with robes, chanting and carrying on," said Jacqueline from Operations. "Sick in the head."

"Come on guys," said Eddie. "Back to work."

Deon had to Google it all when no-one was looking. He'd been watching the game last night, and then gone right to bed. There was blurry footage of strange humanoid creatures sailing down the streets of Sheffield. Where they landed, the tarmac seethed and broke apart. Some people wearing long robes with heavy hoods walked the streets, chanting. Others ran screaming, but still taking the time to film everything, and upload it to Instagram later.

When Deon saw the creatures pull a branch of Barclays to the ground, he found his sympathy was with the robed figures.

The next day, Chloe was back on the Underground platform. She shuffled her feet as he walked up to her.

"I missed you yesterday," he said.

She looked up at him. "Really?"

Her relief caught him off guard. "Yeah," he managed around his own stumbling tongue. "My commute. It's . . . you know . . . more . . . fun when we, erm . . . Yeah."

She beamed. "Come on," she said and put her arm through his.

They walked and talked then about his English degree, and the works of George Orwell and Iain Banks, who apparently they'd both loved since back in school. They talked about the village they'd grown up in, and the schoolmates who'd never moved away, and how weird that was, to just be content with that one idea of what the world could be. They talked about their parents' expectations, and the weight of them, and how they just wanted the space to figure themselves out a bit, and if they just had that they'd be able to present it back in a way that made sense. Or maybe with that space they'd realize that those expectations didn't matter because the world hadn't lived up to its potential so why should they?

The streets, Deon realized, were more crowded than usual. There was a blockage up ahead. People milled about, seeking exits.

"Oh man," he said. "It's going to take me forever to get into the office today."

"Want to grab a coffee and wait for it all to clear?" Chloe said and Deon did. Somehow, they'd ended up laughing a lot while talking about the state of the world.

His phone buzzed though. "I'd love to," he said, "but I really should get into the office. There's this guy . . ."

"What guy?" Chloe asked.

So, he told her about Bryce.

"Yeah," she said. "I totally know a Bryce."

"Really?"

"At meetings. Except mine's a Trevor."

"Ooph," said Deon. "I've heard Trevors can be pretty bad."

"It's not as classic douchebag as a Bryce."

"More like a stealth douche."

"He's totally a stealth douche."

They'd managed to push their way through most of the crowds now. They could see a police cordon, and beyond that a circle of figures in dark robes all holding hands and chanting.

"Is that the same people from up in Sheffield?" Deon asked. He looked to the sky, but nothing dark and mysterious swirled there, only a page of *The Sun* newspaper. He looked back to the robed group. Now, one of the figures was pointing at Chloe, and making urgent beckoning motions.

"Ugh," said Chloe. "Bloody Trevor."

"Wait," said Deon. "*That's* the guy you were talking about?"

"Yes."

"Were you up in Sheffield?"

"Yeah. With my group. We're doing street activism right now."

Deon checked the skies again. "Were you up in Yorkshire recently?"

"God no," said Chloe. "They put gravy on their chips up there."

"Right," said Deon.

"Look," said Chloe, "let's just walk round the other side of this whole mess. You'll get to work, and I'll catch up with my guys. Sound good?"

Deon looked at the chanting circle again. "You sure you don't . . ."

"Nah, they're fine without me."

They walked around. They talked more. When they parted Deon said, "This was fun. Nice getting to spend more time together."

Chloe beamed her big bright smile again. "Yeah," she said. "Good luck with work."

His face must have fallen because Chloe's softened. "Maybe something terrible will happen to Bryce," she said. "You never know."

Deon laughed and waved goodbye.

O

It was during a coffee break that something black, and liquid, and bat-like, and howling from a hundred mouths smashed through an office window, and tore into Bryce.

Alec from accounts was nearby, and dropped to his knees and started howling in tongues. Jessica in Project Management turned and fled so fast that she ran into a wall and knocked herself unconscious. Terry from editorial started to eat all of his pencils, chewing through wood and graphite in great jagged mouthfuls.

Bryce mostly just bled everywhere.

Everyone was sent home after that. Over Eddie's protestations.

Deon was surprised to find Chloe standing outside the office building. She was on the far side of the street looking out over the Thames.

"Hey," he said walking over.

She turned around, and her face split open in a broad grin. "Oh wow," she said. "Twice in one day. I should play the lottery."

"Your street activism all done?"

"Yeah," the police broke it up, Chloe said.

"You OK?" Deon quickly checked her for bruising or blood.

"Yeah." Chloe shrugged. "I think everyone's just on edge after Sheffield. And it won't stop us anyway." The way she said it sounded a little ominous. But then she said quite brightly. "What are you doing out so early?"

"Well actually," Deon said, "something completely insane just happened." And he told her about Bryce.

"Woah," she said when he was done. "That's a weird coincidence. You tell me today about what an asshole he is to you, and then he gets attacked."

"Yeah," Deon said. "Crazy right?"

"Better be careful not to tell me about anyone else hassling you, right?" she said.

Deon laughed. "Coincidences are crazy, right? Did you know that the number of Nicolas Cage movies that come out in a year correlates to the number of people who drown in swimming pools each year?"

"But," Chloe said, "sometimes there might be a causal relationship."

"Well," said Deon, "not between Nic Cage movies and drownings."

"No," Chloe agreed. "But between other things."

"Yeah," Deon said. "But the whole point is you can't be sure just from correlation."

"No, I get that Deon." For the first time, Chloe seemed a little frustrated.

Deon decided to maybe cut his losses and run. "I should probably be heading home."

"But if you all got sent home because of the attack," Chloe said, "you must be free for a coffee, right?"

Deon genuinely felt bad this time. "I wish I could, " he said. "but my boss wants us all on a phone call in-" He checked his watch. "Shit."

"Seriously?" Chloe said.

"He's a bit of a ball buster sometimes," Deon said. Then he grinned. "Oops. Shouldn't have told you that. Don't want something terrible happening to him, right?"

But Chloe didn't laugh at that either.

The next day, Deon couldn't take the Underground because the whole line was shut down. "What's going on?" he asked the disgruntled woman in a high-vis vest standing by the station entrance.

"Unspeakable horrors rising up out of the deep and destroying the train tracks," she said, already bored with the conversation.

"Seriously?" said Deon.

"Maybe," she said. "Honestly there was a lot of screaming and it was a bit hard to make it all out."

"Bloody hell," said Deon and decided he was probably just going to have to call an Uber.

"Hey Deon!"

He looked up. To his surprise, Chloe was standing on the other side of the street. He went over to her. "Do you live round here?"

She shook her head. "Just in the neighborhood."

Deon looked from Chloe to the Underground entrance and back. He thought about Sheffield and people in black robes.

"What were you doing in the neighborhood?" he asked.

"You want to ride-share into Southwark?" she said.

"Erm . . ." said Deon.

"Too far to walk," Chloe said. "Unless you want to."

"Nah," said Deon. "Splitting an uber sounds good."

Their driver was called Alex and his radio blared panicky news stories about strange beasts shuffling out of the Thames and running amok through high-end shops. Outside, black shapes like vast eels writhed in the air above the Thames.

"It'll be the bloody Muslims," Alex said without looking back. "You take my word for it."

When they got out, Southwark seemed abandoned. All the tourists that normally gathered near the Globe and the Tate Modern were gone.

"Are you sure it's OK to be out?" Deon asked, although he was mostly thinking about the email Eddie had sent saying everyone's presence in the office was mandatory.

"You'll be safe with me," said Chloe. Here eyes were shining again, and an almost giddy smile on her face.

"You look happy," Deon said.

She shrugged. "I don't know," she said. "Some days things just feel... possible. Like maybe it's not all inevitably shit. Like, maybe we can make a difference. And maybe it's not a big difference because it's a big world and all of us can maybe only do something small. But if we're all doing small things, if we're all trying to change the world... maybe together we can do something big."

"You're going to lose some serious goth cred talking like that."

She squeezed his arm. "Worth it," she said. "Speaking of possible things. I mean..." She shuffled her feet. "Coffee?"

Deon felt genuinely terrible this time. "I know like I seem like I'm actively avoiding it at this point, but my boss . . ." He pulled out his phone and waved it vaguely through the air. "He's been emailing like an absolute a-hole and-"

"It's OK," Chloe said nodding. "I get it. Little steps."

"Sorry," Deon said again.

"Deon," Eddie said, "dude, we're going have to talk about your punctuality here. This is two days in a row."

"Sorry," Deon said. "The Underground is a bit of a mess today."

"Bryce was here on time," Eddie said. "And he lost two pints of blood yesterday."

Yeah, Deon thought, *well that's because Bryce is a tool with no life who would sell his soul for the chance to lick your boots, and if that's really all you want out of someone who works here then maybe no-one should work here because the real tool is you.*

But he didn't say that. Because this was his job, and this was his boss, and this was what he'd spent a lot of time in university aiming for, and...

And then none of those reasons seemed very important anymore. So, he did say it after all.

Eddie looked at him with wide eyes. He opened his mouth, and Deon thought that this was going to be difficult to explain to his parents, and was going to make paying rent a lot harder, but that honestly it was worth it in the long run, because maybe the first step in fixing the whole world, was just fixing his world. But Deon never got to say that because at that moment a massive tentacle struck the building.

Everything shook. The tentacle was black and a hundred meters tall. Through the office window, several others swayed into view. One crashed against the building wall. Glass shattered. The floor lurched. Eddie shrieked and made a dash to the elevator bank. Deon staggered to his knees. He kept staring out the window.

On a rooftop opposite, he thought he saw a figure in a black hoody, with a small cherubic face, and lips painted the color of Halloween. She waved to him.

More glass broke. He heard metal tearing, and concrete being smashed.

When he could, Deon made it to his feet and ran for the stairs.

Chloe was waiting for him outside. Most of the tentacles had retreated back below the torn up tarmac. She wore a rueful expression.

"Hey," she said.

"Hey."

Around them, people ran for cover. Above them, smoke and flame filled the air.

"I probably owe you some answers," Chloe said.

"Probably."

"So," Chloe said. "My group. Well, I guess we're a cult. We just don't like that word. It's very loaded. But yeah, we're sort of summoning up ancient Gods to . . . Well, it's a lot of what we've been talking about. This idea of course-correcting the world. I mean, we're being murdered by our own hubris, and we've got to do something about it. So, we are. Not just small steps, but big steps too. And yes, I was in Sheffield. And yes, I was in Yorkshire, I don't know why I lied about that. I just . . . I didn't want to freak you out. But we never had time to talk about it properly because of your work, and that douchebag Bryce, and . . . ."

She trailed off and Deon took that in for a while.

"Actually," he said, "what I was really wondering is . . . did you really just happen to be in my neighborhood this morning?"

"Oh," said Chloe, and shuffled her feet.

Deon waited.

"Well," said Chloe after a while, "we really had planned to disrupt the subway lines with the raising of Berusshalom the Dark Whisperer, but I may been the one to suggest we do it in your neighborhood, so that you might need to . . ." She bit her lip. ". . . share a cab with me and stuff."

"Do you even take the same subway as me?" Deon asked.

Chloe took a breath. "No," she said. "But I heard you'd just moved here, and you were the only person who was ever nice to me in school, and it's really been hard to make friends in London, and Trevor has been such a pain at meetings lately, so I just thought . . . I thought it might be nice to reconnect, you know?"

"And you summoned a demon that attacked Bryce?" Deon checked.

"Technically it's a Lesser Extrusion of the Stalking One," said Chloe. "But basically, yeah."

"And you just summoned a bunch of tentacles to tear down the building where I work?"

"Well technically—" Chloe started, and then just said, "Yeah."

"Why?" asked Deon.

"Well, I thought if you didn't have anywhere to work, then, you know . . ." She shuffled her feet. "Maybe you'd be free for coffee?"

Deon looked up and down the street. Most of the people had finished fleeing by now. "I'm not sure the coffee place is going to be open," he said. "Because I think this is the apocalypse."

"Just a little one," Chloe said. And then she said, "Small steps," and Deon laughed maybe a lot harder than that deserved. But it had been a long morning already.

"Also," Chloe said when he recovered, "I brought a thermos."

"Oh," said Deon, and he thought about that, and about what Chloe had done, and about the world, and his world, and her world, and the ending of things, and the start of newer things as well.

"Yeah," he said finally. "Yeah, I think having a coffee together sounds really brilliant actually." And she smiled, and Deon thought that it really was a very pretty smile indeed.

⊐

Final Cycle

~ *L. E. Daniels*

hot flashes
Whip-cracks of heat and a great expanse opens;
Five decades of orbit recalibrate without apology:
Our final cycle, a solitary transit with compromised tech.

dental changes
"You grind," dentist says. Everything tastes like iron.
In his office, a headline reads: *Fifty Is The New Forty*
But we only want forward, our course set: the furnace of a star.

brain fog
We are matter, contracted into form for a pulse,
And releasing again as stardust without shadow.
Why are we in the kitchen? Who wanted what? No.

existential sex
New mouthguard taut; husband looks afraid.
From an entropy of winding sheets in glittering dark,
Self-aware, this system spirals outward until it breaks.

birth death birth
Our bones spur and crackle toward fractals.
Doctors illume but we know what they'll find:
Nebulas collapsing into protostars. Again. And again.

tentacles
Hydrate. Hands look old first. For one hundred thousand years
Ice comets pummeled the earth—seeding polyps, watering potential.
Everything is from somewhere else, including us, including octop-us.

hearts made for breaking
Now—if there is now—our hearts open, ringed with cenotes,
Pounded by impacts. We jettison the skulls of all the drowned girls
We once were, leaving them weightless, spinning: a trail in our wake.

final cycle
At last, repose. We are blinded by the mouth of this star,
We are a ship's manifest carved into ore with names of the dead,
And like everything else before and behind, we burn, we burn, we . . .

⊐

The Unknowable Ones

~ Ken Hueler

Emily watches the gasoline rainbows migrate across the dark sclera and irises of Hubbard's eyes, tracking her as she sets the water glass on their bed table. Hooking his neck with her right arm, she tips medicine into his mouth. She lowers him onto the pillow and waits. After five minutes, the eyes turn grey, then white. Only the pupils remain dark, death leering through peepholes.

What is left of her Hubbard? His hair—still a glossy brown—and his angel-wing ears. Even inside is desiccation, the mental brilliance she'd married rotten from obsession and mania. She should be checking the pot on the stove, but sometimes, just after taking the medicine, Hubbard peeps out, familiar, reactive. Those moments sustain her.

The black in his pupils stretch and soften. "Em?"

She strokes his cheek. "I'm here. I'm here. I need you. Can you stay with me?"

Of course not. Nonsense spills out: Rituals. Old Ones. "*They are the Grand Unification Theory,*" he'd declared, back when he was round and bright-eyed and still her Hubbard. "*They walk the stars, move things. If we know Them, we know the universe.*"

She never understood anyone's desire for that quest. Back in school, when a teacher explained their insignificance in the universe, she'd gotten mad. Why make a kid feel small? She already had bullies and cramps and hands to deal with. Instead, she learned to focus down: on herself, her town, her friends. Be happy, content.

"Make the connection, Emily," he rasps. "Call Them to me. Only They can save me, Their faithful servant." Then he begins reciting the steps, which she memorized many iterations ago.

Her Hubbard, he'd had a mind. Smart. Never a strong man, he was sloppy, quick to ail, forgot to eat when overexcited, but he was kind, fun to listen to, attentive, and a doer. She wanted that back. And her, she'd seen a place to be useful. She'd taken care of him, and for years he thrived. Where is her man now? As Hubbard's energy winds down, Emily pulls the blanket up to wipe his chin, but the doorbell chimes. She waits. A second ring. Stella knows she is home and will keep ringing, the sound digging into Emily's sense of obligation until she is forced to let her in.

"Out for a walk and brought a few things," Stella says, sweeping into the kitchen.

"Thank you for that," Emily replies, fetching two mugs.

"Oh, I can't stay today. I'm going to my sister's down in Bloomington for the weekend. But I'll swing by Monday to check in on you."

Stella's hair is glossy and recently cut. Her clothes are not rumpled. She has time. Her partner is not dying, and her career isn't onerous. Because of her, Emily can stay in the house to tend Hubbard.

"I didn't see an email," Stella is saying. "Let me know what you need from the market and I'll pick it up when I go tomorrow."

Emily notices the discrepancy: Stella can't bring groceries if she'll be out of town this weekend. Emily smiles. "I will, thanks."

Stella plops two snap-lid containers on the counter. "Some vegetable broth for Hubbard and leftover lasagna for you. It's delicious. Oh, and this." She puts a paperback book on the table—saturated primary colors, big letters. "You've got two people to take of, Emily, and I feel you're neglecting one."

"I know. I know."

Stella surveys the kitchen. "One day next week I'll come over and we can give this place a good cleaning. I know how exhausted you must be." She squeezes Emily's hand. "Hubbard will pull through. He's a good man."

As Emily closes the door, she wonders: Does Stella really believe that? What do neighbors think, say? *Emily, she's got a crazy husband, stays up all hours, goes into the woods alone at night. Lot of pets gone missing. Something wrong behind those eyes.*

They are not wrong.

Emily admits she never understood Hubbard, not really. If so, she'd have seen this coming.

She checks the pot on the stove, puts both of Stella's containers in the refrigerator, and shuffles back to the bedroom. Hubbard is mumbling, straining to talk to his Old Ones. He is sweating, tensed like a powerlifter. Why has his cult abandoned him? He's so earnest. Did they decide he was weak? Used up? Not fervent enough? They should see him now. She has come to picture those cultists as snowbound hikers willing to eat one another—but there is no snow.

"Emily," he croaks.

She stiffens. He does not call out to her often, not anymore.

"If you won't take me downstairs, go yourself. Tell Them I need Them. They will know."

Her heart sinks. Hubbard doesn't understand her. Nothing in her wants to touch whatever did this to him. Is it the madness, or did he never know her? Had Hubbard tried to grasp the universe but not bothered to learn his own wife?

A thought comes. "Hubbard," she says, stroking his rough face—she'd apply lotion later, "I did the ritual, two weeks back, and nothing happened."

His face twists, the flaking skin on his cheeks rising like goose pimples. The oily colors burst through the pupils. "Liar."

He means it. Something in her face or voice gave her away. A feeling of helplessness pushes her back, and she storms out of the bedroom. Has she been nothing but an attendant, a convenient companion tending him? How dare he?

Turning down the burner on the stove, she notices the book. What did other people, like Stella, think of her, tending a crazy husband and barely stepping out of the house? Stella must see her as a project, or a charity case. Or maybe Stella really is this kind. How could anyone ever know?

Emily picks up the book. Stella has been a godsend but sometimes, like today, also finds ways to avoid her. Then it hits: Stella is like her, living in moments. Stella parcels kindness in digestible chunks, so she doesn't choke. Was that what she meant when she told Emily to find time for herself? Emily carries the book to the living room, sits, reads the opening paragraph over and over. She can't. She just can't.

Something in her brain pops like a knuckle: She will do the ritual, she will say his plea. All this time she has been tending Hubbard's body, but not his mind, and Hubbard is his mind. Her husband is believing himself to death, but maybe he can believe himself to life. She won't reach his Old Ones, but he will read in her face she tried, and he might get hope, feel less abandoned. Hope drove people. Cured them, sometimes. She has no expectations, but even false hope brings comfort, and like throwing bottled notes into the sea, she is taking action. She'll do the ritual every damned day if he starts improving.

She shuts off the burner, pees, and carries a glass of water to the basement. Everything is still set out, dusty and waiting. Whenever she lays eyes on the cult's paraphernalia, she thinks: gaudy, self-important. She reviews the ritual in her head.

She starts. The words are alien and hard to pronounce. She keeps her nose to the page so she does not miss a single letter. She pauses to execute the steps Hubbard has described. As she concentrates, the world falls away—no dying husband, no bills. She feels cleaner, freer. Near the end, sourness begins fermenting in her belly, but finally she stumbles through the last collection of consonants.

Rising to call out Hubbard's request, she lurches sideways and falls. Her lungs strain to collect oxygen; the floor tilts. She slides down an uneven surface and collides with periodic metal. She is on flagged stone, pressed against a railing. Between posts, mesmerizing ironwork patterns shift like Magic Eye pictures, or an image of two faces that melt into a vase and back to faces.

Hubbard never succeeded, why has she? Because he is Hubbard, focused on his goal, and with something like this, the process matters so very much. His eyes saw only success, and he'd stumbled on the path's unnoticed roots and rocks. Without her watchful help, he'd failed. Every time.

Gripping the railing, she stands on the inclined balcony. She is high above a wasteland of stones, varicose scrub, dust, and twisted trees battling themselves—their trunks struggle skyward; their branches cringe toward the ground. She glances up. A pollution-free sky draws in a misshapen moon, nebula smears, and a smothering profusion of stars. She feels smaller than ever in her life. Her eyes drop. To her left, standing with its back to her and gazing up into the universe, a being as tall as . . . she cannot tell. Galaxy-spiral tentacles writhe from the neck, and the surface of its body ripples.

Her brain tingles painfully, a limb falling asleep. If Hubbard's brilliant mind is collapsing, what chance does her ordinary one have? She inhales the thin air. Understanding is not her goal; unlike Hubbard, she will focus. She shuts out the shifting railing; she does not look at the mis-angled building behind; she does not wonder what the tree branches fear that the trunks do not. She calms, somewhat. The universe shrinks to one point, the creature: semi-solid, ugly, confusing, terrifying, but now isolated.

"He's no use to you now," she screams. "Let him go."

The being shivers. Does it understand? The creature digs one clawed hand into its torso and pulls out something wet and screaming. A flick of the wrist—from which chunks separate and drift down—sends the object heavenward, where it becomes spinning light and vanishes. Seconds later, along the object's trajectory, a bright flash sparks impossibly far away, near a nebula, which collapses into utter darkness. Nearby stars shift toward the absence of light.

Then, out of that darkness, a featureless head emerges, then angular, boneless limbs.

The creature on the ground's writhing head lowers and, incrementally, it begins to turn, but before their eyes meet, Emily is on her basement floor.

She feels victorious, slightly mad, disappointed. Richer air takes the edge off her dizziness, gives her body strength. What she'd experienced should have crushed her, but, like most people, she'd been able to reduce a vast unknowable god to a helpful biped, and even now she was narrowing that strange ordeal the same way she breaks down the endless looming years of tending a fading husband into days, and then hours, and finally one moment followed by the next.

She has no idea what the creature meant. Or if it was even communicating. Human brains like hers, which didn't even understand one other, are incapable against anything that vast. They might imagine mining an asteroid, traveling planet A to B, or colonizing space, but moving stars and dragging objects and creatures across the universe? No one could ever grasp what she has seen.

The clock shows she's been gone an hour, though she was on the other world at best fifteen minutes. How? From traveling, she decides. Nothing unusual, just traveling. A to B and back.

She gathers her wits. She has to lie to Hubbard, and in a way he won't suspect. She sifts through her husband—his strengths, weaknesses, abilities, mental state—and then hers. She climbs the stairs, glancing back once to make sure nothing has followed her back. She heats Stella's broth, adds medicine, and carries it to the bedroom.

Hubbard is sleeping. He should be awake, hungry. She puts the mug down, shakes him. The lids slide, the color slick drifts. She lifts him, eases the broth down.

Hubbard surfaces fast, gasps. "You saw!"

She strokes his face. What tells him that? "I visited, yes."

"Only our priest has seen Them. How? Never mind. What happened?"

"I gave your message."

"Describe everything. Every detail. Tell me!"

She rises for the dangerous part. Hubbard's brain is flooded with hope, finally alert and clever, again. He sees the goal—himself where she stood—and just might be too focused there to spot the lie here.

"That's all you get. If they reach out, I'll tell you."

They won't reach out. She knows this. Whatever went down, whether happenstance or meant for her, Hubbard is even more insignificant than she is. He is near dead, abandoned by his cult. No, They would be done with him. "Rest up, Hubbard."

She leaves. Lingering would give him more chance to examine her. She needs him hopeful.

His ravings tumble after her. She pauses. He is not talking to her, he is demanding. She is an instrument to his goal. She hears no gratitude, no desire for her to join him. Just need.

She heats the lasagne and sits at the kitchen table, picking away at it. The sourness in her belly has faded, but she is not hungry. She just needs something to do with her hands, her mouth. Hubbard has stopped shouting, at least.

The concealing moments fall, briefly, and she endures the wide vista of a hope-strengthened Hubbard prolonging her servitude. 'In sickness' will become 'and in health'. Will his goal be to leave her behind for his beloved Old Ones? Worse, will he want to bring her? She pushes the thought away, savors a mouthful of food, disappears into its flavors. Stella is right, it is delicious.

A sound in the hall. She looks up. Hubbard's hands, then arms, then face drag into view. Where did he get the strength? A pain flits: Her dying father, when she'd announced her brother was coming, rallied for the three days, and immediately after her sibling left, he declined and died a day later. Hubbard has gained this burst from the hope he will finally see Them.

He tries to speak, but he is used up. His head lolls between his arms, oily eyes pinned to his wife. He sighs and his body collapses, his torso sinks and does not rise. Utter stillness.

This shouldn't be happening. Emily knew this moment had to come, but the arrival is a slap. Later. Always later. Now is supposed to be action, later is hope, but now both are silent and still. Emily feels dizzy again: Death is the vastest thing a human can know—it never ends, will outlast the sun, the universe itself.

Emily tears away from the thought. She focuses: A lot has to happen now. Paperwork. A funeral. Notify Hubbard's family, former friends. She must call the hospice agency. The agency will send Moira to verify the death, call the funeral home, prepare the body—how will Emily explain Hubbard's body lying prone in the hall?

Too much, too much. Call Stella. She will help. Has to help—Hubbard's gods won't, and, anyway, what use is a god when you need comfort and the relatives are the ones crying? What is the universe when your home is suddenly too big? Stella will know what to do. When Emily fails—and she will—Stella will prop her up. If Emily shuts herself in room to cry for days, Stella will drag her out, will keep her going.

She will call Stella. But not yet. She needs time alone. Soon she will have attention, questions, visitors, casseroles, cards.

With a start, she realized that she should check that Hubbard is actually dead. She approaches, and his corpse breathes blackness at her; a thumb-sized blend of opalescence and dark exits his mouth, creeps toward her across the floor, folding over itself like a cresting wave.

Emily takes a mason jar from the cabinets, unscrews the cap, fingernails the lid off, and sits on the floor. She waits. As the thing nears, she places the jar on one of the beveled rectangle sides and tips the lip to the floor. The thing, drawn by the living hands around the glass, crawls inside. She screws the lid tight.

She places the jar on the kitchen counter, showers, combs out her hair, brushes her teeth. She chooses comfortable clothes, puts the jar into a tote bag, leaves. Outside is humid. Already she feels sticky, dirty.

The neighborhood is the same: bright flowers, children running through sprinklers, neighbors firing a honk and a wave. She turns down Ivy, follows it to Cote. At the intersection, she slows. Stella is in her garden, fussing over roses. Emily waits, and when the woman turns her back, she darts across the road. She crouches, opens the jar, and tips the thing out.

She scampers back across the intersection, returns the jar to her bag. She can make out the small black thumb in the grass. It turns— Emily is now too far away. It inches to the hedge, wiggles through to the garden. Stella is on her knees, backside to the road, weeding.

Emily heads home. Sweat wicks into her clothes and her damp hair thickens, but inside her the humidity is evaporating. She smiles, waves back at a car.

⬚

A Study of Metamorphosis Calamity

~ Tania Chen

Concrete on thorax,
the apocalypse shaped sound reverberates on impact.
Lashes of wet rain,
metal scented as the butterflies' insides trickle out.

You watch them breathe and slow.

Routes replaced by gorges,
rendezvouses an impossibility as you sit on your patio.
The world falls sideways,
drunk and violent convulsions as you knead bread in the kitchen.

Nyarlathotep reaches through
the mourning croons of pigeons the colour of peeled salmon.
Raw pink peering past
serrated sides where the scales were stripped.

Ache from the pit, you breathe and slow.

Ozymandias' pyramids echo in concert
while your consciousness pools into the abdomen.
Outside the air is glittering gold desert-filled,
you hold the bitsy bug body tenderly in the palm of your hand.

Using sewing kit in your living room,
reteach wings stitched together with the colour out of space to beat.
Falling false perceptions give way,
the porous blades of newly born grass fill your heart.

Together you breathe and slow.

⊐

The Purple Emperor

~ Eric Shanower

Since my husband passed away five years ago, I've developed a strong enthusiasm for gardening. I've grown many varieties of flowers—irises, tulips, dahlias. But the flowers I enjoy most, the blooms in which I take particular pride, are roses. All sorts delight me. All colors—red, yellow, pink, orange, and white roses. But the rose I'm proudest of is the darkly luscious blossom I named the Purple Emperor.

Only one of the several seedlings I crossed to create this hybrid survived. But, oh, how the survivor thrived! The bush is strong and sturdy, the thorns thick and long. The blossoms have only eight petals, but their color is a glorious, glossy dark purple, warmer than violet.

The Purple Emperor takes pride of place in my rose garden. The bush rises majestically in the center of the bed, taller than my other rose bushes. Its many dark blossoms send forth a bold, sweet perfume. I admit I show it special favor, tending, watering, fertilizing, pruning, deadheading, confiding in it. Not that I don't care for my other rose bushes—I love them all. Call me a silly old woman, but the Purple Emperor is the child I never had.

So when something attacked my Purple Emperor, a bolt of alarm struck through me. Early one morning, as I knelt plucking tiny weeds from the edge of the raised bed where my roses live, I heard unexpected rustling. I looked up to see the Purple Emperor rose bush shaking.

It stopped. I frowned at the bush, puzzled. I stepped in among the rose bushes, toward the Purple Emperor. It shook again. I stepped closer and saw an arm clad in a long white sleeve. It extended from a gap in the lattice that enclosed the skirting of my back porch. The hand had gripped the main stem of the bush close to the ground and was tugging it back and forth.

"Hey," I croaked, my throat constricted with confusion. "What're you doing?" My voice grew confident as anger supplanted confusion. "Leave my roses alone!"

My Purple Emperor bush swayed wildly as the arm wrenched it. Leaves scattered.

"Get out of here!" I shouted. "I'm calling the police!" I'd left my phone inside, charging on the kitchen counter, but I hesitated to leave my roses and let the damage continue.

With a dull ripping sound, the Purple Emperor rose bush jerked upward, shedding petals. The intruder was uprooting my rose bush.

"Stop it!" I screamed. "Stop it!" If my roses had voices, they would have screamed, too.

I snatched up my trowel and weeding hook from where they lay nearby on the grass. I sank to my knees beside the Purple Emperor, ignoring buffeting blossoms and tearing thorns as it whipped to and fro. With a grunt, I drove the sharp tines of the weeding hook into the biceps of the strange arm. Purple blood welled around the tines, staining the white sleeve. Such a satisfying sight. But the arm wouldn't stop tugging.

It tore the root ball free. Springy roots showered me with soil. I stabbed my trowel into the forearm. Into the wrist. I ripped the weeding hook through flesh. But to no effect. The arm dragged the bush toward the lattice skirting of my porch. Thorns swept by, raking me. The arm and the root ball disappeared into the lattice before the bush stuck. The small opening couldn't admit the entire rose bush at once.

I dropped my tools and grabbed two of the stems. Thorns pierced my palms and fingers. I ignored the pain and pulled as hard as I could. Whoever was pulling the other end was stronger. By fits and starts, the bush dragged me across the litter of leaves, petals, and broken stems. I swung my legs to brace my feet against the lattice skirting. Beneath my feet the lattice shattered.

The bush pulled my arms into the opening. As my head jerked closer, I saw something strange. The opening wasn't actually in the latticework. My Purple Emperor was being drawn through an opening that hung in the air—close to the ground and near the porch skirting, but not part of it. I didn't understand.

With a tremendous tug, the bush pulled me through the opening. I fell several feet, sprawling on top of the Purple Emperor bush into a candlelit room. Thorns pricked my body. I lost hold of the stems. As I rolled away, I caught a glimpse of a white-clad figure pulling the bush through a doorway.

I lay on the floor, trying to catch my breath, wishing I were as spry as I once was. My shoulder ached where I'd fallen onto it. All my muscles felt strained.

A coffered ceiling of warm wood, shining with reflected candle-light, rose above me, higher than the few feet I'd fallen into the room. How could that be? No roof of a half-buried structure rose in my backyard or anywhere near my home. Where was I? In a neighbor's basement somehow? It didn't smell like a dank basement. A delicate fragrance of roses hung in the air, barely detectable, light and sweet, not at all cloying.

I groaned and pushed myself to a sitting position. Luxurious fur-nishings surrounded me. A wooden bedstead carved with sprays of wooden flowers rose high against the far wall. An embroidered bedspread covered the bed. At its foot stood a heavy wooden chest flanked by richly upholstered chairs. Candles glowed in sconces and in candlesticks set on small tables lining the wood-paneled walls. Hanging paintings featured still lives of roses in many shades of purple. In a tall wooden bookcase, uniform volumes with purple spines lined the shelves.

I was in a bedroom. But whose? And where?

Grunting, I climbed painfully to my feet. Blood from my wounded palms and fingers dripped onto leaves and petals torn from my Purple Emperor and onto a thick carpet, where the blood disap-peared against an intricate design of dark purple roses. I clenched my hands just below my collarbone in an attempt to staunch the blood.

Where was the opening I'd come through? I studied the wall above where I'd fallen. Candles in nearby sconces shed plenty of light, but I could detect no irregularity. I rapped on the wood, high, low, and to either side. Nothing about the wall seemed unusual, but here I was. How had I come here and what was this place?

"Hello?" I called. "Hello-o!"

No answer.

Was I caught in a dream? If so, the clarity of it was like no dream I'd had before. Besides, the sharp pains in my hands and the dull aches in my body argued against my dreaming.

Was this some sort of supernatural experience? Or had I been abducted by aliens? Or was this a drug-induced hallucination? That morning I'd consumed only two cups of tea brewed from rose petals

I'd harvested from my garden. And no one else had been in the house for days. No one could have drugged my tea.

A sense of dread collected at the borders of my mind. Could I be going crazy?

I didn't want to believe that. I was only sixty-seven. Still in good health. My memory wasn't always what it used to be, but my mind was clear. I could recite the names and planting order of not just my roses, but every flowering plant in my garden. I never had to grope for computer passwords, never found myself lost while driving to the grocery store, the bank, the post office, or the local nursery. Was I the victim of sudden dementia?

I pushed back the fear. Think, I silently insisted. If I knew where I was, I could figure out how to get home. But the walls of the room held no windows to see out of, no view to orient my location. I needed to find the front door. Or a back door. Or someone to ask the way out.

Two doorways led from the bedroom. I headed for the one that I'd seen the bush-napper disappear through. One person, at least, had gone that way. Maybe I'd find others. Maybe answers lay that way. Maybe my Purple Emperor, too.

I wanted my stolen rose bush back, but determining where I was took precedence. I recoiled from the thought of losing the rose bush, but if I had to pay that price to regain security, so be it. The Purple Emperor was the only rose bush of its kind in existence. But maybe a root large enough to grow another plant had been left in my garden bed. To see about that, I'd need to get home first.

The next room was also a bedroom. Larger than the first. Just as beautifully appointed. Tiny purple fabric flowers sprinkled the smooth white bedspread. More paintings of purple roses hung on the walls. A glass-doored bookcase held three more shelves of books with identical purple spines. Candles burned all around. But I found no one to help me, so I walked into the next room.

Another bedroom. Was this building some sort of luxury hotel? Or a palace? The furnishings certainly looked top quality. The décor featured more roses. And more purple rose paintings. More of the same purple books, too. Whoever furnished this place enjoyed a narrow taste in reading material.

On I went, through chamber after chamber, eventually losing count. All bedrooms—not even a single bathroom—each more opulent than the last, each incorporating a rose motif, and each holding shelves of purple books, identical in size and color.

Candles burned. Surfaces shone dust free. The bed linen appeared immaculate. Even if no one actually slept in any of these bedrooms, someone must see to their upkeep. A caretaker—at least one, more likely an army of caretakers—must enter the rooms regularly. Their condition demanded it. But I met no one.

After a while, the wounds in my hands stopped bleeding. Dried blood started flaking off. At last, I indulged my curiosity about the books and slid one off the shelf, a compact volume, heavier than it looked. I frowned at the gold leaf on the purple leather spine announcing the title: *The Purple Emperor.*

What? This could be no coincidence. A dream? It must be. How else to explain it?

I opened the book. The thick, gilt-edged pages felt like parchment rather than paper. I marveled again at the title, *The Purple Emperor,* stamped perceptibly by letterpress across the title page. Below the title appeared the author's name, one I'd never heard before, *Lescelius.* Then the lines: *Privately Printed for His Excellency by Kammern in Mainz.* And below that, what might have been intended to be a date in nonsensically arranged Roman numerals, *XMIL.* On the next leaf began the main text.

At first, I couldn't distinguish the words. They blurred before my direct sight, while at my vision's periphery, the printing appeared clear. But when I shifted my gaze, the clearer section of the page blurred and the first section, now on the periphery, became clear. As I concentrated, however, the letters under my direct gaze grew distinct, so that I could slowly read the text. It read like a play script, though without stage directions.

Grograntides: Anger not the Purple Emperor, for his resentment stretches beyond the farthest heaven.

Bertarin: His displeasure outlasts the days unnumbered, long after humanity has shriveled to dust, weightless, dry, and justly forgotten.

Grograntides: Vast and even vaster.

Bertarin: Fast and ever faster.

Grograntides: Thus always has it been. Thus always will it be. All creation bows low, all the gods above creation bow low, and all gods of gods beyond creation bow low before the throne of the Purple Emperor, whose fragrance penetrates all dark reaches of time and space, whose all-seeing eyes read our inmost thoughts, those foundational secrets held dear and drear and dreadful, hidden even from their holders. The Purple Emperor drinks in all, though the strongest, spiciest flavors he oftentimes finds too weak and sickly to inspire even the tiniest pleasure. Jaded by disappointment, he seeks a goad to something greater.

On the script plodded in the same vein. Tedious. Plotless. Colorless, except in the repetition of the title character's designation. My vision clear now, I skimmed page after page discussing how powerful and impressive the *Purple Emperor* could be. On the surface it seemed like drivel. At the same time, I harbored a niggling suspicion that the author intended to communicate a vital subtext not immediately apparent. Twice I sensed a hidden meaning unfolding in my mind, but as soon as my mind tried to seize it, the meaning slipped away, leaving me frustrated. If I could only grasp what was concealed within the text, I suspected I might find the answers to where I was, how I got here, and how to return home. Below that suspicion grew a sense of dread that I couldn't explain. But I felt it, just the same, so that, while I longed for answers, I feared to learn them.

Near the end of the book, lines of dialogue printed in purple appeared interspersed among long paragraphs of black type. The lines in purple were all capitalized, all attributed to the title character, and all identical, like this:

Purple Emperor: BRING ME MY TEA.

I shuddered. I don't know why. I didn't want to read any further. Without glancing at the final pages, I closed the book and slid it back into place on the shelf. My stomach felt as though I'd swallowed heavy stones.

"I'm dreaming," I reassured myself. "This has to be a dream."

But a rising worry bit away pieces of my reassurance. The words I'd read swept through my mind, twisting, haunting. I needed distance from that book. In the next room, a canopied bed streamed heavy gold and purple draperies. Candlelight blazed from a gorgeous, spreading chandelier strung from a lofty ceiling. But bookcases held dozens more copies of *The Purple Emperor*. I needed to leave that book behind. Feeling nauseated, I turned my back on the bookcases and staggered on wearily.

Bedroom after bedroom I passed through, all bedrooms, each fancier than the previous one. The ones as large as ballrooms provided some relief. They stretched so wide that I barely noticed the bookcases filled with the awful purple volumes as I passed them in the distances. I feared that I traveled in circles, but each successive room grew in opulence, so each must have been new.

In one room, my foot bumped an object on the polished hardwood floor. I looked down to see a rose blossom of eight petals, dark and glossy purple. It had evidently fallen from my own Purple Emperor rose bush, the bush I loved, the bush that had been stolen from me. I raised the blossom from the floor. Though slightly crushed, with petals bent, it retained its freshness. I breathed in its robust scent, stronger than the fragrance that perfumed the splendid maze that trapped me. I slipped the broken stem into my hair and perched the blossom over one ear. I welcomed the prick of a thorn in my scalp. The slight pain might keep me alert.

Whoever had stolen my rose bush had passed this way. But which of several doorways had the thief taken? I chose one at random and continued on. More than learning the fate of the Purple Emperor, I needed to escape. Somewhere, somehow, this infinite chain of rooms must end.

My thirst, my hunger, and my urge to urinate grew. A dressing table bore a large glass vase filled with red and yellow fresh-cut roses. I'd passed many similar vases on many similar dressing tables. I tossed the flowers onto the table and lifted the vase to my lips. The water tasted pleasant, like a subtle, rosy perfume.

I set the vase onto the carpet. I glanced around at the open doorways, but, of course, spotted no one. I lowered my jeans and panties, squatted down over the vase, and peed. When I finished, I wondered what to do with the vase. The yellow liquid complemented the purple carpet design handsomely, so I left it sitting there.

Roses were edible, so to placate my rumbling stomach, I pulled a petal from a red rose I'd evicted from the vase. I nibbled the edge. A delicious fragrance filled my mouth. I popped the entire petal in. The texture was similar to a delicate artichoke leaf. I chewed, swallowed, and picked up a handful of the cut blossoms to eat as I tramped on, searching for the exit.

Fatigue overcame me. Rest—I needed rest. Everything else faded— the pain from my wounds, my aversion to the purple books, my concern for my rose bush, even my desire to escape the unending bedrooms. I flopped onto a bed, curled into a ball, and sank into slumber.

Sharp fear woke me. My heart beat hard in my chest. A flood of adrenaline surged through my veins. How long had I slept? Did it even matter? I stretched my limbs, groaning at my stiffness. I massaged my shoulders and arms. Small scabs had formed over many of the wounds in my hands. I swung my feet over the edge of the bed and stood, listening to the silence. Watching. The fine furniture, the soft bedcover, the wood-paneled walls, the bookshelves lined with purple bindings—all around me lay just as it had when I entered the room.

Or did it?

No, the candles had burned low, wax massing at their bases.

The sweet scent of pink roses hung in the still air. Had those bowls of fresh flowers stood on the bedside tables when, bleary and exhausted, I'd first entered the room? I couldn't remember.

All I could do was move on. Nervously, I made what morning ablutions I could and chose a handful of pink roses to eat for breakfast as I walked.

I'd long discarded the stems of my breakfast when I heard a faint, irregular knocking in the distance. As I advanced, it swelled to a chorus of knockings, intermittent and disunited. Grinding noises joined the knocking. I hurried forward, eager to discover the source of the sounds. Other sounds grew distinct, rustlings, faint thumps. Through a doorway ahead, I spotted what appeared to be cardboard shipping boxes stacked three high.

I increased my pace into the next bedroom, then stopped in surprise. From an open cardboard box on top of the pile, a figure dressed in a white coverall drew several identical purple-bound books and added them to the stack held in the figure's other arm. On one side of the room another white-clad figure pulled candle stubs from sconces, tossed them into a wheeled bucket, and from another wheeled bucket drew unlighted candles to replace the stubs. A third figure snapped pristine bed sheets above the stripped bed. Each figure wore a plain, round white cap with a flat top. The figures looked bald, but as long as they wore caps, I couldn't be sure.

"Oh," I sighed. "I'm so glad to see someone at last."

None of them paid attention to me. The figure with the books moved to a half-empty shelf and placed them within.

I stepped further into the room and spoke louder. "Excuse me. I'm sorry to disturb you, but I need a little help here. Can you tell me how to find the exit?"

All three figures turned their faces toward me. I couldn't tell whether they were men or women. I didn't care as long as they could help me. Something else about their faces seemed unusual, but I couldn't put my finger on it.

I spoke louder and more slowly. "Where is the exit?" I walked my fingers through the air in front of my chest, hoping they understood. Maybe they didn't understand English very well. Or at all.

They each raised an arm and, as one, pointed to an open doorway on the other side of the room. Their meaning seemed clear: the exit lay that direction. As my hope surged, I realized what made their faces so strange. They had no eyebrows. I could see that the one nearest to me had no eyelashes, either. Maybe their bodies lacked all hair. That condition had a name, but it escaped me, and a more important matter beckoned.

"Thank you," I said.

I strode through the doorway into another room of white-clad figures performing maintenance—changing sheets, arranging flowers, dusting, even vacuuming. I wondered how the vacuum cleaner's power cord was plugged in. I couldn't recall seeing an outlet anywhere.

"Which way to the exit?" I shouted above the noise. I had to ask three times before they all silently pointed to an open doorway.

I hurried onward. In each room I found more figures and repeated my question, then forged ahead as directed. The sounds of knocking and grinding grew louder. I came to a room where white-clad figures brought in furniture—chairs, tables, bookcases, a bedstead. At one end of the room, two figures knelt on the floor, unrolling the final few curves of a thick purple carpet. At my repeated question, they pointed me onward.

In the next room, white-clad figures used white cloths to polish wood paneled walls and hardwood floors. Several figures were using a ladder to hang a huge chandelier from the ceiling.

In the room after that, I found some of the source of the knocking sounds. Figures used hammers to tap nails, fixing carved panels and wooden trim to the walls. Instruments perched on tripods and levels of various lengths surrounded them. More workers lined the walls of the next room and more the next.

The walls of the following room were still under construction. Spaces between upright wooden posts revealed views to further rooms being built. Figures in white coveralls hammered and planed and measured. They cut wood with table saws and circular saws, which accounted for the grinding noises. I dodged around stacks of lumber and stepped over buckets of screws.

In each room I yelled above the din, "Where's the exit?" repeating the question until someone heard me and responded. Always they silently pointed me onward.

I entered another doorway—just a doorframe, really—and hesitated. No floor extended in front of me, just a skeletal structure of wooden joists and beams. Hammering echoed all around, punctuated by the whine of screw guns. Workers hopped from one horizontal joist to the next, carrying long boards and fitting them into place. Below, through the spaces between joists, more workers labored in other unfinished rooms. I clung to an upright post, part of what wasn't yet a wall, and stepped gingerly to the next joist. I worked my way around the edge of the room, pausing at each step to ensure my balance, always keeping one hand clamped to an upright post while reaching for the next.

Below me stretched more levels of the skeletal structure than I could count, teeming with workers busy at building. Above me towered further levels of construction, as far as I could see.

In front of me, however, only a few skeletal walls stood between me and the end of the building. Night sky showed beyond crisscrossed planks. Joy flooded through me, drowning the sense of dread I'd grown used to. I was almost out!

Clinging to posts, shuffling from one joist to the next, I struggled forward, fearful of slipping between joists before I could reach the exit. As I entered the final room, a sense of dread crept back into my heart. Night sky filled not only the meager doorframe ahead, but through numerous gaps in the construction, more night sky appeared. Empty space stretched both upward and downward beyond the final doorway. There was no horizon. Only empty space. No, not quite empty. Here and there, rounded shapes formed of misty, bright streamers floated lazily, like jellyfish, flashing blue and white in the blackness.

I reached for a wooden post of the final doorframe and pulled myself forward to stand in the doorway. I leaned slightly forward to look out over the edge. No deck or landing or step blocked the view. There was nothing that I could step onto. Even if there had been, there was nowhere to go. A wall of unfinished doorways stretched downward, no end in sight. On both sides the wall of doorways continued. I looked up. The wall of doorways rose high above me, on and on.

This was no exit.

One of the swirling, misty shapes swung closer, washing me with intense light. The streamers that corkscrewed and undulated within the bulky shape had looked white and blue from a distance, but now I saw countless pinpoint prisms of color sparkling within the mist. The swirling shape loomed huge as it glided past, its endless tiny lights twinkling hypnotically, a captivating sight of intense beauty.

Dizziness overwhelmed me. I swayed, suddenly unable to summon my sense of balance. Panic rose. My arms flailed. One hand caught the wooden post of the doorframe. I clung. My body swung against the post and my other hand joined the first to clutch it. The Purple Emperor blossom slipped from its perch over my ear. It plummeted into emptiness below. I squeezed my eyes shut, forced my breathing to slow, punched the panic back down.

"Hold tight if you don't want to fall," said a ringing voice behind me.

I opened my eyes and turned my head. Across the room, a white-clad figure stepped easily from joist to joist, approaching. The figure carried a golden tray, set with a large golden teapot spouting steam, a golden teacup with saucer and spoon, and a golden platter of what looked like cucumber sandwiches.

I gasped. "How do I—how do I get out of here?"

"You don't," said the figure, joining me in the doorway. The figure stood calm and poised, while I clung desperately to the frame, my hands damp with sweat.

"I only want to get back home," I said. Tears welled in my eyes.

"You have no home," said the figure. "Long ago it fell to ashes— after it, your world—and then your galaxy. Now your universe dies before your eyes."

The figure bobbed its head downward. I followed its gaze. Far below us, one of the floating, swirling shapes dimmed its brilliancy. Great swaths of lights within it vanished as I watched. It curled and crumpled in on itself, as if an immense hand crushed it. The misty shape turned smoky gray and shrank until I lost sight of it.

Had I just witnessed the death of a universe? Had I gone insane? Tears spilled down my cheeks. "Leave me alone," I groaned.

"I'm here to announce tea time to the Purple Emperor," said the figure. Its mouth formed an "O." Out burst a short musical note, so beautiful in tone and quality that all my confusion, terror, and despair collapsed before the overwhelming desire to bask in that single note forever.

The note died away.

The black night of endless space shifted. I saw now that the darkness wasn't night, but a giant form, clad in robes of purple, so dark that they'd looked black. I'd been looking at that form and not recognizing it for what it was.

It twisted, rippled, seemed to come toward the wall. Or maybe the wall moved toward it. Shapes like tentacles reached from within the midnight robes. Not tentacles, but tendrils—thicker than my waist and covered with thorns. They whipped forth across the vast interval between the giant form and the wall, shooting directly at me. They wrapped around my body. Huge thorns pierced my limbs, my abdomen. My mouth opened to scream, but the speed with which the tendrils yanked me from the doorway and back toward the giant form tore my breath away. I flew upward, drawn by the imprisoning tendrils. High above, at the pinnacle of the giant form, a dark purple rose emerged from the darker blackness, a rose so immense that the floating, swirling universes were dust in comparison—a rose colored in glorious, glossy purple darkness, warmer than violet. A rose of eight petals. The Purple Emperor.

As I flew toward the beautiful blossom, the petals spread apart. Huge stamens stretched wide. The pistil protruded from the center. The stigma at the pistil's end gaped open like a mouth. Row upon row of pointed teeth lined its interior.

I'd eaten roses before. Now it would be the other way around.

As the tendrils flung me toward the waiting teeth, I caught the scent of bold, sweet perfume.

They always served a bite to eat first—crumpets or small cakes or sandwiches with the crusts sliced off. This time the Purple Emperor found the tidbit extremely slight and unsatisfying. However, it was merely a brief spark on the palate, heralding the taste he craved. He steered his vast, all-encompassing consciousness away from the minor disappointment. He'd long anticipated the glory coming next.

They'd found a new rose, one that promised to furnish a taste more gratifying than all others he'd tried. And he'd tried them all. They'd found this new one and waited for it to mature to the peak of potential perfection. They'd drawn it here from its universe and plucked its petals and prepared it in the most careful manner, mindful always of the Purple Emperor's particular preferences.

Excitement thrilled through him. He could hardly wait to experience this new taste, this new delight, the finest of all. Time meant little to one who continuously experienced every moment of existence simultaneously, yet the Purple Emperor chose to single out this moment to savor everlastingly.

"BRING ME MY TEA," the Purple Emperor commanded.

A Child's Christmas
in Innsmouth
(with apologies to Dylan Thomas and H. P. Lovecraft)

~ Kevin Wetmore

During the winter of 1927-1928, officials of the Federal government made a strange and secret investigation of certain conditions in my hometown, the ancient Massachusetts seaport of Innsmouth. I am going to defy the ban on speaking of what happened that season, as it was, perhaps, the most magical Christmas I remember.

One Yulemas was so much like another, in those years around the sea-town corner now and out of all sound except the distant chanting of the voices I sometimes hear a moment before sleep, that I can never remember whether six Deep Ones dragged off a victim under my bedroom window when I was twelve or whether twelve Deep Ones dragged off a victim under my bedroom window when I was six.

All the Yulemases roll down toward the two-tongued sea, like a cold and headlong nightgaunt bundling down the sky that was our street; and they stop at the rim of the ice-edged fish-freezing waves, and I plunge my hands in the sea and bring out whatever I can find. In goes my hand into that wine-dark, yuggoth-cold water, and out comes a human hand, gnawed upon. Realizing I cannot regift it, I toss it back in the waves, an early present for some fish, perhaps.

It was on the afternoon of Yulemas Eve of 1927, and I was in Mrs. Pickman's garden, waiting for cats, with her nephew Richard Upton, visiting from witch-haunted Arkham for the holidays. It was snowing. It was always snowing at Christmas in Innsmouth. December, in my memory, is as white and gray as was my uncle's skin before he finally returned to the sea. But there were cats. Richard and I often pretended to be ghouls. Patient, cold and callous, our arms wrapped in towels as if winding sheets, we waited to prey upon the fuzzy little corpses in the snow. The wise cats never appeared. We youthful ghouls would go hungry, then descend into snowball fights until Mrs. Pickman declared it was time to go in and that I should run off home.

Just then her voice arose in a shriek. "Fire!" Mrs. Pickman cried.

We ran from the garden towards Gilman House. It's a hotel that's often mostly empty. Smoke poured out of the dining room, smelling of burnt wood and seaweed. We charged towards the blaze.

This was better than all the cats in Ulthar standing on the wall in a row. We bounded up to Gilman House, laden with snowballs, determined to use them to help put out the fire. Running past Mrs. Pickman, a siren on the sidewalk, wailing for all to ear of the imminent tragedy unfolding. We stopped at the open door of the smoke-filled room.

Something was burning all right; perhaps it was Mr. Gilman, who always slept there after midday dinner with a newspaper over his face. But he was standing in the middle of the room, saying, "A fine Yulemas!" and smacking at the smoke with an oar he kept on hand for emergencies, though more likely a rowdy flatlander than a fire.

"Call the fire brigade," cried Mrs. Pickman from the sidewalk. "They won't be there," said Mr. Gilman, "it's Yulemas." There was no fire to be seen, only clouds of smoke and Mr. Gilman standing in the middle of them.

"Do something," he said. And we threw all our snowballs into the smoke - I think we missed Mr. Gilman - and ran out of the house to the telephone box in the square.

We called the fire brigade, and soon the fire engine came and three squat men in helmets and raincoats brought a hose into the house sprayed salt water all throughout the room. "Nobody could have had a noisier Christmas Eve," cried Mr. Gilman.

The firemen turned off the hose and stood in the wet, smoky room staring at him. One mumbled in the local dialect, "Obed Marsh be a-sayin' only dull sheep go a-prayin' to the Christian heaven as it don't help 'em none." He stared, unblinking at Mr. Gilman. "Didn't see you at the solstice out by the reef."

Just then, Mr. Gilman's sister, Richard's aunt, came downstairs, peered into the dripping, smoky parlor, and asked, "Would you like anything to read?" She always said the right thing, always.

○

Years and years ago, when I was a boy, we played in the caves down by the shore, the insistent sound of the incoming tide echoed throughout town—I do not ever remember hearing the sound of the tide going out. We would sing and swim and fish and live our lives to the susurrus of the incoming tide.

I remember that year of the fire, before the government came in and destroyed the reef and we all moved across the country to another coast, it snowed and snowed and snowed. I excitedly told my uncle when he came to visit that it snowed the year before, too. I made a snowman and Emily Marsh knocked it down and then I knocked Emily Marsh down and then Mrs. Gilman, Richard's aunt, served us tea and talked about how to properly behave and told us that the snow falling was not the same snow from years past, as in Innsmouth the snow does not just fall from the sky but joins with the damp on the ground and comes shawling out of the ground and swims and drifts out of the arms and hands and bodies of the trees; snow grew overnight on the roofs of the houses like a cold, silvery seaweed.

In the nights before Yulemas, the bells in the steeple of the Esoteric Order of Dagon rang their tidings over the bandaged town, over the frozen sea foam of the powder and ice-cream hills, over the crackling sea. And if you looked out your window, because you could not sleep, you would see the strange men in peacoats or slickers, shuffling through the streets of Innsmouth, huffing and puffing, making ghosts with their breaths. Some would carry wrapped packages and you did not know if they were gifts for solstice or Christmas or maybe strange things from the South Seas. But you knew it was Yuletime, and it was wonderful to be a child in Innsmouth at Yuletime.

It seemed that all the churches boomed for joy under my window as the end of the year grew closer. Under the tree of harpoons in the living room we would wake to find all kinds of presents. There were the useful presents: scarves to cover gills, mittens for fins, tam-o'-shanters for misshapen heads, balaclavas that stay on underwater, made from aunts who always wore wool next to their scales and wanted the children to stay warm. Then there were the useless presents: a Mother Hydra doll, hardboiled toffee and sardine crunch, bright tin sailors and toy boats, and easy games for little hybrids, complete with instructions that can be played on land or underwater, and once, by a mistake no one could explain, a ship's axe.

My nephew once asked me if the Yulemases of my childhood had a lot of uncles, like he experienced. There are always uncles at Christmas. The same uncles. The ones that would pass around a bottle and share stories of Obed Marsh, sitting by the decrepit chimney, eating peppermint-infused fish heads. As a boy I would fall asleep in my bed to the low murmur of the uncles, still downstairs telling tales of Father Dagon into the night.

The one memory I have that brings no pleasure—some of those mornings an old man trod the piling streets, a fawn-bowlered, red-faced, bushy-bearded, watery-eyed old man in nondescript rags. A very aged but normal-looking man who lived at the poorhouse on the north rim of the town and spent his time walking about or lounging around the fire station. I was surprised he had not followed the firetruck to the Gilman House when it has its blaze on Yulemas eve. His name was Zadok Allen and I hated him on sight and sound. I remember hearing the uncles speak of him. He drank, but not like them, not good South Sea rum but something they called "rot gut." And when he drank he would talk. He would say things, all sorts of things, even to flatlanders. If I remember it was around that Christmas that was the last we saw of Zadok. Not long after I heard the uncles tell my mother that he had, "Gone to be with Father Dagon."

I remember going out with bright new boots that Yulemas, running through that white world as the tide came in with my mates Jim and Dan and Jack, leaving huge footprints in the snow behind me.

"I bet people will think Deep Ones ran through the town."

"What would you do it you saw a Deep One coming down the street?"

"Deep Ones come down my street all the time!"

"Your Uncle's a Deep One!"

"So what? So's yours!"

"Let's write things in the snow."

"Let's go to Mr. Olmstead's house and write 'Mr. Olmstead looks like a shoggoth' on his lawn!"

"Let's push a snowball through his letter box!"

We walked on the white shore and watched the fishes watch it snow. The silent one-clouded heavens drifted on to the sea and we wandered along the incoming tide until Dan's uncle came out of the sea and encouraged us to go back home before the sky grew too dark, which always happened sooner when it snowed.

We returned home through the poor streets when there wasn't the shaving of a moon to light the way, trudging uphill away from the waves lapping the snow-covered sand and rocks. Our Christmases would end in the cries of the dock birds and the hooting of ships in the whirling bay out by Devil's Reef, and I was lucky that year as one of my uncles poured a bit of rum into my clam juice because, "it's only once a year and you're no longer a fry."

Always on Christmas night there was music. An uncle played the concertina, another the fife, a third flipped over a bucket to drum upon the bottom. It was very warm in the little house. Auntie Hannah, who had got on to the kelp wine, sang a song about a sailor who married a fish; and then everybody laughed again; and then I went to bed. Looking through my bedroom window, out into the moonlight and the unending smoke-colored snow, I could see the lights in the windows of all the other houses on our hill and hear the music rising from them up the long, steady falling night. Beyond that, I heard the sound of the tide coming in. I blew out the oil lamp, I got into bed, I said some words to the close and holy darkness and to Mother Hydra and Father Dagon, and then I slept.

⌗

Splinterbone

~ Megan Lee Beals

The splinter in Beth's palm comes out longer than it entered. The end she holds pinched between fingers is the gray wood of old boards. As it exits it thins from the size of a toothpick down until it is no finer than a hair, and it turns the milky white of living bone. It is longer than the depth of the palm she pulls it from, as long as her middle finger when it finally comes away, and when she holds it to the light, she finds that the end is translucent.

Her husband, Greg, gags at the sight and looks away from her, but she barely notices. Greg hasn't really looked at her in months, only at her distended belly. He touches it with his open hand and feels the taught skin as if she is nothing more than a membrane, a thin barrier between him and his child.

"Are you worried?" he asks. There is spittle at the corner of his mouth. He rubs it away with a thumb. He still does not meet her eye.

Of course she is worried. She is eight months pregnant and she has not spent a single waking minute without worry. They haven't finished turning the spare room into a nursery. It is filled with half finished sewing, guitars in varying states of repair, and seasonal décor. There is no space to assemble the crib, nowhere to put the diaper pail. There is hardly even space for Beth herself, which is why she had sequestered herself in the room's tiny closet and cried and cried until she spotted a little seam in the paint, where the height of the ceiling did not match that of the ceiling beyond the closet door.

Beth did not know her house had an attic when she bought it. It was painted shut long ago, to seal away the attic mother. She did not know of the attic mother, either, because they are often shut away. An unspoken necessity for women like Beth. Women who are alone and afraid and unprepared. An attic mother is a blessing, and though she did not recognize the signs, Beth knows a blessing when she sees it.

She cut through the seam with her box knife, pulled down the hidden stairs in a shower of dust, and found new space in her home. A place to store deferred dreams. A place to tuck away all the parts of herself that no longer fit inside her expanding body.

There is always space in the attic.

"Beth?" Greg had asked her something. What is he asking?

She is still holding the splinter. There was an arrangement of splinters near the chimney when she crawled into the attic. They were in neat little rows like tally marks, or letters on a child's practice book. Tidy and straight, bone-white and needle thin. She could almost read something in them. She wanted to read something in them. As she crept near on her hands and knees, her hand scraped against the rough edge of a board and a splinter lodged deep in her palm.

She must have shrieked, because Greg came barreling up the stairs. He crashed into that hallowed place, flinging dust without a thought for its decades of careful accumulation. He directed her down from the attic, chastising small choices, *you should have waited for me, what if there's mold, you shouldn't be climbing ladders in your state and now look, you're bleeding,* and suddenly Beth is in the bathroom and holding the splinter between her fingers. It was wood when it entered her palm. It is not wood anymore.

"Are you worried?" he asks again, a sharpness in his voice and a wide animal fear in his eyes.

"I'm fine," says Beth. Why should she worry? All the doctors say the pregnancy is going well.

Greg tells her to be more careful. It's an old house. Who knows what's hiding in the attic? He suggests she call the doctor and insists when she brushes it aside. What if whatever she picked up from that splinter hurts the baby?

And so Beth calls the doctor. Greg always has such a level head about these things. And with the pregnancy hormones muddling her thoughts, the insomnia, the nausea, and the letters written in splinters that she could almost but not quite read, maybe there is mold in the attic. Perhaps it was an animal nest, as Greg suggests when he sweeps it aside and hauls their storage up to clear the nursery. But the bone-white splinters were lain so carefully. Like samples in a lab, or artifacts in a museum; a precious collection on display.

Tests are run and returned and the doctor assures her that all looks well. Beth is congratulated on her caution and advised to forget the splinter and the animal nest and everything she stored in the attic. Stress isn't good for the baby.

She tries to forget, but she has opened her home to the attic mother. She wanted to accept the contract. It would be better for Beth if she would just accept the contract. But she's scared, and she does not understand the attic mother for the blessing that she is, and so the attic mother resolves to wait for Beth to change her mind.

It follows her through the deepest hours of night, into the small hours of morning. A dark shadow, tall enough to scrape the ceiling and whip-thin as the willow branches outside her bedroom window. It waits for her in the hallway, always at the nursery door.

Beth tries not to see it. She tries not to leave the safety of the quilts on her bed. But the baby is always pressing on her bladder, and so she must brave the hall and waddle her way to the bathroom, past the great shadowy thing that whispers incessantly; *sussurrow sussurrow.*

When Beth finds enough courage to look, the attic mother is gone.

The baby comes. They name her Adrienne but call her Aidy. She is beautiful and perfect and she cries with a volume that banshees could only dream of. Beth feels as though her ears are breaking, but the internet assures her that it always feels that way. That she should delight in the cries, because the sound comes from healthy lungs. And her family tells her to wait until the girl is older and walking, because that's when the trouble really starts. *Enjoy these days when she's young and perfect, you'll never get them back; enjoy this time because the teen years are the hardest; enjoy every moment, every single moment.* And so Beth ignores her breaking ears and the fine white sand that gathers in the wax. And when Greg's voice sounds like he speaks from underwater she tries to listen harder because she hates to see him so frustrated but she cannot make out his words.

Mornings are hardest, when a sound like *sussurrow sussurrow sussurrow* drones from the closet in the nursery. She avoids him then, because he speaks louder and louder, enough to wake Aidy from her tentative sleep. And with him shouting and the baby crying and *sussurrow sussurrow* she can't remember how to speak. And later when

Greg comes home sullen and tired and he sees that what he asked of her has gone unfinished or ignored, he sighs and finds some other place to be, leaving her alone with the baby and the shadowy attic mother.

It is better to not see him in the mornings.

The attic mother is always in the periphery now. Its terrible cracked fingernail hands stretch across the carpet whenever Beth feeds Aidy. She holds the girl close and pretends that the hands are anything else. An unfortunate shadow cast through trees, or an imperfection in the paint. She knows they are not, because branches do not vanish when looked at directly, nor do they loom behind her, bent crick-neck at the ceiling.

Beth stops looking in mirrors, or through windows. She averts her eyes from all reflections, and when Aidy stares beyond her shoulder to the thing that isn't there because Beth will not allow it to be there, Beth turns the girl's head down and holds her eyes fiercely in her own. She sings lullabies against the monster, plucks at guitar strings from around her daughter, and the attic mother retreats to her space in the shadows for some time.

Beth will come to it eventually. She can't walk this tightrope forever.

When Aidy is two months old, Beth trips on the stairs. It is a minor stumble, but she nearly drops Aidy. Breathlessly, she bundles the girl into her bassinet, and when she slows to think, Beth begins to catastrophize. She sees every horrific outcome, the ways that Aidy could have been hurt, the ways it would be her fault. She cries, and Greg tells her she is overreacting. Nothing happened, the baby didn't even notice, but Beth keeps playing her fears over and over in her head until the stumble turns deadly, and the thought of Aidy dead breaks something inside her ankle.

It feels like a needle scrapes against her bone with every step. She limps for a day while it twists through the ligaments and presses at her skin from within. Beth grits her teeth—*it was just a twisted ankle*—and ignores it. Later, she sits with her feet under her legs and a splinter drags against the couch. A little drop of blood weeps down her skin and leaves a bright spot on the dingy gray fabric that could have used a cleaning thirty spit-ups ago.

Beth wipes the blood off her foot and her fingers catch the splinter. She gasps, but it is more surprising than painful, and it comes out easily with a steady pull. It is long as a sewing needle and just as sharp, and her skin closes behind it, unblemished but for a little rusty stain on the thin blue-white skin of her ankle. Aidy watches this with interest, then begins to cry, and Beth sets aside the splinter to ponder it later.

It is gone by the time she thinks of it again.

Her ankle no longer hurts. She does not limp, and it is difficult for Beth to remember why she thought to keep the splinter at all, save for the odd sensation that something inside her is missing. She feels so hollow that she almost misses the pain.

Of course she should call the doctor, but she can't afford the time. And yes, she should talk to Greg, but he is always tired. His shifts are long and his sleep is constantly interrupted as the baby cries and as Beth gets up on creaking floorboards to feed her.

The splinter resurfaces at 3 A.M. to the sounds of *sussarrow sussarrow* pleading from the shadows. It pokes out from the baseboards at the top of the stairs, angled slightly upward, just long enough that it might catch somebody's toe. It looks so enticing. It looks like frozen milk that would melt against her tongue and cool her chest which is burning with the weight of her tiny daughter clinging to her and clawing for a breast. She bends and tucks the splinter back under the baseboards where it can't pierce her family's flesh. The whispering quiets for a moment.

Beth's nail hooks on a stray splinter of wood at the bottom of the baseboard as she withdraws her hand. It tears from the wood, and she instinctively draws the nail into her mouth to suck it away. As she swallows, the whispering returns. It takes shape into words.

Splinterbone splinterbone.

The attic mother is behind her.

Beth hugs Aidy so tight that the girl squeaks and she runs to the nursery where the lights might dispel the shadowy thing. Her ankle does not fail her. The hollow feeling is gone.

Beth might have noticed the strength she gained from that splinter of wood, if the tasks of motherhood weren't constantly accumulating.

But the strength of wood flees quickly, and it will eventually fail. Only bone may replace bone.

Adrienne grows and learns to laugh and coo. Her newfound joys cast her cries into greater, deeper dimension. The girl discovers anger, and her anger cuts deep into her mother's bones.

The doctor says sometimes babies just cry. Greg says you can't stop everything that might upset the girl. He tells her to ignore it. Eventually she will exhaust herself.

She takes their advice. The cries split Beth's fingernails to the quick. They splinter her bones and sometimes a little white needle will work its way out of her skin and stick in the carpet or the bedsheets or in her socks. And when she sheds these defective parts of herself, Beth peels another splinter from the bookshelves and swallows it whole.

The wood props up her faltering bones. It hardens her muscle. It makes her better. She is an excellent mother; attentive and kind, always aware, never tired. She never utters a complaint. Even her hearing improves. Greg's words are clear again, and the thing that whispers *splinterbone* never speaks outside of the small hours of the morning.

Greg cannot see the shadow. He cannot hear it whisper. And he has so little time at home, little time with their daughter, with her, that she doesn't want to worry him.

There's nothing to worry about. She can handle it all herself.

Beth grows thin as food becomes unpalatable. She snacks on dried grass and toothpicks and shards of glass. Anything but the flood of bone-white splinters the attic mother offers her, arranged in little rows at the edge of the nursery door at midnight.

The attic mother offers them with a pleading cry of *splinterbone splinterbone* in a voice that sounds like a chorus of women.

She answers once.

"No."

The thing is absent for days after. When it finally speaks again, the word sounds as though it is drowned in tears. The attic mother hovers over a single white bone at the top of the stairs. Beth almost feels sorry for it, but her daughter is in her arms.

Aidy stares down at the splinter of bone as if she could accept the invitation herself, and Beth kicks it back into the dark space where the floor meets the wall. She pulls a handful of woodchips from her pocket, surreptitiously taken from the playground, and chews thoughtfully. She resolves to strap Aidy to her chest and vacuum every dark corner of the house.

At three months, Adrienne's nails are long and strong and they cannot be filed away with an emery board. Beth should be more careful with the clippers. She should wait for Aidy to sleep, but Beth is impatient, and Aidy twists away from Beth's arms as the blades sink down and clip the soft end of her finger.

Flesh offers a different resistance than keratin and Beth knows her mistake before Aidy can register the pain. Blood begins to well. A small spot, just a little chunk of skin. It could be worse. It could be so much worse. Aidy screams, and all of the bones in Beth's arm shatter.

The muscles in Beth's broken arm twist around to hold Aidy like a tentacle. Needles of bone drip from her wrung out fingers and clatter to the floor. Beth runs to the bathroom and rifles through the first-aid kit with her good hand. She throws swabs of cotton across the sink as she searches for the Neosporin. Aidy screams with red-faced rage and scatters droplets of blood as she thrashes, and Beth shakes the last of the splintered bone from her arm to wring her ruined hand over the wound and pinch it tight with a cotton swab.

Beth sweeps the clatter of splintered bone to the baseboards with her feet as Greg runs into the room. He is shouting something, a question, but she can't think enough to hear. She turns from him, keeps her twisted arm covered with the good one. She cries as she stumbles through her words—*Aidy is hurt I can't find the bandages*—and he steps around her to produce the first aid kit seemingly from the air. He's still speaking and Beth nods nods nods without hearing him. Her bones shift inside of her. They splinter apart and wander through muscle to build up what she lost in the arm. Greg is taking Aidy from her and she lets him. His careful hands will protect their daughters finger, will correct her terrible mistake.

He tells her to get some air and she runs outside and paces the yard as she waits for air to return to her. Her teeth feel like needles, and when she stares blankly into her reflection in the window she finds most of her teeth have sunk down through her jaw to fix her arm.

Her eyes are black pits. Her teeth are cracked and sharp. And when Greg speaks to her, to tell her he's got the bandage on, that he even tucked the girl's hand into a mitten so she won't disturb the bandage, he does not notice that she cannot speak back to him. Every word slices her tongue on the shattered teeth. She smiles with closed mouth, thanks him with a nod, and goes to find her pincushion on a high shelf in her bedroom. She eats needles by the handful and does not stop until the pincushion is picked clean.

The needles help. She carries Aidy easily. Stops cries before they begin. But she can't bear the taste of the disparate materials that make her teeth, and so she stops speaking to her husband and daughter. She can feel the striations in the way they scrape her tongue.

Beth only makes noise while singing now. She sings in open vowels and while Aidy naps she plucks gently at the guitar with nails made of steel and wood and glass. She sings hardest in the mornings, when the attic mother watches woefully from the corner of the room.

The splinters shiver inside Beth as she walks. They rub against each other in the fragile remains of her rib cage with every breath. They threaten to fly apart at the smallest disturbance. Beth brings her house under meticulous control.

Alarms are dampened. The dripping sink is wrenched to a hard silence. And when a guitar string breaks against Beth's sharpened nails, she sets the instrument aside and stops its strings with an old shirt that she used to love.

Aidy is tended to faultlessly; all her expressions understood and all her needs met before the girl can ever cry.

Beth does not sleep. She eats nothing. She meets the gaze of the attic mother who cries *splinterbone* from darkened corners of the house and stares it into silence.

At four months, Beth must drive alone to Aidy's visit to the pediatrician. She hums and hums as she sets Aidy in her car seat, humming to sooth, to plead with the girl to stop squirming. She misjudges the slack she needs for Aidy's growing body, and when the buckle clicks into place, it pinches Aidy's skin.

Aidy cries, and Beth falls apart. Her skin falls lifeless to the ground, pierced and shredded by thousands of shards of wood and metal and glass. The girl is crying still, and Beth can do nothing. She is empty, hollow, dead. The attic mother sweeps into the room, and Beth gives into the dark as she watches it take her daughter.

Beth is in the attic. A little LED lantern washes the space in cold white light. A massive woman crouches over Aidy. Her skin is thin as muslin, her eyes are black pits, her arms are bent with too many elbows and her neck is broken against the rafters. Beth tries to reach for her daughter, but the splinters that held her together are gone. She is limp. A puddle of flesh, unable to lift her head.

Her eyes roll in her mushy face and settle against the floor. Thousands of bone-white needles cover the unfinished plywood, set in careful rows.

The attic mother shifts Aidy to a single arm. Her many jointed, many fingered hand cup around the girl's bottom, and the tips of her longest fingers stroke gently at the base of Aidy's neck.

She picks up a splinter of bone from the ground and stretches it toward Beth's open mouth. She places it on Beth's tongue, and it melts into her, buttery and sweet like icing.

It had been hers. It is the splinter Beth pulled from her hand after she found the hidden attic.

Some women crack, some women survive, none come through unchanged, the attic mother says with a chorus of voices. She sounds so kind. She sounds like forgiveness.

She places another splinter on Beth's tongue; this one gray with age and green with moss. It might be as old as the house. Beth swallows and pulls herself to sitting. She reaches for her daughter, but the attic mother holds her at bay.

Eat. You are not well.

The wood and metal had failed her. She eats another splinter and knows it did not come from her. It was lost sometime in the 80's, when the house had been a rental and a young mother burned the carrots that were meant to be baby's first taste of solid food. Another from the '40s when a child rolled off the bed and hit the floor.

The splinters taste like heartache, like failure, like sleepless nights and quiet tears. But they taste like comfort, too. Like lessons and wisdom and the knowledge that if she eats she will never be alone.

She keeps eating. Where the wood and glass and metal fled her, the splintered bones slip in. They make her whole.

The attic mother reaches out to caress her face, then vanishes as her hand meets Beth's skin. Beth's arm cracks, it bends with an extra elbow and she catches Aidy in a hand with far too many fingers. The girl burbles and laughs in the cage of Beth's hand. Aidy stretches her legs against the wrist and nuzzles her head against Beth's caressing fingertips.

Beth swallows another bone, then two at once, then handfuls as her strength returns. She gorges herself on bone, then creeps down the ladder with a chorus of other mothers swimming in her head.

Beth no longer sees the attic mother. Nothing follows her in the small hours as she quiets about the house. Her reflection has black pits for eyes and her face is stretched strangely to fit the extra bone, but she looks fine in the mornings. Great even; fully rested with time enough for a little makeup. And her arms can stretch across the house to peel an orange in the kitchen while Adrienne drinks blissfully from her breast as they both lounge on the couch.

Beth always puts herself back together before Greg gets home. He doesn't feel the way her bones shift beneath her skin as she rests against him. He never sees the striations in her teeth made from decades of different bone. His eyes are always on their little girl.

"It seems like we're doing better now that we've adjusted," says Greg.

Beth agrees in a voice that is not her own, because another mother can speak sweetness to him while her mind wanders through her foreign body.

"Beth?" he asks, and she realizes she had gasped in pain.

Adrienne has bit down on her nipple. She pulls the girl away and finds a spot of blood on her breast, and a slender white needle poking up from Aidy's gums.

"Is that a tooth? Already?"

"No," she coos down at her daughter. "It's nothing, dear." It is a splinter. Aidy's first. Beth wiggles it from her mouth, and tucks it in a pocket to save for later.

⌗

The Sheep Rancher's Husband

~ Corinne Hughes

*We firmly believe that the happiness and overall well-being of our
beloved sheep flock is vital to the success of our farm.
—from the website of Jeanne & Jem's Sheep Farm*

That there were failures cannot be the end of this story–
I was in love
      like how the knitter craves the yarn, which craves the needles.
When the call began, I realized it had already begun earlier,
during coffee with my wife and daughter–
my daughter just three, the peak age to lose her father–
so I had heard it all the day long

while kneeling in the pasture to watch Jem's toddler hands
disappear into the dense, black wool of the Brecon Cheviots,
a sheep breed known since the Iron Age;

while making love one last time to my wife, her awkwardly
shy at first, then ravenous, then defiant, and finally settled and sweet,
as if we had just traversed the story of our relationship;

while internally screaming during the long tirade that
was my daughter's meltdown over losing an opal gemstone
that may, in fact, never have existed in the first place.

My wife told me the day of my daughter's birth that I had
three years to live before a black ram would send out a call,
which would possess my body to come to it, no matter where
in the entire world I was, to be eaten alive.

I had often imagined I would simply black out, so why leave;
my wife, daughter, and I, were snuggling in the big bed
with all the special pillows, yes the plushies, and a different gemstone,
but then, I remember waking up and removing my clothes,
I remember the cold, frigid air forcing all my blood to my belly,
I remember the look on the ram's face, his mouth too wide,
and in one fleeting moment–
I remember my daughter at the barn door,
watching.

⊐

A Napkin Upon Your Glass

~ *Shanna Germain*

Ordering drinks you don't like the taste of just because the names would get a giggle out of a thirteen-year-old boy is an action that Sheb is beyond the ability to comprehend. She has, to steal the popular nomenclature, run out of spoons for such things.

So far tonight, she's made three *Sex on the Beaches*; two *Slow Comfortable Screws*; two *Pop My Cherries,* one *Silk Pink Panties*, and of course, the ever popular *Sex With the Bartender*. Almost no one drinks more than a sip or two because most of the recipes are ridiculous. Over-the-top, cloyingly sweet, full of weird tastes and textures. Just like most of Sheb's experiences with actual sex, if she's honest. It makes it easier, at least—all these boys and girls who flex for her, shake their hair and their asses—and she doesn't have any interest in any of them. Serve them their stupid-named, unoriginal drinks and send them on their way.

The bar's finally emptied out a bit, nearly everyone moving toward the dance floor to psuedo-hump beneath the undulating beat of a popular song. There are only a few people still sitting at the bar, maybe too nervous or too tired or too caught up in their own existential existence to join the throng.

Sheb takes the opportunity to clean up a little, wiping down wet spots and getting rid of any glasses abandoned long enough to develop a rime of ice sweat. The others she tops with napkins marked with the bar's logo; if someone comes back, she wants them to know that someone has been keeping watch.

She's got her back turned toward the sink when the big guy slides up to the bar, but she can smell him—a wet and musted odor, like a wool sweater long forgotten in the washer. His strange smell, although it makes her nose wrinkle, is almost a comfort. And truly not that much worse than some of the dancers when they come back off the floor, stinking of feverish want and unmet desires. Plus she knows he won't order anything stupid and then wink or smirk or giggle at her, like he's the cleverest person to ever sit at her bar. Not that she thinks he's actually a person.

"Evening," she says as she lays a napkin on the counter in front of him. She's surprised every time by his bulk, the way his clothes sag and hang from him like sloughing skin, the way the actual skin on his face also sags and hangs, wet rivers and furrows that slide down and down. She's never asked his name nor he hers. "The usual?"

"Please." His voice is wet pebbles sieved through a screen. It comes to her under the thrum of the music in a way she understands is not possible based on what little she knows about how sound works. Like being under the ocean and hearing someone whisper your name.

The usual means whatever she feels like making him. She's been practicing this new drink since last time he came in, a few weeks ago now. It's a tricky and complicated one, but she's pretty sure she's gotten the recipe right, the way the sweet blends with the sour, the slight umami that lands a moment in the back of the throat before it deepens. She adds a few drops of flavored bitters she brought from home, and gives it a gentle stir before she sets it before him. It's an inky-purple swirl of liquid and ice, nearly glowing in its dark presence.

"On the house," she says. "For your services."

"Obliged."

It's a ritual of sorts, this thing that they do, speaking the known as if it is the unknown.

He lifts the drink to the bar lights, admires it the way someone might a perfect diamond or a perfect kiss. "Beautiful." Sheb's heart lifts a little, takes some of the weight off her breastbones. "What do you call it?"

She's been reading up on things, studying the language and the cadence. It's a stab in the dark, really, but a stab that feels like it's close to hitting something vital. "*The Lamp of the Familiars*?"

In response, he takes a sip, closing his large dark eyes and showing her the extra set on the back of his lids. His second eyes watching her like this while he drinks what she's made feels intimate in a way that most things deemed intimate do not for her. It's almost too much, her pulse high in her throat, her need to rub her fingers together.

The song ends, and nearly as one, the crowd undulates back, dripping with salt and musk, wracked with thirst and and a hunger unmet. They're over being clever with her now, their prey's moved to different quarters, and they ask for water, for rum and coke, for tequila shots, all while looking away, tracking their possibilities.

He's the only one that still looks at her, both sets of eyes as he blinks and drinks. She lets it rest on her, that heavy gaze, that intense regard, as she fills glasses and takes money, slips tips into the jar, refers the drunkest among them to the numbers of the car services she's written on the blackboard behind her.

Sheb's no fool. She knows what he is, what he does. The services he provides for this bar were explained to her when she was hired on, by the thin little man called Charles who she's never seen since. The woman who runs the place day-to-day, or rather night-to-night since the Cave's posted hours are Dark to Light, doesn't talk much, just smokes endlessly in the little closet beside the walk-in.

Sheb doesn't know what she wants from him. Maybe nothing. Maybe everything. Maybe just this, again and again, the break from the repetition, the lift in her heart when he gazes upon her, the way his presence makes her feel like her job, like her life, like *she*, matters.

No. Not that. Exactly *not* that.

His presence reminds her that *none* of this matters. Not this milling throng, not the way she sometimes pockets what she shouldn't or makes the wrong drink on purpose or feels squeamish at the thought of someone touching her. Not the 3 A.M. wake-ups with her pulse thrumming in her neck, not the way the edges of her skin go soft sometimes, amorphous blobs of not-her that she doesn't know what to do with, not the dreams that drowned long ago and now wash upon the shores of her subconscious at the pull of the moon.

He protects her from the danger of her own thoughts by sitting at the bar the same way she protects others by putting napkins on their glasses. It's not part of her job or even part of her purpose, but she does it anyway, because she can, because it means nothing to her but it might mean everything to someone else.

He is done with his drink and somewhere the moon is falling down and she knows what comes next. "Pest control," Charles had said. "Keeps the place clean of vermin."

Of course, she'd thought rats, mice, scorpions, spiders, the creatures that crawl through the dark and hidden places of the world. But that was before she'd met him, before she made him his first drink and watched him watch her like she was starlight dancing on a dark ocean.

"My thanks," he says to her as he slides the now-empty glass across the bar toward her.

"It was my pleasure," she says, although it wasn't, exactly. It is more a momentary absence of dread, which is perhaps as close to pleasure as she has.

He slides away, intent now on his doing job. She has never seen him hunt and stalk and feed in the morning gloam, in the wee hours after last call, but she can imagine it. *Has* imagined it.

She thinks, as she often does, about following him into the darkness. But there's something there that is still too heavy for her to witness, too much like drowning when all she really wants is to sink for a while.

"Last call," she says into the throng. No one can hear her above the din, but it doesn't matter. They all know what she knows, beneath their last-ditches for life and love.

Closing time is coming. Closing time is here.

⬙

Gnocchi

~ *Simone Cooper*

Darling, I am dictating this record for you, since I'm not sure how soon I'll lose the use of my hands, or which of us will change first.

Our last dinner together as members of the species *Homo sapiens* will include gnocchi. That's always been your favorite. I usually buy them premade, because the slight difference in result never seems worth the effort. But now that our assimilation is imminent, why not? What I do for love is the only meaning I have left.

I shopped in the early afternoon, when there were only a few other shoppers. They seemed calm. Normal. They didn't know what I knew. I could have run through the aisles screaming, "Wake up!" but they wouldn't have understood. Then I'd be spending these last hours drugged and raving, or cooling off in the drunk tank instead of working this dough, shaping the tiny pillow dumplings, inhaling the sensual aroma of olive oil and basil and bursting roast tomatoes.

I paid at the self checkout and packed the produce in a reusable bag that will never take up room in a landfill.

The envoy, It who Embodies Time, whispered to us first through dreams. In the world after the assimilation, words like pollution and garbage will be meaningless. There will only be matter and energies, life and unlife, thought and color. This dream made everyone in town weep, off and on, for days, without knowing why. Only you remembered the dream. Even I did not, until you reminded me.

POTATOES: Here are the potatoes, russets the size of a double fist, a little soft, a little old, like the muscles on the undersides of my arms that are beginning, just beginning, to wobble. Bake the potatoes long

and slow until they are cooked through. Take them out and cut the
skins open to release their steam. Close your eyes and breathe in the
miracle.

The envoy, It who Embodies Purity, told you not to worry, and
you told me. There will be potatoes again, after the assimilation. Perhaps that word was not exact, it admitted. Tubers was closer. But they
will be pleasurable, those tubers. Like potatoes, they will open with a
burst of heat and the scent of earth and plant sugars. Your mouth will
not be a mouth, but it will ingest the tubers just the same.

FLOUR: Add the flour to a large bowl with the cooled flesh of the
potatoes. Leave plenty of room.

I bought flour, just in case, but of course I didn't need it. There's
always an unopened bag of flour at the back of the cupboard that I
never remember is there. Now, there are two. You used to tell me, for
a woman who loves cookies, I don't do enough baking. I'd answer,
my belly is big enough as it is. I was wrong. I should have made the
cookies. Brown butter pecan would have been a good flavor, if I had
to pick something to remember being human by. That, or your lips,
or the salt air I would gulp cold, pre-dawn, watching the mist rise
from the shore of the bay, and listening to the seagulls gossip.

The envoy, It who Embodies Communion, showed you the seagulls
we will know after the change. They will all be connected, the same
as they are now, except instead of by sound it will be by threads of
digesting mycelium, and when they fly, it will be all together like a
single, great, undulating wing. The vision of them will be so beautiful,
we won't need eyes after we see them. Your own eyes curdled opales-
cent, just thinking of it.

RICOTTA: The brand of ricotta we can get in the local store is too
bland and too grainy. I'd complained at the checkout before, but still,
this time, I bought it.

Scoop the ricotta from its container and add it to the potatoes and
the flour, white on white on white.

The sound of the spoon in the plastic tub brings Bugle the beagle
from his bed by the door. He's mostly blind and smelly, and I let his

nails get too long, and sometimes I can't get him outside fast enough to do his business, which embarrasses us both. But I had him before I even met you and long before the sky in the corner of the window changed color, so even though the recipe wants a whole cup, I let him have the last spoonful. I imagine in this moment he is, again, every time, the happiest being on our whole, sad, planet.

The envoy, It who Embodies the Starless Void, said there will be no division of dependents and caretakers after the assimilation. We will all be animals and we will all be people, and those who cannot care for themselves as individuals will be loved and upraised by all through the ecstasy of eternal consumption. I was skeptical and joked to you that Bugle would be okay with that, so long as eternal consumption tasted like cheese. You laughed, but prismatic light came out of your mouth instead of sound, which embarrassed us both.

PARMESAN: Is any cheese more adulterated and abused by the New England grocery store than parmesan? Luckily I still had the wedge we bought with your mother at the good cheese shop in Scarborough.

Grate the parmesan. Make the traditional knuckle sacrifice to the grater. Add the cheese to the bowl. Near the rind of the cheese, where even the tiniest sliver coats your tongue with buttery richness, the cheese may be oily and hard.

Honestly, I had nearly half a cup by the time the whole wedge was grated, but I decided to use it all. The gnocchi might come out too salty, but at least the cheese won't go to waste.

The envoy, It who Embodies The Space Between, revealed to you that the assimilation is only the first stage of our evolution. Eventually, the energies and colors of our bodies will be food for the food of those like the envoy, like grain is food for our chickens, and then even those beings will be food for beings more infinite and more unknowable. What fulfillment, what beauty there is in such singular purpose! *Iä! Iä!* you said. *Cthulhu fhtagn!*

EGG: Just one egg. Crack it into the bowl with all the dry ingredients.

What if I don't stir the ingredients together? What if I don't let time progress, and the birds fly on and Bugle lets out more aromatic sighs and your mother calls to say she's out of her favorite aged gouda again, would we like to join her? Would the white marbles of your eyes clear back to brown? Would your laugh return? Would you kiss my neck while I'm cooking, even if I was the one who stopped and all the world went on?

But that is not how it will be. I have mixed the dough, haven't I? My fingers remember the feel of it, silken and dry on the surface, sticky inside. I remember marking each dumpling with the tines of a fork, as humans mark all things, as the envoy marks us. I've roasted the tomatoes and garlic and the greens from beets we ate last week. I've opened the oven to the heaven of their smells, pulled out and set aside the sizzling tray.

Before I can put the dumplings on to boil, my hands are gone. So is my mouth, though my thoughts spool on.

The elements that form forks and bowls, houses and grocery stores, shorelines and water birds smear together like oil paints across a palette. As I join them, I recognize one specific shade of indigo. It's you! That ochre, scampering? An old beloved dog.

For an instant I am only joy.

I made you gnocchi. I loved and was loved.

Enough.

⋈

Blood and Glitter

~ Jessie Kwak

Sell me to the witch, I told the trader.

She'll come to you dressed all in black, I told the trader, *fingers stacked with silver rings and eyes sunken into dark smudges from long years of service to the Masters.*

It will be impossible to mistake the witch, I told the trader.

And it should have been impossible. But somehow, instead of the witch, the idiot trader has sold me to a goth girl fresh from a shopping trip to Claire's.

The goth girl drops me unceremoniously into her book bag where I wedge between an Algebra 1 textbook and her Walkman, and I curse the trader's soul into the depths of oblivion.

He can't hear me.

No one can.

I'm trapped inside glass.

The witch was supposed to free me on this full moon night, calling my presence into this plane with her own cursed blood. The ritual was meant to be the fulfillment of her entire life's work; she would die screaming in agony at the pinnacle of the ritual, of course, but she would die knowing she'd ushered in the reign of the Masters by releasing me, their Spawn.

I have waited aeons for this night, when I am meant to take my rightful place on this plane. I have outlived stars waiting to hear the humans scream and watch them cower before me, blood running from their eyes and teeth gnashing tongues to ribbons.

This *cannot* be happening.

I will make the best of this.

I *will* ascend.

I take stock of my surroundings and assess the damage.

The good news: The false witch girl has blood in the cartilage of her right ear from a new cheap piercing. If I can get her to fidget with it and then touch this glass vessel I will still be born into chaos and screams of eternal torment, witch or no. The ritual is important, but the blood is more so.

The bad news: The false witch girl has company. Her older brother is picking her up at the mall with another of his soccer teammates already in the passenger seat of his Geo Metro. The teammate who I can sense this girl has recently developed feelings for.

It is disgusting, to sense these feelings of humans. But soon I will burn them all away.

"Krissy get in!" her brother shouts, then laughs. "You look like a psycho. You look like you made out with Marilyn Manson and his clown makeup rubbed off on your face." Her brother grins wide at his own joke; I can feel the girl's embarrassment emanating secondhand through her book bag, and it sparks against my own frustration.

Woman, you hold destiny in your hands, I scream through the Void to her. *Smite him! There is no room for hesitation, no room for shame!*

But I'm powerless in this form. Krissy the false witch can't hear a thing.

"Fuck you," she says to her brother. She flips him a middle finger beringed with obviously (*obviously!*) fake silver.

"I'm telling mom you swear," says the brother.

"I'm telling mom you jacked off with her nice hand towel," says Krissy. "Hey Seth," she says to the hot friend, who had not laughed at the brother's joke, but does laugh at hers.

"Hey, K," says hot Seth.

The car peels away from the curb. As it does, I see the witch hobble-run out of the mall, clawed hands waving in the air as she searches for the one who bought me. If she spots Krissy, she can save me. She can complete her life's work of servitude to the Masters. My rule of dominion on this plane can finally be realized.

I'm here, I scream, but the glass bottle thwarts.

The witch doesn't see Krissy's brother's Geo Metro, and I feel her presence stretch, snap. The witch vanishes from my awareness.

I will not wail in disappointment and despair.

I will *not* wail.

But if I can't ascend on this plane I am doomed. I have been raised for this moment, the Masters who spawned me ceaselessly reminding me of their expectations and obligations. If I fail, I will be worse than a disappointment to them, I will be Grounded, confined to the eternal tortures of the Void, to the agonies of—

Fuck. Fuck, *fuckfuckfuck*: now Krissy's brother is blasting Nickleback.

This can't get worse.

I will find a way out of this disaster.

I have learned a new human ritual tonight.

It is called a "slumber party," and I hate it.

Krissy's brother didn't drop her off in the heart of the woods to summon the Masters' Spawn in a circle of waiting cultists. Instead, he dropped her off at another adolescent human's dwelling.

This one is called Nicole. Where Krissy is gangly with dramatic makeup and dyed-black hair (it *is* witchy, I suppose), Nicole is soft and small with shockingly unstable red curls and a Scooby-Doo T-shirt. She likes musicals. Her bedroom is plastered with posters labeled *Phantom of the Opera* and *Cats* and *Little Shop of Horrors*. She insists on playing a CD of something she calls *Joseph and the Amazing Technicolor Dreamcoat* until the others show up.

Krissy and I both hate the outrageous cacophony, but I obviously can't say anything about it and Krissy chooses not to. I don't understand why.

Perhaps it is because Krissy has been friends with Nicole since they were in second grade, and her will to survive has been worn down by the musicals over the years. Or perhaps it is this more complicated thing I am sensing: that Krissy likes to see Nicole happy because they are friends, and musicals make Nicole happy even though they make Krissy want to stab a knife into her own eardrums.

I did not realize humans developed such friendships. Fascinating —but immaterial. Soon humans will cease to have free will.

Krissy and I both are saved from symphonic torment when the rest of the coven arrives. There are two more adolescent girls in this group: Tracy in a lavender babydoll tee with her blond hair held back in mini butterfly clips, and Samantha in her burgundy corduroy pinafore dress and long black braid. The coven greets each other in a round of nauseating hugs.

"I almost had to bail," Tracy says in greeting. "Toby wouldn't drive me over."

"But we've been planning this for weeks," Krissy says. "He knew that."

"He thinks we haven't been spending enough time together."

"Yeah, right," says Samantha. "You spend every minute together, and you've bailed on us the last three times we were supposed to hang out."

"He's just jealous," Tracy says. "It's cute."

The look the other girls exchange behind her back as she sets down her bag says they don't find it cute. I tend to agree.

"Ooh!" Tracy exclaims; she's spotted me. "Nail polish! Let me guess: it's black and moody. Must be Krissy's."

"It's not *moody*," Krissy says, picking up my little bottle and shaking it. "It's cool. Look at it in the light, it's got little specs of glitter or something in it."

"Look!" Nicole says, pointing. "It's changing color where you're holding it. Like a mood ring?"

Krissy shifts her grip and I press against the glass, hoping for a taste of her blood. "Oh cool, it is changing colors! The guy who sold it to me said it was really special, that must be what he meant." She grips the cap and readies herself to twist. "Who wants to try?"

I surge with hope.

"I do," says Nicole.

"My mom would ground me," says Samantha.

"Toby doesn't like it when I wear black," says Tracy.

"Nobody cares what Toby thinks," points out Krissy, but before she can free me from the bottle another human voice drifts down the stairs to the basement.

"Girls! Pizza's here!"

I am forgotten in an instant.

The girls rush to bring down greasy boxes and cans of a revolting green potion labeled Mountain Dew, arranging themselves on the overstuffed couches of Nicole's rec room to devour their meal.

I watch them shriek as they singe the roofs of their mouths on scalding pizza. I watch them and I scheme. I watch them and I *hunger.*

That pizza smells so damned good.

When I am free I think I would like pineapple with pepperoni.

○

I learn much while the girls eat.

Nicole's parents have enrolled her in accelerated courses next year that will award her college credits. She is nervous that she won't do well enough to please them, though I don't know why because she seems like a perfectly capable young woman, and no one will be attending school next year when my rise brings about the destruction of humankind anyway.

Tracy and Toby are coming up on their three month anniversary, which Tracy is excited about though the other girls in the coven clearly are not. The more Tracy justifies Toby's red flags as "real love," the more I side with her friends in their dislike. I am looking forward to smiting him.

Samantha's mother is Mrs. Gonzales, the high school principal, and a human to be feared. Her edicts for her spawn are known to be excessively restrictive. "She won't even let me go to prom *solo*, let alone *with* someone," Samantha complains. "I won't be able to date a boy until after college if she has her way."

I understand bristling against the edicts of your Masters, obviously, but here I tend to agree with Samantha's mother. I have met only three teen boys so far, one only by reputation. Teen boys are no real prize.

Speaking of, Krissy's brother is universally agreed upon to be a loser—though he is apparently quite idolized by Krissy's parents for his involvement in sports. It is revealed that Krissy's parents attend every single one of her loser brother's soccer games, but missed her theatrical debut because it wasn't "serious."

"They think I'm a disappointment because I won't wear pink and go out for the volleyball team," Krissy says. She tries to sound like it doesn't matter, but she's clearly hurt.

I don't know what volleyball is, but I understand Krissy's pain. If human parents are anything like the Masters, the threat of their disappointment must be hideous. I find myself impressed by Krissy's rebellion. And a tiny bit jealous.

I get my second chance at freedom when the greasy pizza boxes have been piled in the corner of the rec room, near the stairs to be taken back up to the kitchen.

"Did you bring . . . the board?" Nicole asks Krissy, and the other two girls' eyes go wide.

"You *didn't*," says Samantha; "Oh. My. God," adds Tracy.

Krissy sits up straighter. "I might have brought it," she says, but she can't contain her smile, and when she opens up her book bag I cannot believe my luck.

"It" turns out to be the first thing to go right tonight.

Perhaps I have mislabeled Krissy as a false witch. Perhaps she is indeed a practitioner of the arcane despite her youth, because she has brought with her a device for communicating with beings on other planes. In fact, her board is even more sophisticated than the mouse bones and entrails I have used to communicate with the witch who was supposed to bring me through the Veil tonight. The board is imbued with power from arcane symbols, labeled with a double row of letters, a row of numbers, the words *Yes* and *No*.

The Masters insisted on mouse bones and entrails, but if the witch had had this board, maybe we could have avoided this tragic miscommunication. I find myself wanting to roll my eyes at the Masters' rigid traditionalism, and their insistence that they always know what's best for their Spawn, but I don't have time to say *I told you so*. The coven have gathered around the board.

"No way," says Samantha. "I'm not touching a Ouija board. Mom would kill me."

"Then don't tell her about it," says Nicole, reasonably.

"You can just watch," says Tracy.

"You *can't* just watch," Krissy says. She leans in. "If you're not actually touching the planchette, you're not protected from the ghosts. One of them might possess you."

Samantha's eyes go wide. "What?"

"The planchette is like a ward," says Krissy. "It protects you."

This sounds like bullshit to me, but I don't know much about ghosts on this plane. Perhaps Krissy has a witch's knowledge after all.

Samantha doesn't quite look like she believes Krissy either, but she does finally join the group around the ouija board.

Nicole lights a strawberry-vanilla scented candle and dims the lights. The girls squeeze in shoulder to shoulder, giggling as their fingertips come to rest on the planchette. Samantha's are the last to join, but once her tender flesh touches the hard plastic, the room crackles with energy. The nervous giggles hush.

"Let us begin," says Krissy, suddenly straight-shouldered and formal, though a touch of nerves causes her voice to quaver. "Are there any good spirits who wish to speak with us?"

The ouija board has done something to the energy of the room, and although I am still hemmed in by the glass bottle, if I try hard I can push my will through just a little. I strain, funneling every bit of my energy into the planchette.

It edges slowly but surely towards *YES.*

The girls squeal in delight.

"What is your name?" Krissy asks.

I hesitate, then write: *S-U-Z-I-E.*

It's not what the masters called me, but in truth I never liked the name they chose. I've always wished to be called Suzie, but until this moment I didn't have the courage to say so. Perhaps the small rebellions of these human teenagers are wearing off on me.

"Hello Suzie," says Krissy. "Are you a spirit?"

Am I a spirit? I am not. I am a multidimensional being. I am an ancient elder entity. I am a numinous cosmic abomination.

That will take forever to spell out with the planchette.

YES.

"Did you die in this house?" Tracy asks.

Nicole yelps in horror. "Don't be an idiot," she says. "This house is only like ten years old." But still she shivers.

"Suzie could have been buried under the house," Tracy points out. "Like murdered and buried in the foundation."

"Are you crazy?"

"Suzie," Krissy cuts in. "Were you murdered and buried in the foundation of this house?"

"Oh my gosh," Samantha breathes. "Oh my gosh." Her eyes screw closed.

I push the planchette to *NO.*

All the girls give a relieved laugh.

"Who *were* you, Suzie?" Krissy asks.

"Who were you" is an odd way of asking the question, and it catches me off guard. Who was I? I was a Spawn of the Masters, intended to come here and enslave the human race and pave a path for the Masters' return. I was the product of years of their upbringing, as fearful of them as Samantha is of her mother, as nervous about meeting their expectations as Nicole is of her parents, as hemmed in by their demands of me as Tracy is by Toby's.

But I am no longer in their plane. Here, I could be anyone—even a rebellious Krissy, shrugging off her own parents' disappointment with black eyeliner and a cartilage piercing and a laugh.

In my stunned realization, I have not answered the girls. And it is Samantha who finally gets up the courage to ask me another question.

"What do you want, Suzie?"

I want freedom. But not just freedom from this bottle—I want real freedom.

I spell out: *N-A-I-L-P-O-L-I-S-H.*

The girls murmur the letters in unison, frowning at each other in confusion. "Nail polish?" Tracy finally says. "Weird."

"The special nail polish you bought," Nicole says to Krissy. "The guy who sold it to you said it was special, right? Maybe it's haunted."

"Nail polish can't be haunted," says Tracy.

Krissy frowns down at the planchette. "You want us to paint our nails, Suzie?"

YES.

Krissy shrugs. "Then we should paint our nails."

"I am *not* painting my nails that color," says Tracy.

"Because of Toby?" Krissy shoots back.

"Because this is stupid. You're the one moving the planchette."

"Seriously?" Krissy laughs. "If I wanted to paint my nails, I wouldn't bother asking your permission. Or a ghost's. Or some boy's." She lets go of the planchette and reaches for me, still laughing, but Tracy has been stung by the comment.

"I love him," she says. "He doesn't get a say in what I do."

"But you act differently now," points out Samantha. "That's all we're saying."

"I do not."

"You totally do," says Nicole. "Suzie, is Toby an asshole?"

I push the planchette hard towards *YES.*

"You're the asshole," says Tracy. "You're the one that's been moving the planchette this whole time. I'm done, this is stupid." She shoves away from the board, shoulder knocking into Krissy as she turns away, and my glass bottle slips from Krissy's grasp.

The bottle tumbles and falls, arcing through the electric energy of the room towards the ouija board on the tiled coffee table. Nicole shrieks as Krissy lunges for me. She's fast, but she's too late; she lets out a curse and snatches her hand back as a shard of glass pierces her finger and her bright blood spills into the void of my essence.

I am free.

I have been imagining this moment for aeons. On this plane, I can take any form I wish, and I have been trying on different ones to decide which abhorrent visage will be the most terrifying. I've imagined the screams of humans in a beautiful chorus rising to the heavens. I've imagined them clawing at their own eyes to obscure my monstrous horror. I've imagined them falling to their knees, made senseless by my glorious, horrific maw.

I take the form of a teenage girl.

It's not perfect. I've not tried this form before, and it glitches just a touch. My hair moves of its own accord, but gently, like a knot of sleepy serpents. My eyes are pools, the same hue of black blood and glitter that the girls saw captured in the bottle. My skin glows faintly, but I can't help that.

The girls stare at me in shock. I raise my hand and give a little awkward wave.

"Suzie?" Krissy asks.

"Hello," I reply. My voice resonates with multidimensional tones meant to bring anguish to human ears, and all four girls flinch back. I clear my throat and try again. "Sorry about that. Hi, I'm Suzie."

"Are you a ghost?" Krissy asks.

I ponder that a moment. What *am* I, indeed?

I was supposed to be a destroyer of worlds, one who eases the path for the Masters. Somewhere in the ether behind me, I can hear them yowling in disappointment—but it's no longer terrifying. They can't reach me on this plane unless I let them in. And at the moment, I'm not inclined to do so. Here, the Masters are no longer the boss of me.

I've spent untold aeons doing what they wanted me to. Living the life they raised me to live. Don't I deserve an aeon or two to figure out who I am on my own? To eat some pizza with pepperoni and pineapple, or to dye my hair ridiculous colors, or to make friends?

"I'm not a ghost," I say. "I'm just a girl—it's kind of a weird story. Can I hang out?"

The girls look at each other.

"Sure," says Krissy.

"Um," says Nicole. "Do you want a soda?"

"Is there any more pizza?" I ask, and Samantha goes to rummage through the boxes.

"Your hair is really cool," says Tracy.

"Thanks," I say. I accept a paper plate from Samantha, and a poisonous-looking Mountain Dew from Nicole. Krissy smiles at me and I smile back.

If I'm going to have dominion over this plane, shouldn't I get to know it first?

⊐

Den Mother

~ Cody T Luff

Melinda was elbow deep in cookie dough when her phone chimed on the kitchen table. She sniffed, glanced at her batter clotted fingers and tried to adjust her glasses with her shoulder. The screen on her phone read *CINDY*.

Melinda lowered her hands, careful to avoid smearing her sweater with premature cookie, and stood quietly for a long moment. The phone joined her in silence, Cindy's name faded into the time and Melinda's heart ached just above the place her apron strings were tied.

"It's been a long time," she said to her empty kitchen. Her memories filled with the sounds of Cindy, years tumbling from the patter of toddler feet to the angry slap of her teenage daughter's flats to the finality of the tap tap of Cindy's hard soles finding their way out of Melinda's life.

"A very long time . . . " Melinda puffed a curl of gray hair away from her sweaty forehead. "Time . . . oh, no no no . . . " Her glasses slid to the tip of her nose as she turned back to her phone, eyes widening at what she saw there.

"3:40, I only have . . ." Melinda's mind ticked off hours and her heart fluttered in her chest. She needed six batches of cookies, one batch lactose free, by evening. Her gaze rolled to her counter, mixing bowls filled with sweet stuff, dismembered chocolate bars littering the old tile top . . . she could do it. She'd pulled off bigger challenges in her day . . . the bake sale at Mullen's, the barbecue Larry had invited everyone to that she only heard about the morning before . . . Melinda adjusted her glasses, her left thumb smearing dough over a lens. *Damn it.* She allowed herself a small sigh and got to work.

The kids arrived at 7:30. Each in their blue uniform, slightly too large cap, and a smattering of yellow and red triangle scarves. New merit badges adorned their vests, a few noses were wiped at the curb, tired parents waving to Melinda as their children made their way up the little walk and into Melinda's living room. She loved the first few minutes of every meeting. She loved watching the kids talk about games, school, their families. She loved the way they loved each other in these moments. Perhaps not always friends but always friendly with one another. For a solitary moment, Cindy's face bloomed in Melinda's memory. Her daughter at eight, her own troop uniform freshly pressed and merit badges double sewn into permanence on her vest, and tears, so many tears, always.

"All right, settle down please." Melinda waited as the children continued their chatter. Every chair in the room was filled with a grinning, wriggling trooper. The pre-meeting cookies were a major success, chocolate smears on lips and hands were proof of that. She considered asking Carl and Lucinda to be careful of the couch, which of course surprised her. The couch wasn't her responsibility anymore. Danica would have to work a few chocolatey fingerprints from the cream-colored cushions, not Melinda.

"Okay, Quiet Coyote!" Melinda touched her middle and ring finger to her thumb and extended what remained, bouncing her hand in the air. "Remember?"

The chatter dissolved into a room full of children mimicking Melinda's Quiet Coyote, little hands bouncing, a few giggles leaking here and there but that was to be expected.

"Good! Look at you! See? You are learning so well! By next week, I'll bet that Quiet Coyote arrives on their own, right in time for the start of the meeting."

"Excuse me," Shayla rolled to her knees, her Coyote devolving into a raised hand.

"Is that how we do it?" Melinda was careful not to look directly at Shayla, the poor kid was already shy and she knew too much about Shayla's home situation to be overly direct. "Or can someone show me how to ask question?"

Hands rose and bobbled, lips tightly sealed, words gathering and on the verge of exploding into cacophony. Melinda smiled and pointed to Shayla. "Go ahead, trooper. You can show me."

Shayla nodded, a few braids dangling from her cap. "Den Mother, oh Den Mother, I . . . "

"You don't have to do all of it," Lawrence interrupted, his own hand still held up. "You don't have to say all of it."

"That's okay, Lawrence. Thank you for letting us know, but let's hear the whole thing from Shayla." Melinda smiled at Lawrence, a flicker of pity tracing the back of her throat. Lawrence knew all the rules down to the last word, but the poor kid would never make it to a checkered scarf. He didn't have it in him. But Shayla did, Melinda was sure of it.

"Go on, honey. Say it."

Shayla glanced at Lawerence before she said what she sought out to say in the first place. "Den Mother, oh Den Mother, favor me please." Shayla's expression shifted into worry, her eyes wide and pleading.

"You've got it, Shayla. Just a little more, right?"

Shayla gulped and nodded. "Den Mother, oh Den Mother, favor me please. Feed me what I need."

Melinda filled with a pride that made her chest ache. "That was perfect!"

A few little hands reached from the crowd and patted Shayla's shoulders and back. Shayla fought a smile but couldn't keep it hidden as she glanced at her troop mates.

"But all we have to say is Den Mother please," Lawrence sniffed.

Melinda knelt and adjusted Lawerence's cap, her eyes on his. "You are absolutely right. But sometimes the old ways are the best ways."

"Old ways are the best ways," the kids called in unison. She'd taught them the call and response just a few years ago. Of course to them, that was half of their lifetime. But to her . . . she felt a thread of sadness tickle the back of her mind. Melinda frowned, adjusting her glasses.

"You had a question, Shayla?"

Shayla nodded and her small fingers knotted over her belly. "Um, so today is your lasts day?"

Melinda was expecting this question. She painted a bright smile on her face and nodded, "It is. We talked all about it last week. We have checkered scarf trials tonight. After that, Danica will be your new Den Mother."

Shayla frowned. "But I don't want you to be gone."

A soft chorus of yeahs from other children followed.

"Oh honey, it's okay. You all love Danica, right?" There were a few nods but she could see the soft sadness only children were capable of filling their eyes. "I know, I know, but everyone who passes the checkered scarf gets to move up, you'll be full troopers. You'll get to go on the big trips with Father Sam and you'll get to play the big kid games at the All-Meet." Melinda knew that was perhaps a little cheap but her own sorrow burned against the roof of her mouth and she was afraid she might start crying before the kids. She swiped at her glasses, hiding a sniffle behind her forearm.

"You have something on your lens," Lawerence offered.

Melinda grinned, "I do . . . cookie dough!"

The children giggled, which Melinda used as a transition into merit badge time. Each member got a chance to show off their new badges and describe how they had earned them through the week. Melissa's two badges fell off as she tried to demonstrate knife sharpening and Greg made a joke about her suture badge. Not entirely harmless but Melinda let it pass.

They moved onto arts and crafts, but Melinda knew they were distracted by the promise of the checker scarf trial. She found her own excitement building as they finished their friendship brace-lets, whorls of yarn and rounded scissors dotting her living room carpet. She watched Shayla and Lawerence exchange their lumpy twists of friendship, Lawerence's budding crush both obvious and a little painful to observe.

Cindy was at first much more like Lawerence. Her daughter knew all the rules, not just for the troopers but for life itself. Cindy memo-rized the back of shampoo bottles and the small writing found near the seams of cat food bags. She could recite the instructions for the television remotes, a little sheriff in her own right. But slowly Cin-dy's dedication to the rules turned to something else. Her expertise shifted into arguing with the rules, deconstructing them, intention-ally disassembling them and leaving the parts, just like the parts of her mother's heart, scattered on the living-room floor.

The front door opened, a blast of winter slipped inside making the kids giggle and mime shivering. Danica blew in with the cold, her enormous winter coat looked like a ridiculous collection of shiny pillows, a mod-ern-art snowman coated in vinyl. Danica was twenty years younger than Melinda, her face wrinkle-less and her glasses dough-free.

"Hello, hello, hellooooo!" Danica posed, one arm above her head in a vague mimicry of a matador. "It's about time to get scarfed!"

The kids exploded, friendship bracelets tossed away, happy faces all pointed directly at their new Den Mother.

"Get scarfed?" Melinda smirked.

"I like it, it sounds fun. And that's what we need, right? Is some more fun!" Danica twirled, her jacket billowing around her as the kids screamed with laughter.

"Alright, alright. You got them sparked, now get them ready," Melinda smiled.

Danica winked, saluted and pointed toward the Back Room. "Charge!"

The herd thundered off, an end table tipping over as little elbows and knees plowed past. Again Melinda caught herself, her hand already reaching to right the table.

"That's on me," Danica's voice cried from the back.

It is, Melinda thought swallowing a thrum of sadness that writhed in her throat. *They're all yours now.* Melinda found her way to the kitchen, untying her apron as she went.

The kitchen was home. The little table she piled her mail on, the stacked mixing bowls on the butcher's block, the pitcher full of wooden spoons next to the stove. It was at that stove that her husband told her he was leaving and again, at that stove that Cindy told her the same twenty years later. It would be a lie to say that Melinda didn't remember the face of her husband as he delivered his final words but it was the truth that she couldn't remember Cindy's face in the moment. She could stare at the man that she thought she loved as he told her what he thought of her but when her daughter had done the same, she had stared at Cindy's feet. Her eyes simply too heavy to meet her daughter's. The silence that followed was something Melinda had filled with the Troopers and bake sales and volunteering with the Harvesters. And now she would have to return to that silence, her role as Den Mother drawing to a close in short order.

Melinda sat at the little table, folding her hands in her lap. She could hear the first round of chanting starting in the Back Room. Really, the Back Room was just her converted garden shed but Father Sam had been very insistent during renovations that it have a proper name. Old ways were the best ways, after all.

Melinda tried to remember Cindy's checkered scarf trial, flashes of her daughter's face, the bathtub water turning that awful red as Melinda cleaned her child only made Cindy's smile all the whiter.

"For he is in yellow, forever the king, forever in yellow . . . " The children's voices led by Danica's theatrical soprano. Melinda caught herself silently mouthing the words. *He who must not be named, the King in Yellow . . .*

Melinda stood, image of scrubbing a stubborn blood clot from behind Cindy's ear fading as the chanting continued. She thought she could hear Shayla and wondered if Lawerence was staring at her as she chanted. *That poor kid,* Melinda thought. *He wouldn't be strong enough for the knife tonight.*

Melinda unbuttoned her dress, smiling at the bits of dough still clinging here and there. She let the dress fall to the yellow linoleum, dropping her old comfortable bra on top. Father Sam insisted on total nudity and that was fine, she'd already prepared the kids for how she would look on the night of the trial but she couldn't quite force down her embarrassment. Veins and scars and the small tattoo of a bird that Cindy never knew about. *It's okay,* she thought to herself. *They'll be focused on their knives and not my little sparrow.*

"Den Mother, oh Den Mother, favor us please. Feed us what we need," the chorus reached her even in the kitchen. The distortion was rich, the presence of the King heavy in the air. They didn't sound like her kids anymore. They were ascending.

She turned to the door, her arms crossed over her chest, her feet conscious of the cold linoleum. For a moment she stood listening to their call. Her response was inevitable. Her blood, inevitable. She glanced at her little table, the face of her phone glowing blue. She plucked it up, her fingers clumsy on the tiny keyboard. When she was finished, she turned to the door once more, a soft smile on her lips, her hand reaching for the knob.

She didn't see her phone light up, the text blooming across the screen, Cindy's name hovering there.

I love you 2, mom. Forever.

⊐

The Dark Young

~ R. Ostermeier

Mel was adamant the cat they adopted be a rescue; John was equally firm the new addition be a kitten so that it—*he*—grow with them. "I want him to belong to us, to be our tribe," he said. "Not some pre-loved cat bonded to another. I don't want a transplant cat. A graft cat."

Silently, Mel agreed but could not voice her agreement having lost the argument over the desired sex of the pet, although she had 'won' on its colour, ginger. Privately, she doubted they'd get a kitten, and as it turned out local charities had nothing that suited. The Brotherhood had not taken strays in for months as rising pet insurance had seen an increase in the abandoned, and the Cat Hospital and Sanctuary had no ginger cats at all, let alone kittens.

"And almost all ginger cats are toms anyway," Claire at CHS said. "Ginger females are calico or tortoiseshell."

"Oh."

John laughed. Mel ignored him, asked, "We've been to The Brotherhood and Animal Protection League already. Where else is there?"

A younger woman behind muttered softly, "You could always try Miss Aiken's School for the Gifted."

"Don't be mean," Claire said. She turned back to the couple. "She means Miss Aiken over near Cubton. She's an independent. She draws from the wasteland and the farms so she usually has a lot of moggies."

Claire gave them directions to Miss Aiken's house on the other side of the town, telling them the woman didn't have a dedicated building; her sanctuary was in her house on the edge of the woods near Cubton industrial estate, a good half-an-hour's drive away.

"Did you know gingers are mostly male?" Mel asked.

"No," John replied. "Weird though." He paused. "She said *calico*, and it was only when she said the word that I realised I don't have the faintest idea what *calico* is. It's like *gingham* or *periwinkle*. These are words I know, but I've no idea what they actually mean."

Mel smiled, but she was still irked by the unknown detail about ginger cats. She felt as if John had won a tiny fight by accident and therefore unjustly. She'd wanted a *rescue, ginger,* and *female*. He'd wanted *kitten, don't-care,* and *male,* and in a way she couldn't articulate she suspected her husband had managed to get his own way, and this was strangling Mel somewhere at the base of her throat.

The yearning, the excitement was unmarred, however. John had adored cats since he was a child, but an allergic sister—*a buzzkill sister*—had meant he'd never had one growing up. Mel had been a cat lover since she was tiny, her earliest memory the threading of a black tail between her chubby arms as a childhood queen menaced her for ice cream. The presence of a cat spoke of home to her. She pictured her and John in the silver light cast by an old black-and-white film on the television, cat on her lap in a mound of purr, the three of them blissful and complete.

"I'm glad you insisted on a kitten," she said quietly. "You were right."

"I don't think I insisted," he replied after a moment.

"Okay. Whatever you said. Whatever word is right to describe how you said it. It'll be good to have a kitten."

"He'll climb the curtains."

She smiled. "He will rue the day."

They overshot the place at first, passing the sign for Brithemwell before they realised they were at the turn-off for the industrial estate.

"That must have been it," John said, reversing back into the estate entrance. Mel stared into the trees as they drove back slowly through Brithemwell.

"These trees look sick as a dog," she said. "They look like wooden cancer."

The address was an old schoolhouse, redbrick and not sizeable, set apart from the other houses. It backed onto the wood they'd just driven past, and to the left was a building that looked considerably older than the main house. High on the roof was a stone circle in which had once been a cross-shaped hollow, now filled in with grey concrete.

"Did we even look here?" John asked in the silence now that the engine was off. "This would have been perfect. Quiet, but close to town."

"I like our house."

"Yes." He paused. "I do too. I'm just saying, we never even looked here. Are you ready?"

Mel didn't answer. "Are you sure that woman said just to turn up?"

"That's what she said. Claire. She was called Claire."

The afternoon was far advanced, sun low in the sky, rain threatening. John sensed his wife's reluctance.

"This could be it," he said. "What we've talked about for—God, a year. A fire burning in the hearth, jumpers and books, red wine and a little kitten akip betwixt us." He smiled. "What do you say?"

They walked to the door. It wasn't until they saw the plaque under the doorbell reading *Miss Aiken's Cat Sanctuary* they were reassured it was the right place. The house was dark within, however. John pressed his face to the glass while Mel hissed at him to stop, and a moment later—giving him a jolt that caused him to hit the glass— Miss Aitken opened the door.

"I was just looking to see if anybody was in," he said. "It was all dark."

"I do not hold with electric light," Miss Aiken replied.

Hesitantly, they told her what they were looking for, Miss Aiken's eyes tracking back and forth between them.

"We can come back," Mel said when they'd finished.

"Nonsense. I don't post opening hours so how can I truly close?"

The door to the converted chapel was unlocked. With unease, they followed the woman into the interior. There was an unblinking quality to Miss Aiken's gaze, her eyes so wide Mel suspected a thyroid issue and John an abyssal absence of intelligence. She'd a mustiness to her—*A pissiness*, John said—that lingered in the throat. Her hair was tufty and short, thick as the individual clutches of bristles on a toothbrush, each clutch cut at a slightly different height as if her hair had been shorn by the teeth of a ruminant. Miss Aiken appeared to be more bird than human, something chickeny and flightless, close to the earth and happy in the soil.

Inside, the uneasiness grew as there was no light there either, not even a light switch. Instead Miss Aiken lit a candled lamp, and when she replaced the red glass hood over the flame, a deep glow lit the interior space.

"The creatures do not hold with electric light either," she explained. She lifted the lamp to their faces. Her illuminated hand was covered in old scars. "The diurnal round is part of all creatures' existence, and to disrupt it is animal cruelty. No animal has ever had need for false light. Have you ever heard of an animal desiring any other light than the light the universe gives?"

John opened his mouth, closed it again.

"I don't keep good records, I'm afraid," Miss Aiken continued, "but I am certain I have what you desire."

The cages were stacked against the stone walls, high into the chapel rafters, the interior space converted into a clinical environment filled with creatures behind bars. A ladder on wheels—like a set of library steps—could be pulled from the walls on either side to allow Miss Aiken to see into the upper cages.

"It looks precarious if you get a fighty one," John said.

Miss Aiken replied, "The fighty ones go below."

On first sight Mel found the number of animals in the chapel cruel, but as her eyes got used to the red gloom she realised the cages were spacious, each filled with beds and toys and in the corner of each what looked like a tiny black bonsai tree that she assumed was some form of scratching post. From the ceiling of each cage hung a well-chewed teat for water, a network of transparent pipes feeding into each cage. The eyes of the occupants were disconcerting in the dark-ness. When the lamp was not illuminating them, all that was visible was the fluorescent green glow of cats' interiors and the internal purr of a hundred-cylindered feline engine.

The smell was strong but not rank. In the closeness of the old stone this was remarkable. A more troubling odour came from Miss Aiken herself as she wheeled the ladder about the walls, ascending with her lamp to the upper cages, leaving them staring at the dim outline of her cat-hair covered skirts.

On the third try she brought down a kitten that she handed to Mel. The tiny boy was quiet, quaking, curious, hard to hold as Miss Aiken led them to her office at the back. When she lit the lamp in the office, they found the kitten to be almost copper—doubtless the effect of the candlelight—and desperate to be with them. His eagerness was reciprocated; the connection was immediate and their adoration was complete. There was no need to articulate it—

"We'll take him," John said. "If that's all right with you. He's ador-able. He's perfect."

"Yes, he has been perfected." Miss Aiken pulled out a folder from beneath her desk. Her eccentric way of speaking continued as she worked through the papers—

"He's prepared for the world," she said, "as he has been fully born. His name is as yet unspoken, but I expect you will want to give him a name *you* will know him by."

"Jasper," Mel said.

John looked at his wife. They'd not discussed a name. The kitten was tumbling through her hands so swiftly she looked as though she were juggling. "Jasper," he said. "I like Jasper."

Miss Aiken seemed to have taken to them. Once she'd set out the paperwork, she placed Jasper into a basket she called a *creel*. The creel was curious as she had to pull it open. Afterward, this creel appeared to seal itself of its own accord, then she pushed the enclosed kitten into the darkness at the edge of her desk.

"You can take him tonight if you want. I can make my own decisions on adoption, and I think you are perfect." She stared at each of them, those eyes painfully wide. "It's important to note there'll be a visit to check on him." She gestured to the corner of her desk where the kitten's tiny eyes were visible as two green rooms. "A welfare visit. A formality."

"When?"

Miss Aiken paused. "Where do you live?"

"The other side of Cubton."

"Then it shouldn't take more than three weeks for her to get there."

John blinked. The answer was oddly phrased, but before he could ask Miss Aiken had pushed another piece of paper over, a commitment not to return the animal and initialled clauses acknowledging their understanding and agreement that *the colour of the fur might change over time*, and that *the creature's failings were their own.*

"I'll also need the creel back when he is settled."

As they signed and chatted, they felt Miss Aiken warm to them further, and they ended up speaking for an hour while Jasper thundered in his creel. For all her oddness, they found the woman a quirky delight, and even though each was storing her choicer expressions to giggle at later, they enjoyed their time with her, strange though it was to be chatting in an old stone room by candlelight.

It was evening when John looked at his watch. "We need to get back," he said.

"May I show you something before you go?" Miss Aiken said. "I feel we've made such a connection."

She took them out the back of the chapel. It was lighter there, the last of the sunset making the large backyard a warren of shadows. High hedges ran down either side enclosing the garden from outside view, and the trees at the bottom of the garden were impenetrable.

"Those are the trees we passed," Mel murmured. "The same trees."

To the left was a wooden structure like a stable with no fourth wall, the struts filled with molten wax in which hundreds of other candles had given up their strength, the lit candles standing like sentinels on a charnel mound of the waxen dead. On the floor were tin mess plates filled with even more candles, all of them different and each at a different level of burn. These massed candles surrounded a vast sofa raised on hay bales. The seat was double the size of a regular three-seater, the upholstery's design near impossible to make out despite the light from the many candles. *Paisley*, John thought, *A dark paisley or fractals.*

"I can't let you in the house," Miss Aiken said, "but I wanted you to see some of my other charges."

John didn't want to turn his back on the stable. It had the aspect of a manger in a dark nativity, a bestial altar. Miss Aiken tapped him hard on the shoulder.

The window was wide, even more candles beyond the glass illuminating the gloom of what looked to be Miss Aiken's lounge.

"I rarely show these cats as they are not yet complete," Miss Aiken said. "Not everyone is as welcoming as you."

The woman pointed to where a white shape appeared to fall repeatedly towards them. As the form approached, it became clear the cat's front paws had no length of leg. The paws seemed to have been fixed directly to its chest like a couple of soft brooches. The shock of the deformity was profound, and as their eyes became used to the low light, they were suddenly aware of dozens—limbless, eyeless, with misshapen skulls and spines—most simply staring into the darkness. Right in front of John reared a lengthy rope of fur with a wide face and three eyes, the process of splitting into two cats in the womb somehow arrested.

"I thought they didn't live," he whispered, voice tight.

"They live if they are loved," Miss Aiken said.

These deformations kept coming as the cats realised they were being looked at through the glass. A large queen had her front paws too far down her rib cage, and where her paws would normally be protruded another pair of legs turned backwards. Perversely, from near her throat, a tail curled up and over her head, which the cat licked with a split tongue.

A teratoma, John thought, *an imperfectly-separated twin.*

"What happens to them?" Mel whispered.

John could tell she was upset. "Some are not chosen, it is true," Miss Aiken replied, "but others, when they are old enough to be reborn, become more perfect."

"Okay," said John. "Okay, I'm very aware of the time. You've been so kind, Miss Aiken. I cannot express how happy you've made us." He paused. "We never discussed the price. The donation."

Miss Aiken shook her head. "It is forbidden to profit from the dark young. When they go out into the world, they must leave without debt or arrears."

"Okay. Okay then."

As they turned to leave, the view to the black woods was obscured by a creature the size of a bull in silhouette moving from the trees into the garden.

Despite himself, John swore. His body understood the creature as it might a wolf or a bear, a being that deep human memory told him was lethal to his survival. Yet at the moment instinct told him to grip Mel and run, the animal turned and made for the covered stable and the hay bale nestled sofa, ascending to its rustic throne.

"Night has fallen," Miss Aiken said. "She comes home to the birthing bed."

Mel was shaking. The animal was too large, muscular, like a monstrously-swollen goat wealthy with smooth black wool. The creature fell onto the sofa, rolling half on her back revealing udders dark and shiny as molasses.

"She's so beautiful," Mel whispered. "So beautiful and so terrifying."

John's recognition was more disturbing. Now that the initial shock had somewhat dissipated, his sight of the great goat was less the rattling of seeing a wolf, a bear, a deadly snake than the instant rake-step halting of seeing a woman of startling beauty. The creature's monstrous beauty was seductive to him at a level that gave him a dark, dark rattle—

In the car they sat in silence for a long moment. It was full night now.

"That was not what I expected," he said at last. "Did you see the size of that creature?"

Mel didn't reply. After a moment, she told him of a road she used to travel in north London when she was at university. There was a particular road where—if on the top deck of the bus—a person could look over the siding of a research farm to see outsize livestock. *Chickens, pigs. Goats.* The sight had always unsettled her as it was secret, surely in truth experimental animal husbandry but *wrong* somehow—

"The goat was like something I saw on that farm."

"If it was a goat. And her lounge," John added after a moment. "What was that? It was freakish."

"I think that's why the girl at the shelter called it Miss Aiken's School for the Gifted," Mel replied quietly. "Nasty little cow." She paused. "Can we go home now? I want to go home."

The kitten was wrong. They knew it from the first.

This *wrongness* didn't matter, however, as their cottage became his, inhabited, the moment he walked in and his tail shivered erect. They fell in love with Jasper as into an abyss—

"He never blinks," Mel said, "and his pupils are wide as if he's scared all the time, yet he's fearless."

John, not knowing cats as well as his wife did, took her word that Jasper's relentless wide pools of darkness were unusual, although he wondered if part of this might have been that the kitten could not be persuaded to go out during the day, hiding from the light until they drew their lounge curtains and kept them shut.

Jasper moved like a king, assured and aloof, yet his affection for them was undiluted. This affection was part of the *wrongness* as the kitten desired what Mel described as *more than usual* closeness. After a morning run, the kitten had insisted on working his fur into John's sweaty armpits. When John realised this was what Jasper was doing, he raised his arms and the kitten rubbed himself deep into his underarms.

"What is this?" he asked, laughing. "It tickles, but I could get used to it."

"He did it to me too," Mel replied, shamefaced. "Not my armpits either. Don't be surprised if he heads south."

John howled. "It must be a bonding thing. Like with the litter scent marking."

At night, Jasper went out. Miss Aiken had said there was no need to keep him in for a time. *Just scoop his first wet litter and use it to mark the outlines of your property.* This they had done, an horrific task as the used litter smelled like an open grave. Mel had wanted him to stay inside nevertheless, but the creature's unhappiness could not be borne so they put in a cat flap and watched as he sat in their small garden perfectly still and staring at nothing as if he were waiting for a night train.

"He's strange. He just sits there."

"He can't. Not all night. He brings presents so he must hunt at some point."

There were other curiosities to Jasper. As a child Mel had loved working a little finger into the pads to make a cat's paw splay outwards, yet the kitten did not have four toes. Four claws, yes, but instead of them belonging to individual toes, a pair of Nosferatu teeth each sprung from two fused nubs more resembling a hoof than a paw.

"Maybe it's one of those cats from that bloody room," John said. "I suppose it doesn't look odd when you leave him alone though." He caught her look. "I mean when his feet are at rest and you're not forcing the toes apart."

The feet did look wrong though, now they'd noticed it. Jasper had a curious way of moving as if he were in feline high heels, and he was the only cat Mel had ever *heard* walking.

Every dawn as he called to be rescued from the sun, there was a mound of organs at the door sill, none of the kills small, and once a squirrel larger than their tiny boy himself had been torn open, the entrails arranged as if they were the limbs of a many-armed goddess.

The sight sickened, yet it could not mar the love that had settled in them for their kitten. They were infatuated by the way he curled into an innocent ball on their sofa, one paw-hoof over his nose as he slept, rumbling. At full dark, like clockwork, he'd rise and leave the house to sit out in the darkness regarding the night.

"I swear he looks like he's waiting for a train."

When Jasper was in the house, he always returned to the hand-made creel he'd arrived in. Even if they placed him on their covers or the sofa to encourage him, after a while he'd still clop back over the wooden floorboards to the dark nest.

"She said she wanted it back."

John shrugged. "He'll grow out of it."

The basket, creel—whatever it was—was so strange an object. It was shaped like a coracle made of thick, supple branches all bound together, reminding John of a ball of rubber bands. The individual branches that formed the creel seem to have no beginning or end, the thinnest perhaps the width of his little finger, the thickest the width of a handheld bicycle pump. It was a unique construction as there was no door. On placing Jasper into the creel, Miss Aiken had simply pushed her fingers through the gaps to wrench the branches apart, and slowly the branches slid back into place of their own will, enclosing the kitten within.

After a few days, however, Jasper stopped insisting to have the creel reopened, content to sleep beside it, and the humans were pleased not to have to stick their fingers through the branches. The pull as they reformed looked sinister; it was as if the basket was alive rather than simply stretched, sliding back into a comfort the creel had been forced from.

The next day Jasper stopped sleeping next to the creel.

"Give it another day," Mel said, "and if he doesn't pine for it, you can take it back to Miss Aiken." She paused. "I love him so much, my heart hurts."

John nodded. "Yes. It's everything we wanted."

Mel paused. "You don't think the welfare visit will be a problem? The check up? I couldn't bear to lose him."

In truth, John had forgotten all about the visit, and at once he recalled the unease he'd felt on adoption day when Miss Aiken had said, *It shouldn't take more than three weeks for her to get there*, as if whoever was coming was already embarked on a long journey with their cottage as the destination.

"No," he said. "No, it'll be fine."

Mel wasn't in when he returned the next day, but she'd written a note to say Jasper had ignored the wooden creel all day. John left a note to say he'd get a takeaway on his way back then drove out to Brithemwell to return it.

Night had fallen by the time he placed his order at the restaurant and driven on to Miss Aiken's house. No answer came from the front door or the chapel. He didn't want to leave the creel on the door-step—it was so intricate and old a construction it might have been an antique—but neither did he want to return, so he turned the knob on the chapel door. It opened.

Careful to call out as he walked through the unlit interior, he made his way through to the far end, conscious from the low thunder and greenlit eyes that he was watched. At the end of the dark stone inte-rior, his fingers found the rear exit that led to the garden hidden by the high hedges—

The scene looked familiar, yet the sense that sinister presences had moved in was clear to John instantly. He saw some of the trees from the cancered wood looked to have crept into the garden, branches charcoal-black and waving. The moving branches caught John's attention as there was no wind. The candle flames in the covered stable stood upright. For a moment he saw the trees as an audience, a slow-moving congregation gathering. *An illusion, surely,* he thought, placing the creel on the ground and turning to leave—

It was then he saw Miss Aiken—

The woman was weaving through the black growths on the lawn, naked, so white in the dark she resembled a cockleshell, her neth-ers exposed to him whenever she bent down to catch a thing on the ground. The thing was a cat, he realised, one of her special rescues—

The cat had no back end, tapering to a nub beneath its rib cage, but it moved swiftly by dragging itself with its front feet. The cat fought when at last she caught it and carried the hissing length of spite to the stable.

Miss Aiken looked like she'd been in battle by the time she reached the candlelit sofa. John was mesmerised, appalled. The woman's cat-lashed breasts were bleeding, empty—what his brother cruelly called *Hungry tits*—and her dimpled nethers ran with sweat. She was tiny against the creature on her throne—

The great goat—

Unable to move or speak, John watched as the vast animal raised a rear hoof and parked it on the back of the sofa, exposing the reptil-ian leather of her udders. In one swift movement Miss Aiken pushed the frantic cat deep in the great goat's rear, John assumed anus as the woman's fist slid in up to the elbow. At the hole, there was a fizzing, a puckering, before what looked like a tentacle squirted out, past the squeeze of the sphincter, gripping Miss Aiken's elbow like a stiff handshake brace strangers give during photo shoots.

John couldn't move. Words that had come to him that first evening grew malign significance. *Dark nativity. A bestial altar.* What was once only disquieting had turned into an existential threat so profound he feared any attention he brought to himself would result in instant and permanent harm.

Miss Aiken left her arm inside the goat a full minute before she removed it. Her hand came out empty, dripping with what looked like oil or thick ink. The cat had been embedded deep inside—

Naked, coquettish, Miss Aiken nuzzled her white weight into the goat's dark embrace, soon snoring. Even then, John could not move. He stood there for hours, until the candles began to gutter and die, and only when he could not see his own boots did he dare move.

The takeaway was cold when he picked it up. At home, Mel was sitting in darkness at the table, staring at Jasper who was lying flat on his back asleep, front feet and rear pointing straight down. He looked as though he was on a luge. An unearthly rumble rose from him, deeper than expected for a kitten. At first John imagined Mel was lost in the worship of their perfect boy but when he caught her eye he saw she'd been crying.

"He sleeps so completely," she whispered and, after a pause, "I love him more than I thought ever possible."

John put out the food. Jasper didn't stir, his tiny chest rising and falling as if he was sunbathing by candlelight between them. He told Mel what he'd seen, the dark midwifery and grotesque implantation, the sight of naked Miss Aiken forcing her crotch against the great goat's teats—*that caprine Gargantua*—as she snuggled in, the malignant growths that had moved in from the trees as audience—

"I think," John quietly said after a moment, "we have mistaken the nature of the welfare visit we were told to expect. I believe she takes so long to come because she moves so slow."

Mel didn't reply. Instead she told him Jasper's morning gift had included a human hand, pink and pristine but for the gnaw marks at the wrist.

"I buried it. That's where I was when you got home. I buried it at some distance from the house."

"You didn't call anyone?"

"No. Of course not. It was only a baby's hand." She paused. "I love him so much it makes my heart hurt. Look at him sleep. Look at how completely he sleeps."

Mel began to eat, suddenly ravenous to the point of choking, uncaring that the food was cold as a stone. After a moment, John joined her, equally as violently, the meal vanishing in minutes leaving their faces filthy with food.

Jasper slept on. Gently, John closed his palm about his tiny belly, opening his mouth in delight at its warmth, its soft swell. Mel carefully placed her hand over his.

"Who is it that is coming?"

"I don't know," he whispered. "It doesn't matter. He is ours, and we are his. This will be clear to any visitor." He turned his hand to take her hand in his. "We will do whatever is needful to make her welcome."

⬥

CONTRIBUTORS

Devan Barlow

Devan Barlow is the author of *An Uncommon Curse*, a fantasy novel of fairy tales and musical theatre. Her short fiction and poetry have appeared in numerous anthologies and magazines, including *Crimson Bones* and *Star*Line*. When not writing she reads voraciously, drinks tea, and thinks about fairy tales and sea monsters.

She can be found at her website https://devanbarlow.com/ or on Twitter @ Devan_Barlow.

Tyler Battaglia

Tyler Battaglia is a queer and disabled author of horror, dark fantasy, and other speculative fiction. He is interested in subjects that interrogate the connections between faith, monsters, love, queerness, and disability. He has publications with *Crow & Cross Keys, Devout: An Anthology of Angels*, and Atomic Carnival Books' *Greater Than His Nature* anthology, among others.

You can find him on Twitter at @whosthistyler and online at https://www.tyler-battaglia.com.

Megan Beals

Megan Lee Beals writes cozy and fanciful horrors from her home in the perpetually soggy Pacific Northwest. She lives with her husband, her twin son and daughter, and the family's formally feral cat. When she isn't writing or chasing toddlers, Megan is drawing or sewing or building, and generally trying to accumulate hobbies at a truly unsustainable rate. She has been published in *Translunar Traveler's Lounge* and *The Iowa Review*.

You can find more of her various things at www.meganleebeals.com.

Ellis Bray

Ellis Bray is a science fiction author and artist who lives in the vaguely Seattle area, and he really hates the recent addition of a Fire Season to the regular Winter/Spring/Summer/Fall lineup. He is, however, a big believer in "pathological optimism" and strives to show that in his visual and verbal art.

He has a Master's degree in Medieval Scandinavian Studies and if you don't run away fast enough, he will download everything he knows about the Old Norse poem "Völuspá" at you. You can find his nonfiction in *NewMyths* (under SP Hofrichter); his poetry in *Eye To the Telescope* and *F&SF*; and his artwork on Instagram at @idreamofvikings.

Tania Chen

Tania Chen is a Chinese-Mexican queer writer. Their work was selected for the *Brave New Weird* anthology by Tenebrous Press, and has also appeared in *Unfettered Hexes* by Neon Hemlock, *Apparition Lit, Strange Horizons, Pleiades Magazine, Baffling Magazine, Longleaf Review, The Dread Machine*, among others. They are a graduate of the Clarion West Novella Bootcamp workshop of 2021, Clarion West Workshop 2023, and a recipient of the HWA's Dark Poetry Scholarship.

Currently, they are assistant editor at *Uncanny Magazine* and can be found on twitter@archistratego or https://bsky.app/profile/archistratego.bsky.social.

William J. Connell

William J. Connell is currently a practicing attorney in the great states of Rhode Island and Massachusetts. He has also worked as a public-school teacher in the areas of Special Education and History in the same states. He enjoys writing on a wide variety of topics. Most of his non-fiction material is in the legal field, and his work has been published in many law journals. His fiction tends to run to historical adventure, which reflects his love of teaching history, mixed with elements of sci-fi, classic literature, and horror thrown in for good measure! In his spare time, he likes to spend time with his family and Lulu, the family's green-cheeked conure.

You may find him online at: https://williamjconnell.com/.

Simone Cooper

An avid reader and viewer of horror, science-fiction, and fantasy, Simone grew up on a diet of *Creature Features* and *Speed Racer* cartoons on Chicago's WGN-TV. She's played role-playing games since the late 1970's and was a major writer on the 2005 multiple Ennie Award winning *A Game of Thrones* RPG. She currently plays *Amber Diceless* RPG and other dice-light games and has organized more than 30 RPG conventions under the umbrella "AmberCon" in the U.K., Michigan, Portland, and on-line.

Lauren Elise Daniels

L. E. Daniels is an awarded poet, editor, and author. Her novel *Serpent's Wake: A Tale for the Bitten* is a Notable Work with the HWA's Mental Health Initiative. Lauren co-edited *We Are Providence*, which appeared the Bram Stoker Awards® Preliminary Ballot and is a finalist for the 2022 Aurealis Award. She co-edited Aiki Flinthart's legacy anthology, *Relics, Wrecks and Ruins* (CAT Press) with Geneve Flynn, winning the 2021 Aurealis Award. For her poetry, she won the Newport Poetry Award in 1987 and her recent work appears in the HWA's *Of Horror and Hope, Under Her Eye,* and *Mother Knows Best* (Black Spot Books), and *Dastardly Damsels* (Crystal Lake) anthologies. She's finalist for the 2022 Australian Shadows Award. An editor for over 100 titles, Lauren directs Brisbane Writers Workshop.

Daniel David Froid

Daniel David Froid is a writer who lives in Arizona and has published fiction in *The Masters Review, Lightspeed, Black Warrior Review, Post Road*, and elsewhere.

Andrew S. Fuller

Andrew S. Fuller writes and edits horror, fantasy, and science fiction. His work appears in several magazines, anthologies, short films, and the collection *Constellations of Ruin* (2023, Trepidatio). Since 1999, he's edited the fiction magazine *Three-Lobed Burning Eye*. He lives in Portland, OR between two rivers and near several extinct(?) volcanoes.

Visit him online at andrewsfuller.com.

Shanna Germain

If Shanna Germain were a god, she'd be the Benevolent God of Rainbow Sprinkles. Sadly, she's only human. She is also an award-winning writer of short stories, novels, games, essays, and poems. Her work has appeared in places like *Apex Magazine, Best Lesbian Erotica, Best Gay Romance, The Deadlands*, and *Fantasy Magazine*.

She lives in a rainforest with a dog named &. Follow her down the rabbit hole at shannagermain.com.

Maxwell Gold

Maxwell I. Gold is a Jewish American multiple award nominated author who writes prose poetry and short stories in cosmic horror and weird fiction with half a decade of writing experience. He is a five-time Rhysling Award nominee, and two-time Pushcart Award nominee.

Find him at www.thewellsoftheweird.com.

Erik Grove

Erik Grove is a writer, writing teacher, long distance runner, and little dog wrangler living and doing things in Portland, OR. You can find his work in places like *Nightmare*, *Escape Pod*, and the *Space Cocaine* anthology series. He teaches writing and mentors writers with Working Title (www.workingtitle.us).

Check out his webpage www.erikgrove.com for links to his published work, dog glamour shots, marathon training nonsense, and sundry writerly shenanigans.

Ken Hueler

Ken Hueler teaches kung fu in the San Francisco Bay Area, where he also co-chairs the local Horror Writers Association chapter. His work has appeared in *Weirdbook*, *The Sirens Call*, *Space & Time*, *Weekly Mystery Magazine*, *Andromeda Spaceways*, and anthologies such as *The Lost Librarian's Grave* and *Tales for the Camp Fire*. He is co-editor of the game fiction anthology *Winding Paths: A Playable Reading Experience* from Demagogue Press.

You can learn more at: kenhueler.wordpress.com.

Corinne Hughes

Corinne Hughes is a poet and fiction writer. Her work can be found in Cathexis Northwest Press, Grim and Gilded, the Horror Writers Association Poetry Showcase IX, and SMEOP (Hot), an eco-anthology by Black Sunflowers Poetry Press. In 2022, she received the Ladies of Horror Fiction Writers Grant and in 2023, attended the Juniper Summer Writing Institute for poetry. She thinks demons are adorable and currently resides at the end of a long, dark corridor in Portland, Oregon.

Paul Jessup

Paul Jessup is a best-selling video game designer and award-winning short fiction writer. He's also an active Pro Member of HWA. He has three books coming out within a year from Underland Press: *Glass House, Skinless Man Counts to Five and other tales of the macabre*, and *Cancer Eats the Heart*.

Ngô Bình Anh Khoa

Ngô Bình Anh Khoa is a teacher of English in Ho Chi Minh City, Vietnam. In his free time, he enjoys reading fiction and writing speculative poetry. His poems have appeared in *Weirdbook, Star*Line, Spectral Realms*, and other venues. He also writes haiku on occasions, many of which have received honorable mentions and awards in various contests in the US, the UK, Japan, Canada, and elsewhere.

J. B. Kish

J.B. Kish is a horror and weird fiction author living in Portland, Oregon. His work has appeared in *Cosmic Horror Monthly, Metaphorosis Magazine*, and Unsettling Reads' *Still of Winter* anthology. When he's not writing, Kish teaches workshops that help emerging authors design strategies to reach their goals. He has one wife, one cat, and one dog.

Jessie Kwak

Jessie Kwak is the m*****-f***ing pirate your mother warned you about.

Kiera Lesley

Kiera Lesley lives and writes in Melbourne, Australia with her partner and their retired racing greyhound. Her work has won an Aurealis award and can be found in *Nightmare, Andromeda Spaceways, Etherea,* and elsewhere. When not writing she enjoys tea, napping, heavy metal, and knitting.

You can find Kiera online at: www.kieralesley.com or on socials @KieraLesley.

Cody T Luff

Cody grew up listening to stories in his grandfather's barber shop as he shined shoes, stories told to him at bedsides and on front porches, deep in his father's favorite woods, and in the cabs of pickup trucks on lonely dirt roads. Cody's work explores those things both small and wondrous that move the soul, whether they be deeply real or strikingly surreal. Cody's debut novel, *Ration*, was released by Apex Books. His work appears in numerous journals and collections.

Find him online at https://worlds.workingtitle.us and codytluff.com.

E. E. Marshall

E. E. Marshall lives in the Northwest, enjoying the glory of green springs, warm summers, mild winters, and a large community of endlessly quirky and creative people. When not hiking in the mountains and on the beaches, they spend time exploring the history of stories from the first shaman whispering lore around a campfire to the experimental tales written entirely online for the people who only read online. What a perfect time to be alive!

Scotty Milder

Scotty Milder is a writer, filmmaker, and film educator based in Albuquerque, NM. He received his MFA in Screenwriting from Boston University. His award-winning short films have screened at the Boston Underground Film Festival, Cinequest, the Dead By Dawn Festival of Horror (Edinburgh, UK), the Leeds International Film Festival, the Cannes Short Film Corner, HollyShorts (Hollywood, CA), and the HP Lovecraft Film Festival/CthulhuCon (San Pedro, CA).

His short fiction has appeared or will appear in *The Vanishing Point, Dark Matter Magazine, Dark Moon Digest, Black Sheep Magazine*, as well as anthologies from Red Cape Publishing, Yuriko Publishing, HellBound Books, Dark Moon Books, Crone Girls Press, Dark Peninsula Press, Dark Ink Books, Sinister Smile Press, and others.

He has developed screenplays and television pilots with Lin Pictures/Warner Horizon, Fanfare Entertainment/Sony Pictures Television, and Kopelson Entertainment. His independent feature film, *Dead Billy*, is currently streaming on Amazon and Google Play.

He teaches screenwriting and film production at Santa Fe Community College, and he also hosts the *Horror from the High Desert* podcast and co-hosts *The Weirdest Thing* history podcast.

Rajiv Moté

Rajiv Moté is a software engineering director and writer living in Chicago with his wife, daughter, and a tiny dog. He is a member of SFWA and the Codex Writers whose stories appear in *Cosmic Horror Monthly, Diabolical Plots, Year's Best Hardcore Horror vol 5*, and the forthcoming *Monster Lairs* anthology from Dark Matter Ink.

He can be found on Twitter/Threads/BlueSky at RajivMote, and his published work is catalogued on his blog: https://rajivmote.wordpress.com/published/.

Remy Nakamura

By day, Remy Nakamura works in the frightening intersection of the funeral industry and data management. At night (really the early morning hours, and only after a cup of coffee) he transforms into a writer of dark and weird fiction. You can find his stories in *Escape Pod*, *Pseudopod*, and a number of themed anthologies. He graduated from the Clarion West Workshop, served on the Science Fiction and Fantasy Writers Association's Board of Directors, and is currently working on a Masters in Genre Writing. Remy grew up in Greece, Japan, and the San Francisco Bay Area. He currently resides in Portland, where he spends as much time as possible getting cold, wet, and muddy.

You can find Remy online at www.mindonfire.com, remymura@bsky.social, and on instagram as @remy.nakamura.

Kurt Newton

Kurt Newton's poetry has appeared in numerous magazines and anthologies including *Weird Tales, Cosmic Horror Monthly, Spectral Realms*, and *Penumbra*. He is the author of eleven collections of poetry. His 2022 collection, *Songs of the Underland* (available from Ravens Quoth Press), is currently nominated for an Elgin Award.

R. Ostermeier

R. Ostermeier writes for Broodcomb Press and has three collections of strange tales currently available—*A Trick of the Shadow, Therapeutic Tales*, and *Nocebo*—each of which explore worlds of peninsular disquiet from folk horror to more contemporary weird fiction. It might not be for you . . .

Kate Ristau

Kate Ristau is the author of two trilogies for tweens and teens: Clockbreakers and Shadow Girl. She also wrote *Wylde Wings* and *Mythwakers*. This is her first horror story, and she's not sure about this whole 'looking into the maw of the Abyss' thing. Make sure she's okay at kateristau.com.

Eric Shanower

Eric Shanower is the award-winning cartoonist of the graphic novel series *Age of Bronze* (Image Comics), retelling the story of the Trojan War. He's written and drawn dozens of *Oz* projects, including writing *New York Times* best-selling graphic novel adaptations of six of L. Frank Baum's *Oz* books (Marvel Comics). Shanower has illustrated for television, stage, magazines, and children's books, two of which he wrote himself. He lives with his husband in Portland, Oregon.

John Shirley

John Shirley is an award-winning author, songwriter, television, and screen writer. Credited as one of the originators of cyberpunk, his fiction work has spanned multiple genres, including Westerns, science fiction, horror, graphic novels, historical fiction, and horror. His first collection of poetry, *The Voice of the Burning House*, is now out from Jackanapes Press. He's also had an impressive television and film writing career with credits including *Star Trek: Deep Space Nine* and *The Crow* starring Brandon Lee. As a musician, Shirley has fronted his own bands and written lyrics for Blue Öyster Cult, among others.

Born in Houston, TX, he now lives with his wife in Vancouver, Washington. Visit him online at John-Shirley.com.

Tais Teng

Tais Teng is a Dutch sf writer and illustrator with the quite unpronounceable name of Thijs van Ebbenhorst Tengbergen, which he shortened to Tais Teng to leave room for exploding spaceships or clever steampunk ladies on the covers of his novels.

His drawings range from talking teapots to quite beautiful bat-winged ladies with a naughty character. In his own language, he has written everything from radio plays to hefty fantasy trilogies. To date, he has sold seventy-two stories in the English language and two children's books: *When the Night-gaunt Knows Your Name* and *The Emerald Boy*—both with a generous helping of horror. Spatterlight recently published his YA novel *Phaedra: Alastor 824*, set in the universe of Jack Vance.

You may find him online at http://taisteng.atspace.com/ and https://www.deviantart.com/taisteng

Kevin Wetmore

Kevin Wetmore is a five-time Bram Stoker Award nominee, the author or editor of almost three dozen non-fiction books and many, many short stories, including his other Lovecraft mashups, "Tales of a Fourth Grade Shoggoth," "Are You There, Azathoth? It's Me, Margaret," and "The Statement of Eeyore Carter," as well as other Lovecraftian stories in such anthologies as *Fall of Cthulhu II, Whispers from the Abyss 2, Urban Temples of Cthulhu*, and *A Lonely and Curious Country*.

Learn more at www.SomethingWetmoreThisWayComes.com.

Jonathan Wood

Jonathan Wood is the author of 8 novels (The Hero series, The Dragon Lords series writing as Jon Hollins, and *City of Iron and Dust* as J.P. Oakes). When not writing he spends far too much time playing videogames and sharing memes on facebook while society collapses around him.

He can be found online at jpoakeswrites.wordpress.com.

EDITORS

Frances Lu-Pai Ippolito

Frances Lu-Pai Ippolito (she/her) is a Chinese American judge, mom, and writer in Portland, Oregon. Her writing has appeared in *Nightmare Magazine*, Flame Tree's *Asian Ghost Stories, Chromophobia, Mother: Tales of Terror and Love, Death's Garden Revisited*, and *Unquiet Spirits*. She is the founder of game and book publisher Demagogue Press and the nonprofit, Qilin Press, which focuses on diverse, marginalized voices. Frances also co-chairs the Young Willamette Writers program that provides free writing classes for high school and middle school students.

You can find her on IG @francespaippolito, FB Frances Pai, and at www.demagoguepress.com/.

Mark Teppo

Mark Teppo is the publisher of Underland Press. He has written more than two dozen novels across a wide variety of genres, including historical fiction, eco-thriller, horror, western, mystery, science fiction, and dark fantasy. He lives in the Pacific Northwest, where he is busy making things.

His favorite Tarot card is the Moon.

For more information about Underland Press, please visit the website:

underlandpress.com

Printed in the USA
CPSIA information can be obtained
at www.ICGtesting.com
LVHW092308240124
769912LV00037B/1043